Dear Reader,

The editors at Harlequin and Silhouette are thrilled to be able to bring you a brand-new featured author program beginning in 2005! Signature Select aims to single out outstanding stories, contemporary themes and oft-requested classics by some of your favorite series authors and present them to you in a variety of formats bound by truly striking covers.

We plan to provide several different types of reading experiences in the new Signature Select program. The Spotlight books will offer a single "big read" by a talented series author, the Collections will present three novellas on a selected theme in one volume, the Sagas will contain sprawling, sometimes multigenerational family tales (often related to a favorite family first introduced in series), and the Miniseries will feature requested, previously published books, with two or, occasionally, three complete stories in one volume. The Signature Select program will offer one book in each of these categories per month, and fans of limited continuity series will also find these continuing stories under the Signature Select umbrella.

In addition, these volumes will bring you bonus features...different in every single book! You may learn more about the author in an extended interview, more about the setting or inspiration for the book, more about subjects related to the theme and, often, a bonus short read will be included.

Watch for new stories from Janelle Denison, Donna Kauffman, Leslie Kelly, Marie Ferrarella, Suzanne Forster, Stephanie Bond, Christine Rimmer and scores more of the brightest talents in romance fiction!

We have an exciting year ahead!

Warm wishes for happy reading,

*Marsha Zinberg*

Marsha Zinberg
Executive Editor
The Signature Select Program

COLLECTION

# Suzanne Forster
# Donna Kauffman
# & Jill Shalvis

## *velvet,*
## *leather*
## *& lace*

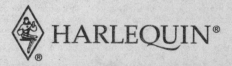

# HARLEQUIN®

TORONTO • NEW YORK • LONDON
AMSTERDAM • PARIS • SYDNEY • HAMBURG
STOCKHOLM • ATHENS • TOKYO • MILAN • MADRID
PRAGUE • WARSAW • BUDAPEST • AUCKLAND

ISBN 0-373-83654-6

VELVET, LEATHER & LACE

Copyright © 2005 by Harlequin Books S.A.

The publisher acknowledges the copyright holders
of the individual works as follows:

A MAN'S GOTTA DO
Copyright © 2005 by Suzanne Forster

CALLING THE SHOTS
Copyright © 2005 by Donna Kauffman

BARING IT ALL
Copyright © 2005 by Jill Shalvis

This edition published by arrangement with Harlequin Books S.A.

® and TM are trademarks of the publisher. Trademarks indicated with
® are registered in the United States Patent and Trademark Office, the
Canadian Trade Marks Office and in other countries.

www.eHarlequin.com

Printed in U.S.A.

# CONTENTS

# A MAN'S GOTTA DO

Suzanne Forster

# CHAPTER ONE

WHEN A MAN STARTED flipping through his black book as if it was the Yellow Pages, he was either desperately in need of a date for some do-or-die social event, or horny. Jamie Baird was neither. All right, maybe that second thing. His workload hadn't allowed him time to date in months, so he was pretty much always horny. But that wasn't what had sent him searching through the black book today. He needed a woman to pose as him. Not for him. *As* him.

Jamie was the CFO of a catalog lingerie company that had stumbled onto a promotional gold mine. Velvet, Leather & Lace was run by women for women, and their slogan was Hot At Any Age, Sexy At Any Size. Jamie had been coaxed into taking the job two years ago by two women friends from college. They'd needed someone with his business background, and his androgynous name had turned out to be a bonus, too. Everyone outside the company had assumed he was a woman, and that impression had never been corrected by anyone at VLL, including Jamie.

He hadn't expected to stay once the company was launched, but he'd been challenged by the seemingly insurmountable odds. Recently he'd secured two wealthy investors, and now everything had changed. VLL was less than two weeks away from their first global satellite fashion show, and their little white lie had caught up with them. The media was closing in.

The press wanted to meet publicity-shy Jamie Baird, the third *woman* on VLL's rags-to-riches dream team, and his two partners couldn't cover for him this time.

Jamie clicked through the steps to bring up his personal address book. His computer system housed what amounted to an electronic black book, an automatic speed-dialer and a speaker phone. Everything needed for instant contact, and Jamie had never needed instant contact the way he did tonight. He had less than seventy-two hours to create a female Jamie Baird, one who could convince the press and the world at large that she was the real thing.

"I need a quick study, a snappy dresser and a math whiz," he told the screen. "That's not asking too much, is it?"

It was dark in his office except for the glow of the monitor, but he was used to being bathed in pale light as he worked late into the midsummer night. You could call him a workaholic, although he preferred to think of himself as a problem solver. Tonight, you could also call him a desperate man.

His partners, Samantha Wallace and Mia Tennario, had already done both television and radio interviews for the show, but now the *L.A. Times* wanted to do an in-depth feature of Jamie in "her" home. Everyone wanted to meet the "brains behind the beauties of VLL," and Jamie had a hunch the story would create even greater demand. Good news, and bad.

His home was a waterfront bungalow on one of the canals in Venice Beach, California, and he'd probably dated half the single women in the area before he'd gone into work-enforced celibacy. Lovely creatures, all of them, but there hadn't been any clicks of the long-term commitment kind, which was totally his fault. He'd been sowing oats, not searching for a relationship. And then the VLL situation had taken him out of circulation entirely. Now he was reduced to making what amounted to cold calls. A couple of the women might even be a little miffed at him for various reasons, but he didn't think so. It had been months. It was now July. Who held a grudge that long over a missed phone call?

He scrolled through the prospects, noting names and wondering what had happened to several of the women since he'd last seen them.

A lovely blonde named Sandy caught his eye. It had been over a year, but he remembered her as lively, fun and well…buxom. His notes confirmed that.

Jamie found himself smiling. A stacked Jamie Baird? The boys at the health club would appreciate that. Not that he'd ever actually told them what he did, and he was hoping Jamie Baird was a common enough name and L.A. a big enough place that they'd never put it together. They would go nuts if they knew that he not only worked for a lingerie company, but had secretly designed some of the sexiest pieces. They thought he was a money manager.

He highlighted Sandy's name and moved on to Frances. Tall, slender and pretty, but apparently, it was her slight overbite that had impressed him the most. His notes said she'd accidentally bitten him, but it didn't say how or why. He did remember where. Still, he had to get better at details.

He highlighted a couple more, and then he saw Lorna's name. She was the last woman he dated before submerging into celibacy. Oddly enough he'd met her in the produce section of the grocery store. She'd helped him pick out a breakfast melon, and by the time they'd found a ripe one, he was wondering why he needed a melon. He'd rather have her for breakfast.

He'd written only three things by her name: 1) smart, 2) a sex goddess and 3) unapologetically voluptuous.

Voluptuous. Everywhere. *Lorna.*

He wasn't likely to forget her. They'd had volcanic sex on their second date, but even if they hadn't, she would have more than qualified as a sex goddess. She was flame haired and green eyed with luscious curves. Perfect for VLL. His two business partners were beautiful women, but they were petite in frame, and VLL was supposed to be dedicated to women of all shapes and sizes. It couldn't hurt for them to have a plus-size partner, especially going into the publicity blitz for the fashion show.

He found a few more names and decided he had enough to start. Moments later he'd cut and pasted all the women's phone numbers to his speed-dialer program. The computer would now dial the numbers for him, and when the women answered, he could talk to them through the speaker phone system.

Jamie clicked the buttons and sat back, waiting for the computer to find him the perfect match. Look, Ma, no hands. Technology did have its benefits, although except for the demands of his work, he tended to avoid it. He didn't have a cell phone, a Palm Pilot or a GPS system in his car. He'd developed an aversion to having conversations with people who weren't there. And probably weren't even people.

"Hello?"

It was Sandy's sweet voice. He should have noted that she had a voice like crystal bells. Details again.

"Hi, Sandy, it's Jamie Baird. Remember me?"

"Jamie Baird?" Her breath sucked in. "The Jamie Baird who got an emergency call from one of his partners and left me in a hotel room, never to return? I was naked, Jamie!"

"Well, Sandy, I tried to call, but you kept hanging up on me—"

CLICK

*…just like that.*

Jamie winced. If he'd been holding a receiver to his ear, he'd be deaf. That was Sandy with the sweet voice? Maybe his program had dialed the wrong number. Or something had taken possession of her body, like a demon from the bowels of hell.

The automatic dialer didn't give Jamie a chance to recover. It went right to the next number.

"Hello?"

"Frances, it's been too long. How are you? This is Jamie Baird."

"Jamie who?"

"Jamie Baird, Frances. I know it's been a while, but—"

"A while? Nine months is a *while?* I cooked a beautiful meal and invited my parents, and what did you do? You stood me up, you lousy good for nothing—!"

Jamie could hear the click coming. He hit the function key to lower the volume, but she landed the receiver before he could bring up the gauge. It sounded like a car crash. Possibly he needed to check his settings. Or possibly this wasn't a good idea.

He turned off the automatic dialer before it got to Lorna Sutton. His eardrums weren't up to it. He fell back in the chair and stared at the computer screen, but nothing registered as he contemplated the utter failure of his plan. "I didn't remember the dates being that bad," he murmured.

He was thirty-four years old and yet still fascinated and baffled by the opposite sex. Maybe he knew something about women on an intuitive level because they seemed to love his lingerie, but when it came to the complexities of their thinking, he was working without a safety net. He'd always figured that at some point Cupid would get him with that arrow, and all would become clear. He would understand the mysteries of love and the secret desires of a woman's heart, but Cupid seemed to have pretty bad aim where Jamie Baird was concerned.

"Women trouble?"

Jamie swiveled to see who'd asked the question. A small wiry man stood in the doorway, a red bandanna wrapped around his spiky gray hair, and a floor mop in his hand. It was the night janitor, and Jamie had spent many an evening with Frank Natori in the last several months. Too many. Natori considered himself something of a philosopher. He loved to be obscure, but every once in a while, he said something that reminded Jamie of Mr. Miyagi of *Karate Kid* fame. It almost made sense.

"Eavesdropping again?" Jamie pretended to sound gruff.

Natori's grin stretched. "Getting rejected again?"

Jamie shrugged. "It must have been something I said."

"Or didn't say. Women need words."

"Words?" Jamie gave him a skeptical look. "If women needed words, I'd be home free. I'm *Webster's*, my man. I'm good at words."

"But not the right ones."

"And what are those?"

Natori's dark eyes twinkled. He propped his mop against the door frame and pulled a feather duster out of his back pocket. "Only you know, and when you say them, you'll get the answer you want."

Jamie cocked a brow. "Are we talking about the word that starts with *L?* Like *l-o-v-e?*"

Natori carefully dusted the breasts and wings of a marble nude. The statue was a Greek goddess, and Jamie had picked her up at an art auction, thinking she symbolized the VLL philosophy of creating your own sensual reality. Jamie took his inspiration wherever he could find it, even picking up ideas from the guys at the gym, whose male fantasies had inadvertently given him the idea for StripLoc, a line of lingerie with breakaway seams.

"Could be a word that starts with *L,*" Natori said, "but not necessarily the one you're thinking. Could be a word that starts with *F.* Only you can know what the right words are, and only if you listen long enough and deep enough."

"To her?"

"To *yourself.*"

"I wish *you'd* listen to yourself for once. You're not making any sense at all. And I don't have time for words, right or wrong. I need a woman tonight."

Natori blinked down his nose at Jamie. "Try the corner of Second and Main."

"Not a hooker! This is a business proposition."

"No difference. If she hears the magic words, you will get what you need."

"And what the hell *are* these magic words? And don't say—"

*"Only you know."* Natori tipped his head and headed for the door where he picked up his mop and tilted it over his shoulder.

"Stop and listen," he said, glancing back at Jamie. "You might hear something. Until then, offer her money."

"Money? Wouldn't that be insulting?"

"Not if you do it right. It all comes back to words."

Jamie gave him a look of disgust, which the janitor never saw because he'd already left.

Words. Money. Hookers. The old guy was losing it.

But Jamie turned back to his computer and reached for the mouse, scrolling down the list of names. He had made a decision. He was going to call Lorna Sutton, and he was going to make her an offer. All she could do was hang up on him. But he didn't think she would. At one point, she'd embarrassed herself by revealing a secret childhood dream, and now, the way things were breaking, he just might be able to help her make it come true.

LORNA SUTTON put a few drops of her favorite aromatherapy oil in the vaporizer and breathed in the scent. Her eyelids fluttered in appreciation. An Enya CD played softly in the background, soothing her even further. For the first time in months, Lorna was in a good place, both physically and emotionally, and her bedtime ritual of cleansing her face with strawberry essence while listening to the sweet strains of a harp was one of the reasons.

She'd worked hard to achieve order and balance in her life, and finally, things were falling into place. As of this morning, she was taking a couple weeks off from her paralegal job, with nothing planned but relaxation. She'd long dreamed of visiting an island in the tropics, any island famous for its trade winds would do, but that was on hold for now. She'd decided on something more practical. She would eliminate the major stressors from her life, which meant men, dating, the L.A. freeways and caffeine. Not cold turkey, mind you. She'd been working up to this for a while. She'd played with the idea of giving up carbs, too, but without men, chocolate was an absolute necessity.

Inner peace was her goal. Inner acceptance. All those warm, fuzzy things that went with the *I* word—but she also wanted to be on more than a nodding acquaintance with the bold side of her personality—her inner vixen, of course. And maybe even her inner *B* word?

Obviously, she needed to work on it if she couldn't even say it.

"My inner bitch." There, she'd done it.

Too much of her life she'd bent over backward for others, and what had it gotten her? Three appointments a week with her chiropractor, and telemarketers calling her every thirty seconds because she was the only one on the planet who wouldn't hang up on them. If she didn't straighten up soon, she would have to join the circus as a contortionist.

She gave herself a sharp nod in the mirror. "Stand tall, girl."

She'd had it with girlfriends who insisted that she would be beautiful if she lost another fifteen pounds, and guys who swept her off her feet and dropped her on her butt. She was beautiful *now.*

She applied her revitalizing night cream, peering at her ultrafair skin and trying to see the visible difference the cream promised. The fine lines around her eyes had smoothed out, but she still had an unsightly blotch on her chin. The spot was probably hormonal, and she might even miss the lines if they disappeared. They warmed up her green eyes considerably.

She turned off the vaporizer and drew on a sexy black lace negligee. She'd ordered the formfitting gown from a catalog company she'd just discovered called VLL. Their lingerie was wickedly gorgeous and came in larger sizes. There was no law that said she couldn't feel sensual and womanly without a man. In fact, who needed them? The phone book had listings for handymen and sperm donors.

She admired the gown's empire lines in the mirror, especially the narrow satin straps and the way the ruched bodice cupped her breasts. The black lace also gave provocative glimpses of nude skin. Very sexy. Enough to make a guy's eyes bug, should he be so lucky as to get a look.

She was just about to apply some oil of wild strawberry to her décolletage when the phone rang. She glanced through the doorway into the bedroom. Who was calling her now? She'd planned to curl up in bed and watch DVDs. Maybe munch on an apple, or if a mood-altering drug became necessary, then chocolate.

By the time she got to the night table by the bed, her phone machine was already taking a message. When she heard the caller's voice, she stopped so quickly the room seemed to tilt like a carnival ride.

"Lorna, it's Jamie Baird, the guy who can't tell a ripe melon from a green one."

"Jamie?" she whispered. Her heart was trying to kick its way out of her chest and take her inner serenity with it. He'd actually stood her up for their third date. A no show. Why was *he* calling her? He was the reason she'd had to rethink her life and her friends. She was searching for her inner bitch because of him.

"Lorna, don't delete me!"

Lorna lifted her finger from the delete button. She looked around the room. Did he have a camera in here somewhere?

"If you're screening calls," he said, "just listen for ten more seconds. What's ten seconds for what could be the sweetest deal of your life?"

He couldn't be serious. He was calling to offer her a

deal? He wasn't going to grovel or get down on his knees and beg her for another date? That was the least he could do—not that she'd accept.

"I need your help, Lorna. Didn't you tell me you dreamed of being an actress when you were a little girl? Well, have I got a role for you. You were made for this role. You're perfect."

She should never have told a man like that her dreams. And he should not have been born with such a husky, baby-let-me-love-you-tonight voice. Damn Jamie Baird anyway, with his wavy black hair, squared-off jaw and sexy quarterback butt. The second she'd laid eyes on him, she'd wanted to have sex with him—right there in the produce section. She'd been showing him how to check melons for ripeness, and dear God, the way he'd handled that fruit. She could almost hear the melons squealing with pleasure. She'd never seen sexier hands, and he definitely knew what to do with them.

Lorna grabbed a magazine off her night table and fanned herself with it. She should not be thinking about his hands right now. She would start melting from the toes up. Her body heat had already hit record numbers. She smelled like a strawberry patch in the summer sun. Yup, it was definitely going to be a mood-altering chocolate night.

"Say yes," Jamie implored.

Now there was a familiar refrain. At least she'd held out until their second date, but then she'd all but attacked him. He could kiss, too. Such heat, such sizzle, such bliss. And afterward, such humiliation. What had possessed her? She couldn't blame it on diminished capacity. She hadn't had anything exotic to eat or drink that night. It was one of those out-of-control moments where you did something you never thought you could and then wished you hadn't.

They'd actually done it in his car before they even got to his house, and then on his porch before they got inside, and then of course, in the living room before they reached the bedroom. In fact, they never got to the bedroom. They were too exhausted.

Bold? She'd been brazen, positively sluttish.

On second thought, the third time wasn't technically the living room. It was the dining room table. Both areas were combined in a great room.

"Say yes," he echoed, "and you'll think you've won the lottery. You can have your choice of a vacation anywhere in the world, a lifetime supply of lingerie, or if you prefer, cold, hard cash. Whatever you want, Lorna, but *please,* be my star."

Now, he was offering money? He could have had her with an apology! The man really knew how to rip out a woman's heart and dance the tarantella on it. He needed to be taught a thing or two, and this might be her chance.

Lorna tossed the magazine on the bed. Jamie Baird had already introduced her to her inner vixen. Boy, and how. Now, if there was any justice in this world, he was about to present her with the perfect opportunity to get in touch with her inner *B* word.

She picked up the phone. "What do I have to do?" she asked.

## CHAPTER TWO

THE SILENCE on the other end of the line prompted Lorna to ask, "Is anyone there?"

Jamie's voice sounded a bit skeptical. "Did you just say yes, Lorna? This *is* Lorna, isn't it?"

She was glad he couldn't see her smile. "Yes, this is Lorna, and *yes,* I said yes. I'd love to help you, Jamie. And by the way, it's wonderful to hear from you after *all* this time."

"Really? Wonderful?"

She could just see his sexy dark brows arching, then furrowing in doubt. Just for fun, she made little kissy noises into the mouthpiece.

"What do I have to do?" she asked him, "knock off a bank? A person? You name it, and I'll do it. *Anything* for Jamie Baird."

"Lorna, are you all right?"

"Perfect. Couldn't be better."

"And you're sure you want to do this? Maybe you should hear what it is first. Some people might think it's a little weird."

"It's you asking. That's enough."

Silence. Sweet music to her ears. He was speechless, and she was the reason.

"Here's the deal," he said finally. "I need you to be me. I need you to pose as me, as Jamie Baird."

"That *is* weird." Lorna sat on the bed, listening with disbelief as he laid out his plan for her to take his place during VLL's publicity blitz, including the interview that would feature Jamie in "her" home. It surprised her that he worked for VLL, especially since the company was supposed to be run exclusively by women. She'd read the VLL story in their catalog. How bizarre that she'd just put on one of their negligees.

"Everything happened at warp speed," he explained. "Our new investors proposed a global satellite fashion show, and the publicity campaign got away from us, but we'll clear up the confusion as soon as the show's over. Right now there's too much at stake to throw the press a chunk of red meat, namely me. If they find out Jamie Baird's a man, they'll go after that story, and it's crucial they focus on the lingerie, not on me. We may not get another shot at this kind of exposure."

He paused, as if waiting for Lorna to react. She didn't.

"Are you still interested?" he asked.

"More than interested. I'm excited. I'm *ready*."

"Ready is good." Another space of silence. "Why?"

"Why am I ready? Because I'm on vacation with nowhere to go, and it sounds like fun." *And because I want to see you sweat, Romeo.*

"So, the timing is right?"

Finally, he sounded as if he was beginning to believe her. "It's perfect," she said. "When do we start? When do I become *you*?"

"I'll pick you up in ten minutes. We'll go to my place."

"Tonight? Now? Your place?"

"The interview's just two days away. I have to get the beach house looking like a woman lives there, and I'll need your advice on that. And you have to take on my entire life, Lorna."

She couldn't ignore her vital signs any longer. They were having a field day. All of her crevices were damp— her cleavage, her armpits and the backs of her knees. Even the one she was sitting on. The effect he had on her was so unladylike. She was getting…steamy.

She grabbed the magazine to fan herself, wondering if she should take it with her. But not for her. For him. "Why don't I meet you at your place in a half hour. No, make it forty-five minutes."

"Great. Bring whatever you need. You're going to be staying until the interior is done. And Lorna, come as you are."

Lorna glanced at her negligee. Beyond the low-cut bodice, it was one of VLL's new line of breakaway lingerie. They'd called it StripLoc in the catalog, and certain essential seams were actually held by a Velcro-like material that let go with a little tug. Lorna had planned to change into jeans, but he'd told her to come as she was.

"See you in forty-five," he said.

"Yes, you will," she answered brightly. "You certainly will."

FASCINATING PIECE of work, Lorna Sutton.

Jamie thought about little else but their phone conversation as he plowed through the rooms of his house, picking up clothes, newspapers, magazines. He was between housekeepers and the place was a train wreck at the moment, especially his bedroom.

*Anything* for Jamie Baird? Her voice had been honey dripping from a stick when she'd said that. And those noises she made in his ear, what were those throaty little noises? God, what a sweet jolt that was. She might as well have applied electrodes directly to his groin.

He crouched in the doorway of the master bath to pick up a men's magazine lying open on the floor. This one had a section on hot gifts for women, featuring lingerie. He only had the magazines around for research, of course. A man who designed women's unmentionables *had* to do research, right? Just like college boys bought *Playboy* for the articles.

"The sacrifices never stop," he said, adding the magazine to his pile. There was nowhere to go with all the junk he'd collected but his walk-in closet, which was already exploding. He dumped everything—magazines, papers and the armful of clothes—into an overstuffed hamper and then slammed the lid on it, praying nothing escaped.

What was that thing she'd said about being ready?

More than interested. I'm excited. I'm *ready.*

Everything coming from her mouth sounded like an erotic invitation, but maybe he was dreaming. He remembered their second date as lightning hot. It may even have equaled in intensity all his other experiences put together, and he'd been with a few women. That kind of chemistry could reach flash point. It could be dangerous.

That had nothing to do with why he'd backed off, though. He would have walked on hot coals to see her again, but he'd been ambushed by the job. He wasn't afraid of volcanic sex, even when it got crazy and emotional, as it had in this case. Hell, no. He'd said some pretty intense things, like asking her where she'd been all his life, and admitting nothing like that had ever happened to him before. And he'd caught the brilliant glitter of her green eyes afterward. She'd sworn it wasn't tears, that she was fine. Actually, she'd been adamant about that, but he hadn't been so sure. They'd both been blindsided, that much he did know.

A quick glance around his bedroom told him his work wasn't done. An Eiffel Tower made of condoms stood on his dresser. He'd won it in an arm-wrestling contest at his gym, but how many women decorated with condoms? Maybe he could stash it in the garage along with the collection of Vargas pinups his partners had given him for artistic inspiration. He also had a signed football jersey on the wall, black satin sheets on the bed and a pair of leg irons hanging from his bedpost, possibly to offset the dressmaker's dummy he used to drape material and the stacks of sketch pads on his work desk, filled with lingerie designs.

He gave the leg irons another look, wondering why a female Jamie Baird couldn't have a pair of those in her bedroom. Might make for some interesting interview questions. On second thought, maybe too interesting. He wanted to keep the focus on VLL. When the guys came over for poker, he kept this room locked tight. Maybe he'd better do that for the interview, too. The press was curious about Jamie Baird, the woman business guru, not the designer. Better not to confuse things. They were confused enough already.

"It's not easy being a girl," he said under his breath. As he left the room, he reached down to adjust himself, probably just to make sure everything was still there. It was a reflex.

Turning the bungalow into a woman's domain was going to take some work, he realized as he walked through the house. It was actually a three-bedroom, two-and-a-half-bath rambler with a swimming pool and spa in the back, surrounded by a huge stone terrace. Apparently, the original owners didn't think there was enough water in the ocean so they added a pool. Jamie liked it for the privacy.

He was in the kitchen, loading the dishwasher when he heard the brass door knocker out front. Lorna? Nothing soft or seductive about that rap. It was all business.

"Come on in," he called out, reaching for a kitchen towel. "It's open."

He'd dressed for the midsummer heat in trunks and a tank top, standard beach gear. He'd also opened the terrace doors and the skylights to let in the balmy evening air that southern California was famous for.

He was picturing Lorna in shorts or a sundress, but a vision in black lace walked through the door. The gown she was wearing looked more like a negligee than a dress, and unless his eyes deceived him, she was naked underneath. He'd never been one of those guys who ogled women's body parts, but her breasts moved when she did, and for a second, he couldn't tear himself away.

She made him burn, just the sight of her. It felt as though someone had struck one of those matches that wouldn't go out.

"Recognize it?" She touched the skirt of her gown. "It came from Velvet, Leather & Lace, your catalog."

"If only we had models who could make it look the way you do," he said. His gaze dropped from her coral-pink mouth to her breasts, again. They needed obedience school. Not her breasts. His eyes.

She smiled and set down the overnight bag she was carrying. On her way back up, she hooked her finger in the side slit of her gown and ripped it up to the top of her thigh.

It took Jamie a moment to find the words. "What are you doing?"

"Isn't this fun?" she said. "It's like Velcro. All it takes is a little tug and your clothes fall off."

Jamie thought his jaw might fall off.

She tugged at her bra strap, and it came apart with a soft ripping sound that he was very familiar with. The black lace cup drooped forward, revealing one lush, creamy breast, almost entirely. Her nipple peeked out at him like a shy child. If she ripped open the other one, she would be topless.

"Want to see what else it does?" She touched the other strap as if she'd read his mind.

"No, that's okay," he said. "I know what it does. I designed it."

"You designed StripLoc lingerie? How clever of you. I'll bet you're making couples all over the country very happy, possibly tonight. Sure you don't want me to demonstrate? I tried it at home."

"In that case, the gown should come with a warning label."

She gazed at him, seeming puzzled. "Why? Have I offended you somehow?"

"No, it's just that you're so... Wow."

Her smile warmed the room. "I'll take that as a compliment."

"Please do. You're a natural," he assured her. "I may have to put you in one of our ads." He was starting to wonder if someone had put her up to this. Maybe one of his partners? Either that or he should add another note in his black book after Lorna Sutton's name: playful exhibitionist.

"I love the gown," she said softly, standing there, more exposed than not. She looked like a luscious dessert made of strawberries and whipped cream. Her breasts were milky white, the nipples pink tipped, and the delicate black material covering her blushing flesh looked like a lace doily. She'd already sucked all the air from his lungs, and she'd only been in the house a few minutes.

It had happened that way before, too. He remembered their second date in haunting detail. It had stayed with him for months. They'd been like flowers and bees, unable to resist each other. He'd actually wondered if they'd been chosen by capricious gods to torment each other. Hell, they'd done it twice before they'd made it through his front door.

Jamie walked over to her, wondering what would happen if he touched her now. Would they both catch fire?

"VLL's lingerie has *never* looked better," he said, picking up her bag. He connected with her startling green gaze and drew a breath. "Now…how about a quick tour of the place."

She put her gown back together, but the damage to Jamie's powers of reasoning had been done. Even when he concentrated he wasn't much of a tour guide, but he did manage to point out that the great room where they were standing was a combination of kitchen, living and dining rooms, with a fireplace as the focal point. He showed her the French doors that led to the pool area, and after that he took her down the hallway and left her bag in the guest room, which also looked out on the pool. In the other direction was the third bedroom, which he'd converted to a workout room, and beyond that the master bedroom, which also had French doors leading to the pool area.

"Your house is charming," she said, sounding a little skeptical, "but we may want to soften things for the interview. The African theme is a bit macho."

"African theme?" Jamie had to think. "You mean

that wooden carving in the living room? The elephant plant stand?" It was Asian, according to the import store where he bought it.

Lorna didn't seem to have heard him. She was already on her way down the hallway toward his bedroom, and he had to stop and watch her go. It wasn't that she swiveled. He wouldn't call it swiveling, but her gown seemed to be moving in a different direction than her hips. Amazing. He hadn't designed it with that effect in mind. It almost made him dizzy.

He had no idea how he was going to be in the same house with her and not want to inhale her like a piece of cotton candy at the fair. He didn't understand her at all, and the confusion felt as if it could do him in. But what a way to go.

When he got into his bedroom, she was at his desk, studying the latest sketch on his pad. She actually reached out and touched the rendering with her fingers, and he could tell she was startled. She probably hadn't believed he actually did design some of the pieces.

"Jamie, look at this sketch!"

He glanced over her shoulder at the model in her butter-yellow silk pantaloons and corset. His mind immediately went to how Lorna would look in the outfit with her lush breasts spilling out of the corset. Spectacular, he realized. *She would look spectacular in anything.*

The idea for the old-fashioned cami-pajamas had come to him after one of his late-night discussions with Natori, who'd said that an undressed woman wasn't nearly as sexy as a half-undressed woman. Jamie had thought about it, and agreed.

"What do you think?" he asked Lorna. "I was going for a *Tom Jones* feel, the movie."

"What do I think?" She turned and pinned him with her big green eyes, pinned him like an insect. "I think it's *me*. Look at that woman, and tell me she isn't me!"

"It isn't you," Jamie said, but when he really looked at the sketch, he felt a hollow sensation invade his chest. Shit. It couldn't be her.

"She's one of the catalog models who works for us," he explained. His voice had lost conviction, but he made up for it with volume. "I liked the way she wore my clothes, and I had her in mind when I designed this."

"A model with a mole on her breast?" Lorna pointed out the sexy dark spot in the woman's décolletage, making sure Jamie saw it. And then she ripped the strap from her bodice, letting it fall open again. There was an identical mole snuggled just inside her cleavage.

"Does your model have one of these?" she asked. "Does any other woman you know have one of these? Right there? Where mine is?"

Her breasts bounced as she thrust them at him. Jamie was beginning to understand the fantasies of men who dreamed of being smothered to death by a woman's bosom.

"You need to keep your clothes on," he said. "People get thrown in jail for indecent exposure." Lame, but it was the only thing that came to him. He'd just realized it *was* her in the sketches. Lorna Sutton was his muse, and he hadn't even realized it.

"Indecent exposure? This from the man who's secretly exploiting me and using my body to inspire his lascivious designs? A man who hasn't spoken to me in six months? Maybe now I know why."

He backed her to the wall. "What are you implying? That my sketches are somehow violating your rights?

If you can prove that's you in those sketches, be my guest. I didn't realize it myself."

She averted her eyes, but only for a second.

"Why are you here?" he asked her, "dressed like that, in one of my designs?"

"Because you called me and invited me!"

"You're not a reporter or the paparazzi? You're not some practical joke sent by my partners?"

"I don't know your partners. I didn't even know you worked for VLL. You called and offered me a deal, which by the way, we haven't discussed. I'll take the all-expenses paid vacation. To Tahiti, if you don't mind. I have a thing about palm trees and trade winds."

"Fine, fine." He stared deeply into her eyes, wondering who this beautiful witch woman was and how she'd managed to derail him twice now. If she was here under false pretenses, he would find out and there would be hell to pay. But right now, it didn't matter what *she* was up to; *he* wanted to be up against her. His hands tingled with the urge to rip her negligee off by its StripLoc'd seams. His groin tingled with the urge to have her ripe, juicy body against his and to kiss her as senseless as she was making him.

## CHAPTER THREE

THE PILLOW WAS TOO WARM and it smelled of him. She flipped it over, knowing that wouldn't solve the problem. It was too warm because of her, and it smelled of him because it was his pillow, and she'd insisted on taking his room.

The mint she detected was probably toothpaste, and the notes of cedarwood and pine were from his cologne. Of course, there was that male thing. Pheromones, she'd read somewhere. They had no discernible odor but supposedly they shot straight to the susceptible part of a woman's brain and toggled on her hormones.

She switched pillows and lay there, eyes open, wondering if she would be smelling other things now. Perfume? Hairspray? This bedroom must be where he brought his women. And with his rock star looks he probably had groupies, whom he loved and left on a regular basis, if the way he'd dropped her was any indication.

She really didn't want to think he was that much of a rogue. But he'd really had her with those sketches. She'd had several sleepless hours to think about it, and she'd realized that Jamie Baird had a lot at stake, and desperation could drive a man to do slimy things. How did she know that he hadn't whipped up a couple sketches of her, thinking she would be flattered to death, and it would close the deal when she saw them? Although, he had certainly done a good job of looking shocked when she'd recognized herself.

He *was* a rogue.

Both pillows landed in a heap on the floor as she sat up. It was too warm to sleep anyway. And at thirty she was too young for hot flashes. She'd taken off the black lace negligee and slipped on a short kimono. She was wearing only panties underneath, and if it hadn't been for her concern that he might wander in to get something he needed, she would have been wearing nothing.

She could see without turning on lights. The moon was full, and the French doors and the skylight provided plenty of illumination as she got out of bed and went over to his desk for another look at the sketches.

It was her all right, and he had talent to spare. He'd made her look sexy and sweet at the same time. Yummy, she thought, which wasn't bad. Chocolate sundaes were yummy, as were purring kittens and the madly sensual shape of a man's behind. Yummy and biteable. Maybe that was the secret of his success. He could make a woman look good enough to eat. Any woman.

After their second date, she'd been riddled with questions and doubts about herself. She was certain she'd been too wild and fast, and she'd also wondered if he was secretly turned off by women of size. Otherwise, why did he drop her like a hot potato? The rejection had almost driven her to dieting, and then she'd decided to hell with that—and him. No man was going to make her feel that bad about herself.

The faint sound of splashing water distracted her from her thoughts. She did a quick visual check of the master bath to see if anything was running, and realized the noise was coming from outside. Both the bedroom and bathroom had French doors that led to the terrace.

She'd left them open for air circulation, and it sounded as if someone was swimming in the pool. What a refreshing thought.

She tied the kimono around her and went out to investigate. If it had been a different situation or anyone else, she would have put on a more concealing robe. But it was him, the rogue, and if he felt any attraction for her naked legs, let him suffer. If he didn't, she would know soon enough.

He was swimming laps. His stroke was smooth and fluid, and the muscles of his shoulders rippled as easily as the water. The moonlight made it all very beautiful, a solitary swimmer cutting through ribbons of black and molten silver. Lorna was surprised at his athleticism. She would have thought him too busy to be in such great shape.

She walked to the edge of the pool, and he suddenly surfaced at her feet, breaking the water with resounding force. He must have known she was there. She didn't think he missed very much.

Silvery water made his facial muscles look powerful and his dark eyelashes long and spiky. He had naturally wavy hair and lots of it. She watched it spring back from the weight of the water and curl at the nape of his neck. He'd always looked good enough to eat, but right now he looked good enough to drink, too. A tall glass of hard lemonade on ice or spiked iced tea. Something cool and bracing, with a kick.

Lord, she was thirsty.

He threw his head back to let the water pour off him. "You're up late," he said.

"I couldn't sleep."

"Neither could I. It's too hot. And that mattress in the guest room is filled with rocks."

*Good,* she thought, *he was suffering.* Not enough, and not for the right reasons, but it was a start.

"How's *my* bed?" he asked her.

"A change of linen would be nice."

"There's nothing wrong with those sheets. They were fresh out of the dryer."

She lowered her voice to a whisper. "You slept in them. I can smell you."

He whispered back. "You can *smell* me? Is that some kind of sexual thing?"

Lorna made the terrible mistake of getting flustered. Normally she was armed and dangerous in a verbal duel, but his searingly husky voice had caught her off guard. Rule number one when obedience training a man, she reminded herself. If you want to put him in his place, do not blush!

Jamie was already undressing her with his eyes. He'd removed her kimono as effectively as if he'd pulled the tie and whisked the silken robe off her in one bold stroke. Still whispering, he said, "No one is forcing you to sleep in my bed. That was your idea."

"No reporter is going to believe that I live here unless I'm totally comfortable," she reminded him. When they had discussed sleeping arrangements earlier, she'd explained that she had to inhabit the entire house as if it were hers, or she wouldn't be convincing, and that included his bedroom. He'd agreed. Yet more evidence of his desperation, as far as she was concerned

"If you want to trade beds," he said, "I'll be happy to oblige. And trust me, the reporter will never know."

"If I want your bed, or anything else—"

"Just whistle," he said, cutting her off.

Obedience training was too good for him, she decided. Someone ought to muzzle him, which was precisely what would happen when she did the interview. She would become Jamie Baird and he wouldn't be able to do or say a thing. She might even introduce him as her assistant. Oh, what fun. If that was her inner *B* word coming out to play, it was about time.

"Say the word, Lorna," she whispered, correcting herself.

They were at the deep end of the pool, and the ladder to climb out was on the wall a few feet away. He swam there and pulled himself out. Lorna almost didn't want to watch. Water streaming over his face was one thing. Water streaming over his rugged body was going to be quite another.

She was already intimately familiar with his chest hair. She'd felt it tickling her skin when they'd made love on his dining room table. By then he had his shirt unbuttoned and her bra pushed up, which had bared her breasts in the most erotic way imaginable, and freed him to do unspeakable things. They never got their clothes all the way off. Who had time?

But that was then and this was now. Did she really want to see his chest hair all drenched and glued to his muscles? His swim trunks clinging to the bulges between his legs?

Apparently so.

She couldn't rip her gaze away as he walked toward her. He was ungodly gorgeous, especially those sexy bulges. Cold water looked hot on him. His chest was mostly smooth except for the crescents of dark hair arcing over his pecs and the feathery arrow between his abs. He was built like a Greek deity, except for the bulges, where he was considerably larger. It looked as if he might be flirting with an erection.

Even the possibility turned her to liquid. She could

hear gurgling in the pit of her stomach. Dammit *all,* she was weak.

She guessed him to be just over six feet, and she was just under five feet six, if she cheated and stood on her tiptoes. She certainly couldn't intimidate him with her stature so she had to find other ways. And she would use every wicked one of them. Thank God he didn't have breasts and she did.

He grabbed a towel from a deck chair and blotted his face as he walked over to her. "Why are we whispering?" he asked.

"Because it's late, and I assume your neighbors like to sleep."

"Sleep, yes, I used to like it myself."

Lorna had never imagined it could be arousing to watch a man raise his arms and towel off his pits. It was with this guy. Hell, she would probably get aroused watching him brush his teeth. By the time he'd worked the towel over his chest and down to his thighs, she was fighting the urge to cross her legs and squirm. Maybe he needed help with the other side? He did have the loveliest rear end. She could remember touching it when he was buried deep inside her. And gripping it for dear life when that beautiful storm came over her.

Why was she attracted to men like this? To rogues and sexual desperados? She needed a glandectomy!

"Why don't you take a swim?" he suggested, tossing the towel aside. "Get comfortable with the pool."

"I'm naked under this kimono," she informed him.

"I won't look."

Sure. Just like *she* hadn't looked. At least she had the attention off his body and on hers, which relieved her anxiety, but not by a whole lot. She didn't normally flaunt herself this way. She'd always been self-conscious about her ample curves, but he didn't seem to be bothered by them. She hadn't picked up any signs of distance or disapproval, and she was very sensitive to those things. In fact, he seemed pretty interested in what she had going on under her kimono.

"Maybe we should discuss the interview," she said. "I'll need to be prepared."

"Tomorrow. I'll coach you on everything you need to know. Right now, since we're both awake, let's relax and get to know each other. How about a drink?"

"Sure. A lemonade would be great. Hard, if you have it." She almost blushed again.

"Hard lemonade? You are an interesting woman."

"It's very tasty," she assured him. "Sour and citrusy. Makes my mouth pucker just thinking about it."

He gave her mouth a smoldering look. "Will Long Island iced tea do? I'll throw in a lemon wedge just to watch your mouth pucker."

She nodded and he headed off to the gazebo bar on the other side of the terrace. She hadn't noticed the bar before, but his backyard was lovely. The pool lights turned the water a vibrant turquoise, and the surrounding gardens bloomed with flowering bushes and trees. The night breezes were sweet, and somewhere beyond the foliage, she could hear the waters of the canal softly rushing.

Lorna felt as if she were lost in a tropical jungle. It might just be the perfect night for seduction. With that thought in mind, she arranged herself on a chaise lounge to wait for him. She let her kimono gape open, knowing what it would reveal every time she reached over to pick up her drink from the table between them.

Jamie returned with the drinks, set them on the table and stretched out in the other chair, still beautifully damp and disheveled from his swim.

Her iced tea had three lemon wedges. She heaped him with polite thanks and reached for her drink. "Have you learned how to pick out melons yet?" she asked.

His moonlit gaze went straight to her deeply plunging neckline. "I'm not as good as I'd like to be," he said. "Are you offering lessons?"

She set her glass down and leaned toward him, crowding her breasts with her arms. She could feel them rise and shimmer with her movements, and the sensation sparked a sweet little gush of excitement in her nether parts, which was not exactly what she had in mind. She wanted *him* to gush.

"It's very easy," she assured him. "The melons need to be firm, yet soft and supple to the touch. It's always good to jiggle them a little to make sure they're ripe and ready."

"Really?" He cleared his throat and took a long drink of the tea.

"Oh, jiggling is a must. It tells you whether a melon is juicy or not. Smelling works, too. And if the fruit is large you can cup it in your hand and tap it with your fingers. Gently, of course. You wouldn't want to bruise the tender flesh."

"Oh, hell, no."

She glanced down at the abundance of her own tender flesh. Spilling out of the robe would be putting it mildly. She tweaked the kimono together, pretending modesty, and then she leaned toward him, and everything popped open again.

His poker face gave nothing away, but she thought she detected a line of perspiration on his upper lip. The effect on his swim trunks was even more gratifying.

"How does one smell a ripe melon?" he asked.

"With your nose, of course. It's a rich, musky odor.

You can't miss it. Melons have a mound, you know. Yes, they do. It's at the warm, swollen end of the fruit. You can find it by handling them. Don't be afraid to handle them to your heart's content. And when you find the mound, you just breathe in, easy as that. Of course, the real test is to give it a little bite and see how it responds, but then you'd have to buy it, so I wouldn't do that unless you're quite sure this is the melon you want to eat."

He set his glass down. "You're telling me to bite a melon? Right there in the store? I'd get arrested."

"Not at all." She smiled. "*Mmm,* I can almost taste it, sweet and dripping with juice. Can't you?"

He let out a tight sigh. So tight it could have been a groan. "It's hot out here," he said. "Are you sure you don't want to go for a swim?"

"No, I'm fine, but please yourself." She ran her fingers inside the neckline of her robe, stroking her flushed skin. She was sticky hot and probably smelled like a strawberry patch. She would have loved a dip, but he didn't need to know that.

"I'll just get wet," he said.

She smiled. "Me, too."

He dived in and swam like a dolphin under water. But when he came up, he clutched his side and gave out a howl.

Lorna sprang from the chair. "What's wrong?" she called to him.

"I don't know. It's my chest. It's tight as a fist. It feels like my heart."

She was certain he wasn't having a heart attack. It was probably a cramp. "Can you swim?"

He went under, still gripping his side and Lorna panicked. She ran around to that side of the pool, but he was drifting to the center, and she couldn't get close enough to reach him without going in, too.

"Are you all right?" she shouted when he came up again.

She couldn't hear his answer, but he was clearly in pain. She could tell by the way he was grimacing. She still wanted to believe it was a cramp. All that talk of melons had overstimulated him. He was probably overheated, and then he'd gulped down the entire glass of Long Island iced tea.

Lorna could barely swim. She should call 911, but there wasn't time. She had to do something. He went down again, and without another thought to her modesty—or her safety—she ripped off the robe and jumped in the pool.

# CHAPTER FOUR

JAMIE FELT SOMEONE fling an arm across his chest and pull him toward the surface. They broke water, and he got a lungful of air before they went back down again. The pain in his ribs was excruciating, like a nail being pounded into his side. It had been bad enough to stop him in the middle of a stroke, but he had no intention of drowning. He'd been waiting for the pain to ease.

Now he *couldn't* swim because she was clinging to him. It had to be Lorna, and she was going to drown them both. He glanced up and saw the bubbles escaping from her mouth and nose. She definitely wasn't a swimmer. She wasn't even holding her breath.

Jamie rolled, trying to reverse their positions. The move brought a stab of pain—and sank them lower. They weren't going to make it to the surface unless he could break her grip, but she had him in some kind of headlock.

He kicked hard and pulled her under, turning her into his arms. His only goal was to get her the hell out of there, but she didn't seem to want to go with him. She tussled with him, and they rolled and writhed like two underwater lovers. Their arms and legs got entangled. Their bodies bumped in the most intimate ways.

Her breasts were all over him. Buoyed by the water, they bobbed and shivered like pale moons in the darkness. They brushed up against his chest. They caressed his arms and his face. They did everything but call out to him "Fondle me!" He'd never seen anything so erotic as this woman's body. It amazed him that she could arouse him at a time like this, when his entire being was riveted on getting her to safety.

As he pinned her to his side and swam for the surface, he realized that she had on nothing but panties. Skimpy black panties. Otherwise, she was naked in his arms, and that awareness nearly sapped his strength. He could feel himself surrendering to the mindless pleasure of her nakedness, and his body responded. Inside him a depth charge had been detonated, and it was heading due south.

He held her close as they burst through the water. She gasped for air, spluttering and cursing. "You could've drowned me!"

"You could've drowned us both," he said as he swam with her toward the ladder. "Now relax. I've got you, and I'm not letting go."

She was quiet only for a moment. "I thought you were having a heart attack," she accused.

"I did, too, but the pain is gone."

"It was a cramp, silly. Not your heart."

"Shh," he told her, "save your strength."

Ignoring him, she continued to speak, even as he helped her out of the pool. He went up the ladder first and then guided her, lifting her into his arms as she climbed. He was a little disappointed that he wouldn't have to give her mouth-to-mouth. Anyone who could talk that much wasn't having any trouble breathing.

"Let me help you to a chair," he said, sheltering her with his body.

"I can do it." She refused his help, but the minute he stepped away from her, she was exposed.

And to his everlasting shame, he took full advantage of it. He didn't get her a towel the way a gentleman would have. He just gazed at her, silently shaking his head and totally knocked out by what a vision she was.

He took another step back and said softly, "My God, Lorna, you're beautiful."

She made an attempt to cover herself, but as she met his gaze, there was an almost audible click between them. Her hands dropped to her sides. "No, I'm not. I'm too—"

"You're not too anything, except beautiful." He cleared the fire from his throat, which seemed to be one of the hazards of being anywhere near her. Fire. She was the source of his glorious turmoil, and he would have sworn that she wasn't unaware of it. She seemed suspiciously fascinated by his struggle.

He couldn't stop himself. Just as he'd had to gaze at her and tell her how beautiful he was, he now had to move. He had to walk to her, touch her.

She made no attempt to stop him as he stroked her cheek and moved close to whisper how desirable she was. She even let him kiss her lightly on the mouth. But she gasped with surprise when he bent to her breast. He dragged his lips over the areola, nuzzling her, and then he drew the nipple into his mouth, giving it a sensual tug.

Her moan of appreciation made him instantly hard. It hit a switch and sent a bolt of current through him. His swim trunks had been loose a moment ago. Now, a pounding erection had taken up the slack. Oh, that ache. It was so wild and sweet.

Her fingers combed into his damp hair. "Not again," she whispered. "We're not going to do this again, are we?"

Her voice was choked with sweet despair. She was

pleading for reason, for deliverance, but she wasn't going to get it. And neither was he. No relief in sight from this insanity. She was crazy with desire, crazy in heat, just as he was.

"How can we not?" He left her breast to sprinkle kisses all over her face. Her naked flesh made him ache, but the bewilderment in her expression called to him like a siren from the rocks. He understood the fear brightening her eyes. Her heart was pounding out of control. The beats radiated through him, inciting his own heart. This was crazy, contagious. People got hurt when they gave in to these impulses.

But how could they not?

He slowed it down. The plan was to let her vital signs return to normal, but she looked up at him instantly, and their gazes connected with irresistible force. The silence deepened. The only sound that could be heard was the soft rush of the canal waters. He brushed her lips with the back of his thumb and stroked her cheek.

"I was wondering if you were ever going to kiss me," she said.

"I've been doing nothing but kiss you," he protested.

"My mouth." She tipped her chin, offering soft, full lips.

Another jolt to the groin. She killed him, this woman. She knew right where it hurt, and she went there. Didn't spare him a thought. He breathed a warm kiss to each of her eyebrows and lashes, to her cheeks and chin. Little kisses everywhere but her waiting mouth. He wondered if she understood the trap that she was baiting for both of them.

"You taste like the county fair," he said, "like cotton candy and ice cream bars with sprinkles."

His diversion seemed to work because she almost smiled. "Then you must be one of those frozen bananas."

"Pretty well thawed by now, young lady."

"Really?" She bumped her pelvis up against his erection, and her eyes widened at the size of him. His eyes got narrow, he was sure. She was playing with fire. Did she know that? He'd obviously emboldened her by slowing things down, but she was still naked, and he was still painfully aroused.

"I did love those bananas," she said.

"I'd be happy to share."

He must have sounded sarcastic, but he longed to drag her into his arms and crush the breath out of her. Just holding her would release some of this maddening pressure. Instead, he stepped back.

She made a little sound of discontent, but didn't attempt to hide herself from him this time. She seemed to be offering up every gorgeous, shivery inch for his inspection. A fertility goddess. Moonlit. Moonstruck? He should be so lucky. It pleased him that he wasn't twitching and salivating like a wolf that had spotted its prey.

She touched her breasts, just a pinky finger drifting along the swollen outside curve. Her exploration was slow and curious, as if she was trying to understand something.

"Is it my breasts that make you hot?" she asked.

The words weren't out of her sweet mouth before he felt another surge of heat to his shaft. He was a bull on a chain. Worse, she was still touching herself. Against his will, he watched her fingers glide over her own nipple and tickle it to hardness. They were hesitant, exploratory. Was she trying to stimulate herself? It was certainly working on him.

He called her on her question. "You seem pretty sure that I'm hot—and you're the reason why."

"Well, yes, unless you're selling tents these days. Look at you."

He gave it his best innocent-bystander shrug. "It's these shorts I'm wearing. They bunch up."

"*These* shorts?" She reached down and stroked him through the cotton. "The ones made of tent material?"

The urgency of her touch hit him like a hammer. It didn't matter that she was slow and languid in everything she did. His heart was a rocket. It took off at the speed of light, and so did his imagination.

"Does this make you hot, too?" She asked the question with a straight face, but she was playing dirty. Her fingers slid down his engorged shaft to his sacs, and she sidled close enough to cup them in her hand. "How about this?"

Her firm grasp took his breath away. "I think we're done taking my temperature." He gripped her wrist and held her away from him. He intended to be gentle, but he needed distance. Her, at arm's length. His control was as thin as thread, and another touch would snap it.

However, he wasn't done with Nurse Sutton. She might be a goddess, according to the notes in his black book, but he wasn't a god. He was all too human and prey to the sins of the flesh.

"How did it feel when you touched yourself?" he asked her.

She didn't seem to know how to answer. "Wonderful," she got out.

"Wonderful, like this?" He brushed his mouth to the delicate outer curve of her breast, where she'd caressed herself. She shuddered with pleasure, and he ached to give her more. But he held off, waiting for her to come to him. He enjoyed the temporary reversal of power. It was good to have her on the ropes, breathing hard. And he loved every second of this wickedness she elicited in him. Or maybe he'd elicited it in her. He didn't know anymore. It was all good.

"Not fair," she whispered. "Exquisite, but not fair."

"All's fair." He teased her with his tongue, flicking it gently.

"Oh, Lord, don't make me do this."

"Do what?"

"Come apart right here in your arms. Don't make me do something crazy like that."

She arched her spine, filling his mouth with her soft flesh. His reaction was instinctive. He clamped down on her nipple and sucked. His hands found the heat of her buttocks and everything inside him tightened with pleasure. He gave her breast another deep pull.

"Don't make me…come…apart…"

Little guttural sounds swam in her throat, and she began to undulate. He moved to the breast he hadn't kissed, which set off a chain reaction of sighs, every one of which thrilled him. She thrilled him, the crazy woman. She tossed her head, moaning and thrusting. And all at once, she emitted a harsh little cry that sounded as if she were on the brink of the orgasm she didn't want.

"Jamie," she gasped, "I think you should stop. No, wait, don't!"

*Don't stop.* That was what he heard.

He dropped to one knee and breathed a kiss of tribute to the mound between her thighs. As his hot breath penetrated her black silk panties, she sighed and squirmed against him. It was one of the sexiest caresses his mouth had ever known. Lord, how he wanted to slide his fingers inside those panties and stroke her to completion. If she was going to heaven, he wanted to make sure she got there and back.

Her whimper sent blood pounding through the chambers of his heart, his loins. He could hardly tell one sensation from another anymore as he seduced her through the silk, tracing her soft curves and watching her quiver. When he delved inside, she was already wet. Drenched in sweetness.

He pulled aside the black triangle to admire her blazing red curls. She looked like a birthday ribbon, all satin loops and ruffles. And beneath the bow was a gift, a secret portal containing drops of ambrosia that could intoxicate a man and nearly kill him with pleasure. A gift, waiting to be opened.

His tongue found the nectar. And she found some kind of nirvana in every wet, delicate stroke. He could hear it in her throaty cries.

"This is wrong," she whispered. "It's just wrong."

"It must be," he said. "Anything this incredible has to be wrong."

He glanced up at her anguished expression—and at the same time caught the rich scent of her female excitement—fiery body heat and sweet juices flooded out of her, the perfume of a goddess.

"You're wet," he told her, "gushing."

"Don't rub it in." She looked almost angry as she sank her hands into his hair and drew him back to her. "Oh, dammit, do. Do rub it in."

He gathered her to him, his fingers luxuriating in her beautiful bottom. But the instant he sought out her secrets, she went rigid. Her hands curled into his hair, forming fists, and he wondered what could be happening to make her legs quake so violently.

"Lorna, are you all right?"

WAS SHE ALL RIGHT?

No. Lorna most definitely was not. She was about to collapse. Her body was building to a crescendo beyond anything she'd experienced, and her legs shook uncontrollably. They didn't want to hold her another minute, but at the same time, she was frozen, fed by the soaring pleasure he gave her. She'd locked her hands in his hair because she was disintegrating, and she had nothing else to hold on to, but his every caress sent a shock wave through her. A sweet shock wave.

"Jamie!" She tried to step back and lost her balance, falling against him as he rose. Maybe he planned it this way?

He whisked her up in his arms, whispering in her ear. "You taste like bliss," he told her, "and I need to know how bliss feels. I need to be inside you."

She knew what was going to happen, and she didn't have the strength to defend against it. Her body had not finished what it started, and it was crying out for him. They would do it in the chaise lounge, in the bushes, maybe in the pool itself. Once it began, it would never stop. There was no holding back this tidal wave they'd created.

One realization hit her after another. Jamie Baird touched needs in her that no other man ever had, and as much as that thrilled her, it wasn't why she was here. She was supposed to be teaching him a lesson about women, and this was no way to go about it. If she made love with him now, he might even think that women were fatally attracted to rogues, and they weren't. She wasn't.

Her last awareness was a revelation about him. He wasn't turned off by her size, not the least little bit. But if that wasn't the reason he'd backed away all those months ago, then what was?

Hunger fired his kisses and burned through his low growls of desire. The sounds were harsh and thrilling, and she hoped they meant that he was as desperate as she was. He had better not be getting off scot-free when she was suffering this agony of ecstasies. He had better not be getting off at all. If she had any willpower, she would end this craziness, tell him never to touch her breasts again—and mean it. Call it sexual aversion therapy, which was just about what Jamie Baird deserved.

But then again, if she did have sex with him, he wouldn't be able to run out on her this time. She was his houseguest, *and* he needed her for the interview. That might be even more painful for an intimacy phobic like him. Watching him panic the next morning over pancakes and eggs, and knowing it wasn't about her inadequacies, would be sweet justice. Squirm, you gorgeous weasel.

If only it didn't require that they have mad, passionate, out-of-control sex first. Her body began to quiver at the thought and she could feel the tremors all the way through to her spine. She couldn't do it.

"Put me down," she said. "Please, just put me down."

He searched her face. "Are you sure?"

"Yes, yes!"

He made a valiant attempt to do as she asked, but there was something in the way, Lorna realized. His erection. It was like a safety net, stopping all things from falling. There was no way not to come into contact with it, no matter which way he turned her body, or twisted his.

"Sorry," he said, rocking her forward.

Lorna had begun to wonder if he was purposely rubbing her bottom against the damn thing to arouse her— because it was working. She was melting inside and out, turning to steam everywhere his hardness touched her. Each little slide and bump weakened her will, and she knew in her heart that nothing could save her. She clenched her legs, but he felt like a branding iron against the back of her thighs, and by the time he'd penetrated the barrier, she'd already lost the battle.

Desire lit her up like a flare. She gasped softly, and suddenly nothing else mattered. Who cared about teaching him lessons? She wanted this man. In the chaise lounge, on the terrace, in the pool, wherever.

When her feet touched the ground, she fell into his arms and kissed him so passionately they both lost their balance. He grabbed her, but they were already tumbling backward, and nothing could stop them, not even his massive efforts.

Lorna's foot came down on the edge of the pool— and then there was nothing. She dangled in thin air for a millisecond, clinging to Jamie before she tipped over backward—and took him with her. They both plunged into the water, and a part of Lorna went into shock, unable to grasp what was happening. She was still clinging to Jamie, still crazy to make love with him and lose herself in that ecstasy. *She didn't want to let go. She wouldn't.*

But another part of her had been shocked awake. The reasoning part of her was already whispering, warning her of the danger she had narrowly averted. That part of her was talking common sense. It was reminding her that she was not as strong and self-contained as she might have thought, not as resolved—and it was telling her to be grateful for accidents.

As she and Jamie spiraled into the cool black depths, Lorna realized that it might be the only way to put out the flames that neither of them could extinguish. She'd already been in this pool tonight, and that dip had nearly drowned her. Maybe this dip would save her.

Grateful? Yes, maybe she was. And very wet. But at least this drenching might bring her to her senses. She'd written off as a fluke that one crazy night with him, but she'd been wrong. He was a challenge beyond her wildest imaginings, a challenge to everything she knew and understood, mostly about herself, and she would need every bit of help she could get to deal with him.

# CHAPTER FIVE

NOON? LORNA COULDN'T believe it. That's what the clock radio said, and the sun flooding through the French doors was so bright she had to peek at the digital display through her fingers. Had she really slept that late? Half the day was gone.

She threw off the black satin sheets that still smelled hauntingly of mint and pine forests, and sat up, wondering why Jamie hadn't awakened her. He might be sleeping, too. They'd had quite a night. The swimming pool had doused the flames, but it didn't get the embers. Her mind had burned most of the rest of the night away— and she imagined that his had, too.

She couldn't stop thinking about what would have happened if they hadn't fallen in the pool. Never mind the sexual bliss. Would he have been in bed with her now, his body curved behind hers, his arm carelessly draped over her breasts?

She whimpered in despair and left the bed. *She wanted it all, desperately. The entire mating dance, everything from eye contact to afterglow. Every sweet thing Jamie Baird could give her. She wanted it.*

Determined to break his hold on her mind, she made quick work of getting herself ready. Action would be her distraction. Smiling at the thought, she popped some rollers in her hair and then headed for the shower.

Twenty minutes later, record time for her, she was groomed, dressed for comfort in white cutoff jeans and a parfait-pink top, and ready to go. Even her hair had cooperated. The long burnished waves looked bouncy and freshly washed.

That must be a sign. A good hair day *had* to mean that the forces were on her side. Fortunately, the mission she had to accomplish would keep her from obsessing over what they'd done last night—and berating herself. He'd been as wound up as she had. Who made up the rule that she was the responsible party, even if she had used some wiles? He'd enticed her right back, and he was the sexual desperado, after all.

She stopped on the way out of the bedroom, curious about the dressmaker's dummy. It was draped with a cream-colored material that was as sheer and delicate as gossamer. She hadn't noticed before, but the design looked like an antique nightgown with a high lacy neck and pearl buttons, except that some vital parts were missing. Two large openings were cut into the bodice, each with a flap that could be buttoned to create the image of a pocket.

The gown must be for nursing mothers, Lorna decided. But then she noticed the skirt. It was tacked together with a panel between the legs, and a cutout where the crotch would have been. A birthing gown? Another opening in the back confused her, as did the false pockets along the side seams. All very strange, and there wasn't time to investigate further. She needed to find Jamie and get started with the coaching sessions.

As it turned out, finding him was the easy part. He was at the dining room table, bent over a legal pad and so absorbed with whatever he was writing that he didn't seem to have noticed her. It was harder to believe he hadn't noticed that this was the dining room table where he'd ravished her on their second date. To be fair, perhaps they'd ravished each other, but she wasn't thrilled he'd picked that exact spot today.

On that night she'd been up against the table, on the table *and* bent over the table, very near the spot where he was sitting. That might make it a little hard to concentrate, at least for her.

"Hey." He glanced up at her, his dark gaze sliding over the summery outfit she wore. "Today, you *look* like cotton candy."

She managed not to thank him for the compliment. He looked like an ad for the military in his camouflage-print trunks and muscle shirt. He could have been working on the engine of a jeep. Now she understood what the word *ripped* meant when it applied to arms and shoulders. She could see the visible grooves in his muscles, even when they weren't flexed. In fact, it was hard to take her eyes off them.

She slapped herself mentally. "Are those interview questions?" she asked, indicating his legal pad.

"Not the actual ones, but I have a pretty good idea what the reporter's going to ask, so I'm making a list of possible questions and answers for you to study. I'm almost finished. Meanwhile, are you hungry? I ordered in."

He got up from the table and showed her the island divider where he'd laid out an array of food. "Help yourself," he said. "There's a place down the street that makes the best *heuvos rancheros* in town. We've also got Spanish rice, black beans, hot tortillas and fresh salsa. Coffee's on the kitchen counter. I just made a fresh pot."

Her last meal had been an early dinner of corn chowder and a green salad. She was hungry.

"These eggs look good," she said, admiring the colorful dish. It bubbled with cheese and a rich red sauce, and the aroma of onions and peppers wafted up to tantalize her. She scooped up plenty of the *heuvos* and rice, heaping her plate. She also spotted a bowl of fresh fruit and some fluffy lemon muffins.

"Cream, sugar?" he asked, apparently intending to get her a cup of coffee.

"Thanks, but I'm swearing off." Caffeine was one of the stressors she'd eliminated in her quest to find balance and inner harmony. But the big one was supposed to have been men. Ha!

She narrowly avoided walking into a shiny metal pole as she went over to the counter to sit on one of the stools. She was not up for eating brunch on the dining room table, *everything* considered.

"Delicious," she said, rhapsodizing over a bite of eggs and Spanish rice.

He smiled, hovering. "Can I get you anything else?"

He stood right next to the pole she'd nearly hit. The floor-to-ceiling device looked as if it had come from a fire station, and a person could actually slide down it. She must have looked right through it when she'd first come into the room. He really did distract her. Last night she'd completely missed that odd gown hanging on the dressmaker's dummy.

"What is that thing?" she asked him.

"A pole."

"I can see that. Why is it in the middle of your kitchen?"

"It isn't normally in the middle of my kitchen, but if it were, it would be for pole dancing."

"You pole dance?"

"Let's just say Jamie Baird pole dances."

Lorna had been kidding. He obviously wasn't. He

shrugged as if to say why not? Wink, wink. Pole dancing is great exercise.

She gaped at him, wondering if she would ever get
her mouth shut again. "Tell me you're not serious.
Please, tell me you're not."

"It's great exercise," he said, slapping the pole.

He was *so* predictable. "If you're a firefighter, yes.
But I'm a carb-loving thirty-year-old woman who con-
siders yoga strenuous exercise, and you're not getting
me near that thing. Forget the vacation in Tahiti. Forget
you ever met me. The deal is off."

She rose from the stool and turned on her heel, but
her swinging foot hadn't even touched the ground before he whipped her back. They could have been taking
a tango lesson. "Jamie!"

"How do you know you won't like it?" he argued.
"You're beautiful, voluptuous and sexy. I'll bet you
could make that pole sweat just by—"

"It is not my goal in life to make a pole sweat. Any
pole, even your— Oh, never mind."

His eyes glinted, hot with male interest. He wanted
to pursue her slip of the tongue, but something else was
driving him.

"I am serious," he said. "You're a shapely woman,
Lorna, emphasis on woman. You could stop traffic. The
405 freeway would be a parking lot."

"Also *not* one of my goals."

"What is your goal?"

"To end this conversation?"

"All right," he said, releasing her. He nodded, as if
coming to his senses. A hurricane-force sigh escaped
him. "You don't have to pole dance. It was probably a
bad idea…but it would *really* help me if you did."

*"Why?"*

"Because it's good business. VLL is featuring the poles in the next catalog, and we're betting they'll be one of this year's hottest Christmas items. We have an entire pole-dancing package, and I'd like you to plug it during the interview."

"Oh, my God," she whispered. "I never agreed to anything like this. I'm not pushing packages for you, especially if poles are involved."

"No one's asking you to push anything." He went to the table and grabbed his sketch pad. "All you have to do is show this design to the reporter, tell him it's VLL's latest creation, and when he asks what it's for, you can show him the pole. There's no shame in that. You represent a lingerie company, Lorna. I mean Jamie. The pole is part of our marketing strategy for the goods we sell."

He held out the sketch pad, which she ignored. "The reporter's a he?"

"A he whose name is Hudley Campbell, and his normal beat is technology. Should be interesting."

"Won't he be angry when he finds out you duped him? Can you afford to make an enemy out of a *Times* reporter?"

"No," Jamie admitted, "which is why I'm going to offer him an exclusive after the fashion show. He'll get to break the real story on Jamie Baird. I'm hoping that will make him happy *and* generate more publicity for VLL. It's a risk, but I don't have much choice at this point."

"A risk because of the timing?"

"Right. An exposé about VLL's closet male could eclipse the launch of the show. It's impossible to control the media, especially when they smell a scandal. That's why I can't go public now. After the global launch, with any luck, it will keep the buzz going."

He'd thought of everything, and she didn't doubt that he would land on his feet. Guys like Jamie always did. "Would I be expected to talk about my designs," she asked, "meaning *your* designs?"

"If he brings it up, just be coy. Tell him we can't give away all our trade secrets. As I just said, I don't want him to break the story about Jamie Baird being a man. It would take the focus off the show and put it on me."

Reluctantly, Lorna took the pad from his hand. Even more reluctantly she admitted that his pole-dancing idea wasn't bad. The drawing wasn't finished. He hadn't completed the model's facial features, but he'd colored in the fabric, and it appeared to be a red velvet leotard, or maybe a cat suit. The lines were fabulous. The plunging V-neck would show off a woman's décolletage and the wrap midriff would support the bust and tuck in the waist, giving the illusion of an hourglass figure.

Now she was thinking like a designer?

Jamie poured himself another cup of coffee and returned. "Campbell will want to see some of the designs that will be featured in the satellite show. Would you be willing to show him this?"

Lorna nodded. "Yes, of course."

"Thank you." Relief was evident in his voice. "You can't tell by the drawing," he said, pointing to the design, "but the material is stretch velvet, and it does more than cling—it holds and controls. See how the fabric hugs the tummy and the butt?"

As he bent over her, pointing out various aspects of the outfit, she could feel the steamy combination of his breath and his body heat.

She glanced up at him. "Is this me?"

"The woman in the drawing? Is she you?" He met her gaze and very nearly stopped her heart. "Right down to the mole on her breast," he said, his voice growing increasingly husky.

"I don't see the mole." She touched her throat.

"Would you like me to draw it for you?" he asked.

Lorna didn't realize where her hand had drifted until she saw his eyes darken, and his face go hot. "It's right here," she said, pretending she'd meant to touch her breast all along. "But thanks anyway."

"Not a problem. Any time." He coughed and thumped his chest with his fist. "I have some calls to make. I'll leave you here with the interview material unless there's anything else you need. Oh, you haven't finished your breakfast. Want me to warm it up in the microwave?"

Lorna had taken exactly one bite. "Thanks," she said.

Just moments later, he had her settled on the great room couch with a lap tray, a plate of steaming food and his legal pad of questions and answers.

"Sorry I took up the whole dining room table," he said, "but this should be more comfortable anyway. And I just happen to have something to show you."

The great room had a large flat panel TV that dropped like a movie screen from the ceiling. Beneath the TV, a glass and mahogany console housed Jamie's video collection. He took an encased CD from a revolving rack in the console.

"This should answer any questions you might have about pole dancing," he said, showing her the case. "It's the video we're including in the package."

"I don't have any questions about pole dancing."

"You never know." He slipped the disk in the player and hit the button, then flashed her an encouraging smile and made his exit.

His teeth were sparkly enough for a toothpaste commercial.

Pointed canines, she observed. Don't be fooled. He probably polishes off little girls like you for brunch.

Lorna had given up on the *heuvos*. And if she had doubts about what pole dancing was, the video quickly cleared it up. The TV screen was filled with the image of a woman slithering up and down the pole and essentially making love to an inanimate object. The whole thing was rather snakelike. Jamie was right about it being good exercise…but only if you had the vertebrae of an anaconda.

Still, Lorna watched and became increasingly fascinated with the woman's fluid grace. She'd never seen anything quite so sensual. It was almost as if the pole were partnering the woman, and they were performing a strange and beautiful dance. They both seemed to be moving, although Lorna knew that wasn't possible.

She smiled as the woman gripped the pole and swung in a wide arc, flinging out her arm as if she were reaching for the gold ring. Next, she hooked the pole with her knee and arched backward from the waist, whipping around, her hair flying. The wicked part of Lorna would love to have tried that move, but not under the present circumstances.

Pole dancing might be the perfect opportunity to bring Jamie Baird—or any man—to his knees. But last night had cured Lorna of trying to teach him a lesson with her womanly wiles. She didn't have enough self-control for that. She would have to find another way to get her point across—and quickly. Scorned women everywhere were counting on her, and she was running out of time.

SHE WAS CIRCLING the pole. Jamie watched her from the terrace, hidden by the French doors. He hadn't intended to spy. He'd left her in the great room to prepare while he'd gone to the guest room to check his voice mail and make some phone calls.

The voice mail had been light, probably because it was the weekend, although some of his staff were working overtime now because of the show. There'd only been a dozen calls stacked up since last night. He'd left messages for his two partners, who were both heavily involved with other aspects of the show, and then he checked in with his assistant for updates, and to let her know he wouldn't be in the next day because of the interview. After that, he'd thought about crunching some numbers, but had decided to get some fresh air first. That's when he'd come outside and seen her through the door's louvers. Naked curiosity had held him fast.

She did fascinate him beyond comprehension, especially after last night. The physical attraction was obvious. She'd turned him into one of those Mayan fertility statues with penises like brickbats. It wasn't enough that his morning erection never went down; she stirred feelings in him that didn't make sense. When he was around her he felt happy and sad at the same time. It should be one or the other, right? What was it with these undifferentiated pangs? How was a man supposed to know if he was feeling good or bad?

It was tough enough to think with a perpetual hard-on. It was impossible with these...feelings.

*Maybe you should actually go crunch those numbers, Baird.*

It reassured him that a part of his brain was still struggling to make sense against the onslaught. He ignored it, of course, and maneuvered to get a better look at her through the space between the open doors. The woman hadn't stopped in the entire time since he'd been listening. She'd gone over the interview material, and then busied herself rearranging the area. He appreciated that she'd tucked away some of the guy stuff he'd overlooked, like his sports magazines and his barbells. When she was done with that, she had actually rehearsed some of the interview questions out loud—and she was good. Very natural. Very chatty and funny. The reporter was going to love her, thank God.

But now she was in the kitchen, circling the pole with an intrigued expression. And Jamie loved that. She looked as though she might want to try a move or two. He knew how sexy she could be. The pole was about to find out.

He drew in a breath as she let her fingers glide over the smooth metal surface. She wrapped her hand around it and tugged, probably testing it for strength. That gave him a couple of twinges, which only deepened as she clasped her other hand and fell backward, swaying.

She began to swing in a circle, drawing her body up and falling back, moving faster as she went around. He didn't fail to notice that each time she came up, her breasts made contact, brushing the pole and gliding along its smooth surface. It almost hurt to watch. If he could have traded places with anything in the world right then, it would have been that goofy pole.

"You really should try it," she said, giggling merrily. "It gets the blood racing, and it's great for erections."

Jamie's besotted brain snapped to attention. He thought she was talking to him. But she was looking the other way, and he realized she was pretending to talk to the reporter. She must be rehearsing again.

"Do I pole dance?" she said. "Oh, you bet. I've got a few moves in me."

Jamie sincerely hoped that she didn't plan to discusss

erections with Hudley Campbell. However, if she did a little demonstration, it should get plenty of attention, which would be good for VLL. He didn't know whether to be relieved or nervous that she was getting into the idea of being Jamie Baird.

Clearly, he was under too much pressure. There was a lot at stake beyond his personal interest in the company. VLL employed about thirty people at the administrative level, which was his baby. But that was a drop in the bucket compared to the work they subcontracted out. They didn't outsource the production of the clothing to other countries. It was done right here in the U.S. by hundreds of workers who needed their jobs. And then there were his partners, Samantha and Mia. He'd never seen two people work harder. This might be the company's only shot at a larger share of the market and he couldn't let their efforts be wasted.

Jamie's focus shifted back to Lorna, and he realized he was smiling. He had the feeling his body was smiling, too, in places it shouldn't be. Good thing she'd studied that interview material because he might just have to corner her a little later and give her a pop quiz.

## CHAPTER SIX

THE NIGHTGOWN was trying to take her hostage. If it *was* a nightgown. Lorna should have left it on the dressmaker's dummy where it belonged. Now that she'd slipped it on over her head, she couldn't tell what went where. Or where she was. She couldn't see anything, including a way out of the endless folds of gossamer and lace.

"Help," she mumbled, turning in a circle.

She tugged and pulled, but very gingerly, trying not to damage the sheer material. She would love to have taken it off, but she didn't have that option, either. She already had one arm through, but couldn't get the other. It wouldn't go past her shoulder. Possibly she was stuck in the leg hole. She'd forgotten about that strange panel sewn into the skirt. Thank God, it was a very *long* skirt. The rest of her body was covered, but barely.

She staggered around blindly, wondering if she should call for help. He would think she was developmentally challenged. She'd been hiding out in her room all afternoon and evening, avoiding Jamie and his pop quizzes. He'd wandered into the kitchen just after she finished pole dancing, and she'd been too winded to answer his questions. Plus, she'd been a little suspicious of his timing. It was also weird that he'd taken a sniff of the pole and said something about how it smelled of strawberries.

Hell, maybe she would just go to bed this way. She should be fine, as long as she didn't smother. Of course, she would never find the switch to turn out the lights. And if the arm that was caught over her head went to sleep, she would probably have to have it amputated.

"Lorna, are you in there somewhere?"

She froze. It was Jamie. And he wasn't calling from outside the door, he was right next to her. He'd let himself in, the sneak. He was probably going to be furious that she was messing around with his designer strait jacket, but she managed to sound indignant.

"Did you forget to knock?" she said, turning in the direction of his voice.

"I thought you were in trouble. You were talking to yourself in here."

"We single women talk to ourselves," she informed him. She could just make out a shadowy form through the layers of fabric. "It's therapy, which we need because we share a planet with certain men who tend to confuse us with fast food."

He hesitated, perhaps not sure how to argue with a person wearing a nightgown on her head. "Just as long as you don't answer, I guess."

"Oh, I've answered you many a time—and maybe you should count yourself lucky I did. I don't think you playboys know how often women, who are much too compassionate for their own good, come up with ways to excuse your behavior. I'm sure you've had more free passes than you deserve, Mr. Baird, if you deserved any."

*"Really?"*

He sounded ready to debate the point, but she had other plans for that discussion. She was saving her bullets for the interview. And he *had* actually explained himself to her on more than one occasion, even though he didn't know it. In her fantasies he had begged her to forgive him and made extravagant promises, as he should have. She should have written up a transcript of that conversation and sent it to him. It might have been educational.

She made one more attempt to squirm her way into the gown—and gave up with a whimpering gasp. "Could you help me with this thing?"

"That depends. Are you putting it on or taking it off?"

"*On.*"

"May I ask why?"

Because she didn't have the option of taking it off. She had nothing on underneath. It hadn't made sense to try a nightgown like this on over clothing.

She gave the material a determined tug and heard a ripping sound. "Oh, sorry! Hope I didn't ruin anything."

"You ruin it, you buy it." He laughed softly. "Now hold still, and let me help you."

She was in no position to argue. When he told her to relax her shoulder muscles and let out all the air in her lungs, she did it, exhaling deeply. But the real obstacle seemed to be her breasts, and no amount of deflation was going to help there.

Jamie grumbled to himself. "I never thought I'd hear myself saying that a woman's body was too much of a good thing. But something has to go."

"My breasts aren't going anywhere."

"I wasn't talking about your breasts, but that's an idea. I suppose we could try cling wrap and butter."

"What?" Lorna let out an astonished yelp. Her arms were restrained and she couldn't stop him no matter what he did. "No cling wrap and no butter! And no touching, either."

"You're no fun. You're probably going to say no kissing, too."

"You kiss it, you buy it."

Lorna heard a ripping sound, and the relief she felt was instant. She could breathe again. "What did you do?"

"Opened a seam. They're just tacked together. Now, let's get you dressed."

She tried to work with him, but it required gyrating in some rather embarrassing ways as he eased the tightest part of the gown over the fullest part of her body. She'd said no touching, but that was impossible. His hands were all over her, touching, tickling, taking her breath away one startled gasp at a time. Worst of all, the sensations were annoyingly stimulating. *Aiii.*

Her breath was steamy hot against her face, and her heart was agitated, and even though she didn't want to, she was making it worse by trying to anticipate where he would touch her next. Every time he did she started like a deer, but somewhere way down deep, she also melted just a little. Under protest, mind you, but she melted anyway.

What could she do? She needed his help, but this was a dangerous way to get it. Her resolve was slipping away, if she'd ever had any. They might both be turned on before it was over, and she was much more worried about herself than him.

Finally, between them, they coaxed the gown down until her head popped through the lacy collar. She pulled a deep breath, her panic easing a little. That was too much like nearly drowning in the pool last night. It took a few more minutes to get her arms in the sleeves and her legs in the right places. The gown was actually designed like a long skort, a combination of shorts and a skirt.

He laughed a little as she shook back her hair and looked up at him. She blushed and averted her eyes, laughing, too. Those hands of his were still hotly lingering on her breasts, at least in her mind, and it was hard to look him straight in the eye. Besides, she felt patently ridiculous for having gotten herself trapped in an article of clothing, even one this complicated.

"Thanks for not letting me smother," she said. "What is this thing I'm wearing?"

"A work in progress. When it's done it will be the sexiest piece in the winter collection. At least that's the plan."

"Sexy? This?" She hated to be the one to tell him, but—

She glanced down at the strange gown with all its lace flaps and pearl buttons, false pockets and seams. More than anything, it reminded her of a gossamer mousetrap. And by the way, where was that seam he'd opened? Was she exposed somewhere?

He stepped back to look at her. "Hot," he said with a nod of approval.

"Warm," she conceded, "but only from the wrestling match."

"You haven't seen what this baby can do." His pride was evident. "It's top secret. Not a word to anyone, especially Hudley Campbell."

She had no idea what the secret was, so it shouldn't be too hard to keep. And at the moment she was more interested in what Jamie was wearing. It looked like a kimono-type robe, loosely tied, and from the glimpses she got of the opening he didn't seem to have anything on underneath.

Had she sighted bare skin? A ripple of inner thigh?

He looked as if he'd just rolled out of bed and thrown on the robe. His hair was all over his head, wonderfully dark and tousled. His legs were great, too. Long and brawny, the muscles softened by downy dark hair. He had some grooves there, too.

Why did he have to show up tonight, looking like a

god awakened from his nap? It seemed the sillier she got, the sexier he got. But apparently what she really wanted was a penis sighting. And she was fascinated enough with the possibility to keep checking the way his robe was tied, wondering if it might come undone.

"I was just admiring your robe," she explained when he caught her looking. "I don't suppose you designed it."

"I don't suppose—and I doubt you're going to like sleeping in that thing." He was talking about the gown now. "Any time you're ready to take it off, I'd be happy to help."

"I can manage." She touched one of the pocket flaps on the bodice. "What are these gizmos?"

"They're peek holes."

Her hand jumped back. "Let me guess. This is not a nursing gown."

"When you're right, you're right." An engaging grin. "It's not for nursing babies, it's for making them."

"And you let me put it on? Without telling me?"

"You can't get pregnant by wearing it."

She glanced down cautiously. "You're right about that." She would have guessed it was for birth control, not fertility.

"It's a Victorian wedding nightgown," he explained. "The flaps and openings are there so the groom can avail himself of his bride's naughty parts without her having to endure the indignity of undressing."

"Really?" Her stomach dipped oddly, but she understood the part about indignity. "What's this thing between my legs?"

"Now there's a loaded question." His gaze brushed over her like a smoldering torch. "If you're talking about the nightgown, the chastity panel between your legs has an open seam in the crotch so the groom can please his bride with relative ease."

"Never mind. I get the picture."

Now Lorna felt as if she'd lost her stomach on a carnival ride. A swirling emptiness filled the pit of her belly, which was a total contradiction in terms. The smart move would have been to lose the gown and end this conversation, whichever way she had to do it. Nakedness seemed less dangerous than the steamy images he was painting in her mind. She'd already tried to block them out, but they were too damn sneaky and subversive.

A battle of wills was waging inside her, and the wrong side was winning. She gave in with a sharp little sigh, allowing herself to imagine what it would be like to be a Victorian bride, seduced in the dark through the openings in her gown. A man's hands sliding through those openings, his lips and tongue...

She fingered one of the pearl buttons on the breast pocket, startled as it slipped through the buttonhole that held it. The flap fell open, capturing her creamy flesh in a lace frame, as if someone had just taken an erotic picture of her breast. Even the rosebud tip was exposed.

She covered herself with her hand and colored hotly. "Are these pockets rigged?"

He shrugged. "Absolutely. A sudden move will undo them. Can't have anything dampening the wedding night fires."

"God forbid she should want him urgently, and he wouldn't be able to service her." She said it with irony, but there was a throaty catch in her voice, and he must have heard it, too. She was not trying to entice him, however. This wasn't calculated. It was just happening. His crazy gown had captured more than her breast. It had captured her imagination.

And his, too, it seemed. His voice was low and reverent as he took in the effect of her fiery modesty. "*That* is incredibly sexy."

She glanced down and wished she hadn't. There should be a law against Victorian nightgowns. She also stole a peek at the opening of his robe, this time hoping she wouldn't see what she'd been looking for earlier. She wasn't entirely sure what she would do if an erection presented itself. Hopefully, ask him to take his toys and leave, but then again, maybe not. The images of her naughty parts being revealed for his pleasure were doing crazy things to her breathing.

His robe was still tied, and everything seemed to be where it should be, except his gaze. It was hungry, restless, roving.

"Why are you looking at me like that?" she said accusingly.

"Like what?"

"Lustfully."

"No… No, this is business." He pretended to be surprised at her claim, but his voice was thrillingly rough and grainy. "The way you look right now—it's perfect for VLL's catalog. I've never seen anything sexier, really. You're ravishing. You could sell a million copies of this gown."

Lorna could feel heartbeats thundering in her chest. He couldn't mean her, could he? He must mean the ad, someone like her.

"Undo the other pocket, would you?" he said. "And then cover yourself, just so I can see if it enhances the effect."

Both breasts exposed? Was it lingerie or porn he was selling?

"Please," he said, "it's business. This could put VLL

on its feet, guarantee work for lots of people *and* help the economy."

She could hardly resist that pitch, true or not. Had he said a million copies? If Helen of Troy could launch a thousand ships to help her country, why couldn't Lorna Sutton sell lingerie?

She gave the other button a touch, and the flap fell open. Now she was cupping both breasts and her insides were in sweet turmoil. It was hard not to swoon. Her legs were weak, and her entire body felt tender to the touch, especially her breasts. Her flesh was hot and soft, aching. Her nipples burned for a firm touch, a man's touch.

And Jamie Baird looked as though he wanted to have her for dinner, but not as his guest. His jaw flexed, as if he'd just had a taste of something so delicious it hurt.

"How does it feel with the gown open that way?" he asked. "Is it what you imagined? Is it arousing?"

She nodded, unable to confirm or deny. Her voice wouldn't work right, and she didn't want to think about the gown anyway. Still, it was hard not to wonder what the various other pockets and flaps were for.

She croaked, "Your customers will be very happy."

"Not as happy as I am."

"Shall I button up now?" she asked.

"We haven't explored what else the gown can do."

"I don't have any more hands."

"You're not going to need them," he said. "I'll be your guide. This is business. It's the perfect opportunity to see if the gown is going to work."

"Absolutely, it will work." It *was* working. She was breathless, perspiring and probably dampening his creation with a secret spring of intimate fluids.

Suddenly he was closer, speaking softly. "Did you find these?" he asked. "You have a false pocket here on either side." He lifted one of the openings with his finger, letting cool air flow over her hot skin. "This is for hands, of course. The groom's hands, if he wants to hold her by the waist or lift her hips. Hers, if she wants to touch herself or guide him."

"Interesting," she got out.

"Of course, they're for foreplay, not sex," he told her, "unless the groom were to get very creative."

He stroked the mouth of the opening while she watched...and waited for him to stroke her. She would have turned to water vapor if he had touched her that way, with such sensual precision.

"Thanks for sharing," she said quickly. "I think I can guess what the rest of it's about."

"Really? This?" There was an opening the size of a silver dollar over her midriff. He dipped a finger in there and caressed her belly button with a soft, circular motion. "Some women find this very arousing."

"Mmm, tickles," she said.

"Maybe this then?" He found openings under her arms that would have allowed him to stroke the sides of her breasts. She stared straight into his eyes, daring him to touch her there. He stared back, scorching her to her depths with the heat of his sensuality. Her nipples hardened and tingled. Her nerves fired with alarm. Her juices flowed.

It was wrong what he did to her. Wrong.

His warm breath eddied in the valley of her throat. That was how close he was. He never did touch her, and her nerve endings were well aware of that. They were screaming for relief by the time it was over. Maybe that was the point.

"This *is* business, right?" She caught her breath, suddenly anguished. He seemed to arouse her so effortlessly.

"Oh, absolutely, this is business."

His voice wasn't any better than hers. He could hardly manage the words, but it sounded sexy coming from him.

"There's more, but this is the best one," he said, reaching around behind her to tug on a pocket on the back of the gown. It covered her derriere and was nearly as wide as her hips. She already knew what that had to be for, sex from behind. The Victorians were a pretty randy bunch, or so she'd heard. Now she knew why. They were being driven crazy by their clothing.

"This opening," he said, playing with things behind her that neither one of them could see, "is so that he can guide her while they're making love, positioning her body for…deeper penetration. It also allows him to caress her anterior cleavage, which I've heard can be very stimulating."

"And I've heard enough." She cleared her throat.

"Perfect timing. I'm done talking."

Talking, maybe, but not walking. He moved around behind her and freed the "anterior cleavage" pocket, letting in another whisper of cool air. Her skin was ablaze. Again, she waited for his touch. Her buttocks tingled and stung, as aroused as her breasts. He did nothing, but she could feel the heat of his eyes, and that was almost as bad.

Eventually he came around to the front, and she realized that her hand had fallen away from her breast. She tried to shield herself, but he stopped her.

"Don't," he said. "You're beautiful. This is what the gown was made for."

He put his hand where hers had been, covering her breast. He moved deeper into her space, and she pressed herself against him. It was hopeless. She loved his touch. She loved every single thrill he gave her.

She lifted her mouth to him, and he gazed at her waiting lips, as if he might actually be able to resist them. She hissed and nipped his lower lip. It got her the kiss she wanted, savage and satisfying.

"Just in case you're wondering," he said, gripping her face with his hand, "this isn't business."

He brushed her lips again and growled, the sound vibrating deeply in his throat. His hand kneaded her breast, bringing her to a crescendo of excitement. Her breath caught. The sensation was almost as painful as if he'd burned her. Everything was surging, running away with her. It was too fast, too fast. If she didn't stop herself now, she never would.

She shook her head and stepped back, searching for the right words, but the look on his face startled her. It ripped through her heart.

His eyes flared and burned out, turning to cinders. He seemed to be unable to grasp what she'd done, and perhaps he didn't even understand his own response to it. She saw confusion and frustration. She saw anguish, and she understood. She wasn't the only one being torn apart.

A second later, she was in his arms, tears brimming. This night was doomed, and she knew it. "I can't."

He drew a breath. "I know."

He released her, and she stepped away from him. But what she should have done was run. She didn't expect her body to react so violently. It clambered for his arms, for everything about him that was male. She let out a little whimper, and it seemed to crush his resolve.

"Jesus," he whispered, "come back."

She couldn't, not yet. But in her hesitation, she saw what she'd been looking for since he'd arrived. His body in full-blown arousal. Beautiful. Maybe it was her hormone-soaked state of mind, but all that raging male muscle looked beautiful to her. His darkening shaft had thrust through the opening of his robe, which was still very much tied.

"That's not fair," she whispered. Why couldn't they have just said good-night? Now, *everything* hurt. *Everything* hungered. She was a sparkling bundle of nerves and needs.

An impulse took her over to him. It made her touch him.

His groan was sweetly agonized. She watched his face contort and knew what he was going through, the deep, hard pulls of excitement. She felt them, too.

"God, too much." He wanted her to take her hand away, but she dropped straight to her knees, her mouth open and wet with desire. She wanted to taste the hardness she'd touched.

"Lorna, if you do that, I won't—"

But her lips had already closed over him, and she was lost in the carnal pleasure of it. Another savage groan came out of him. He gripped her head, trying to be tender, but cursing the violence of his need.

His hands worked in her hair, pulling her into him. He began to move, and her throat ached with the sweetness of it. She curled her tongue around him and sucked on him, gently at first. Within seconds, they were caught up in an orgy of thrusting.

"Stop," he said suddenly. "Lorna, stop."

He held her back, and she looked up at him, still breathing hard. "What's wrong?" she asked. A moan of frustration escaped her as he lifted her to her feet.

"I am wild to be inside you," he said, "*wild.*"

They clung to each other tightly, surging, both of them. Earlier he had touched her in a way that had stirred fantasies, forbidden dreams she didn't even know she had, and they were still burning in her mind. The most intimate part of her body was hotly enflamed, but she doubted he would guess the turn her imagination had taken.

As he bent to pick her up and carry her to the bed, she stayed his hand, turning her back to him. Before he could question her, she felt behind her and found the pocket, surprised to learn that he'd closed it.

She heard him suck in a breath as it fell open.

"Lorna, what is this? You want me that way?"

He dropped to one knee and cupped her with his hands, stroking her bottom like butterfly wings. Lost in sensation, she could hardly differentiate his fingers from his lips and his tongue. He was a magnificent lover, touching, kissing, nuzzling, nipping. He did everything but enter her as he aroused her exquisitely sensual flesh.

Lorna soared to a peak of pleasure, and she'd already begun to tumble down the other side when she felt him exploring with his fingers. He trailed them along the cleft of her derriere on his way to the sweet flood of moisture that dampened her satin curls.

Moments later, she fell over the bed, wet with need and screaming as she felt him behind her. His body pressed against hers, male flesh against female. Throbbing, ready. He entered her with slow deliberation, and she could hardly bear it. She loved exactly what he was doing, but she was crazy for more. Some primitive impulse had taken over her. Helpless, she thrust her hips back, taking him deeply.

He let out a guttural sound and grasped her flanks, as if to control her, but she wouldn't be controlled. She rocked back again and again, and at last she felt him shudder. He began to move and the thrusting was as primitive as her need. She'd broken his control, and it was fast, deep, glorious.

She had never felt such wild pleasure in her life, even with him. But mixed with her ecstasy was a sense of wild despair. She had promised herself that this wouldn't happen. She was hopelessly out of control and yet enthralled with every sweet, terrible thing he did to her. Apparently she had no shame. But worst of all, she had betrayed her convictions. And as he flooded her with mindless pleasure, and she thrilled to every second of it, she began to fear for her sanity, too. If there was a hell for wayward women, then surely she was going there. They were probably preparing the bonfire now.

If there was a hell for rogues, he ought to be there already.

But none of her concerns seemed to matter as he fell over her and cupped her breasts. He held her roughly, tenderly. His body fused with hers as one, and the last thread of her resistance snapped. They came together violently, sweetly and completely.

## CHAPTER SEVEN

A BED OF ROCKS. Could have been a bed of thorns for all the sleep Jamie was going to get. He swung his legs over the side of the bed, rubbed the small of his back and stretched. His yawn turned into a low growl of displeasure.

Moonlight poured through the French doors, so dazzlingly bright it forced him to squint. It was well after midnight, but he'd already made up his mind that his insomnia had nothing to do with his conscience. Or her. Or the interview tomorrow. It was the rocks.

He got up and yanked the louvers shut on the French doors, shrouding the room in darkness. There'd been too much light to prowl and growl. He felt like an animal that couldn't sleep because of hunger pangs or some other unfulfilled lust. But how could he be having pangs after the lust he'd just experienced? What was it about the two of them that led to volcanic sex and other natural disasters?

He stopped and rubbed his back. "Hell, it isn't the rocks," he said. "It's a thorn. One thorn."

She was jammed in his side like a spine with barbs. How had he ever let her get so deeply embedded? This was one of those crazy fatal attractions. He was hopelessly hooked on a maniac. The woman couldn't decide whether she wanted him or hated him. Maybe she hated wanting him. Whatever it was he'd made a mistake in letting things get so far out of control.

Afterward, she'd gone quiet, like catatonic quiet, and he hadn't known what to do. He'd wanted to comfort her, but she wouldn't let him. He'd apologized, and for some reason, that had made her angry—and she'd retreated further. He didn't want to leave her that way. Perhaps he should have been quiet with her, and waited her out. But he'd been shaken up by the sex, too, and he'd wanted to bring her out of her shell so they could talk about it. He'd even tried a confession to lighten things up. He'd admitted that after watching her pole dance he no longer liked the idea of her doing a demonstration for Hudley Campbell.

"Poor guy will make a fool of himself," he'd said. "A man isn't safe around you."

That's when it got bizarre. She'd started to laugh, but she was crying, too. Maybe she'd thought he was trying to blame the sex on her. She'd accused him of being callous and insensitive and a few other things that didn't make sense. Finally when she'd calmed down, she'd thanked him in a razor-edged voice for making it so easy for her to find her inner bitch.

"Please, just go," she'd whispered, "or it really *won't* be safe."

Did he want to write her off as crazy? *Yes.* It would have made everything much easier. But she wasn't crazy. She was hurt and angry, furious at him for something that she wouldn't talk about. It couldn't be because of what had happened six months ago. She would have confronted him about that, right? That's what a guy would do. He'd get it out on the table, deal with it.

*Hey, Jamie, we had a date, didn't we? What happened?*

However, he had to admit that if she *had* confronted him, it would have been awkward. He would have had to say that he'd been swamped with work and had forgotten, which was true, but might have hurt her feelings, and she probably wouldn't have believed him anyway. That was where it got complicated. Feelings.

Jamie stretched and wandered into the bathroom, congratulating himself on his policy of leaving toilet seats up. It was too dark to see, which was the reason they should always be up. Interesting how most women didn't get the infallible logic of that.

As he stood there, absently answering nature's call, he puzzled over how she could have labeled him insensitive. Look at the thinking he'd just done about her, and the effort he would have made to spare her feelings over that missed date, if she'd given him the chance. He would have had to make up some elaborate excuse, like being in intensive care, maybe in a coma, to be safe. Just so she wouldn't think it was her.

And it *wasn't* her.

He hit the lever and left the room to the sounds of swirling water. The woman had been lurking in some dark corner of his mind ever since he met her in the produce section. He'd mentally pushed her away, along with everything else that wasn't about VLL, but clearly she'd been working her magic on him all along from behind the scenes, inspiring his sketches. Obviously, she'd had a big impact on his success, too, but he didn't dare tell her that, given the way she reacted to compliments. She would probably thank him with a skull fracture, courtesy of the dancing pole.

He looked around the bedroom for something to wear, which was a lost cause, given the absence of light and the way he tended to fling things when he undressed. His shorts were in her room.

Tomorrow should be an interesting day. His gut instinct was to leave Hudley Campbell a message and call the interview off, but the *L.A. Times* was crucial to their advertising campaign, and Jamie had a lot of people depending on him, not to mention investors at risk. Still, partnering up with her was a risky proposition. He didn't know how much longer he could handle being at this woman's mercy.

He roamed the dark room, still feeling very much like a restless animal as he stalked the answer to his unanswerable dilemma.

"Ms. Baird, is that you?"

Lorna turned to see a man's face pressed against the glass panel of the screen door. Whoever he was, he'd caught her in the great room, making a last-minute check of her packed bags.

"It's Hud Campbell," he said. "I'm a little early."

Lorna nodded, not quite sure what to do. Campbell was the reporter from the *Times,* but he was more than early. He wasn't supposed to be there at all. Jamie had slipped a note under her door earlier that morning. It said that he'd cancelled the 10:00 a.m. interview and would be out for a while. He hadn't offered any explanation, so Lorna had packed her things, expecting to go home.

She'd hoped he would have talked to her before doing anything so drastic. She'd planned to apologize to him for last night. It wasn't his fault she couldn't control herself. But he wasn't around when she got up this morning. She'd been naive to think that having a roommate would stop him from disappearing. It hadn't even slowed him down. He could have been his own Vegas magic act.

Now she was just hoping to leave before he got back.

"I'll be right there," Lorna told the reporter, thinking she might be able to stall him. But he'd already let himself in by the time she got to the door.

"I hope this isn't too inconvenient," he said, offering his hand.

Lorna didn't know what to do with him. She couldn't say she was Jamie, but she'd probably better not say she wasn't, either. Where *was* Jamie?

She quickly sized Campbell up as they shook hands. Tall and gangly, with tinted wire-rimmed glasses, he reminded her of a basketball star she'd had a crush on in college. She'd been mad for nerdy athletes in those days.

Perhaps he'd liked redheaded women in college. He seemed to like them now, especially ones wearing lime-green sundresses with spaghetti straps.

"It's a pleasure," he said.

He still hadn't released her hand when Jamie walked in the front door a moment later, carrying some shopping bags and a surly expression.

"This is Hudley Campbell," Lorna said quickly.

Jamie could barely conceal his double take. "I left you a message this morning," he told Campbell. Jamie noticed Lorna's bags and pointed at her. "On Ms. Baird's behalf, of course. She's been called away on business and can't do the interview."

"Sorry, never got the message," Campbell said. "Damn cell phone, it's always hiding from me." He peered through his glasses at Jamie and his shopping bags. "And who are you?"

"My assistant," Lorna gushed, "and what would I do without him? He does everything for me, don't you...*Loren*. He even shops for me when I'm busy working. Loves to shop."

Jamie blanched, which gave Lorna more pleasure than she could have imagined. Actually, he looked hunkier than hell in khaki shorts, flip-flops and a black

T-shirt with the sleeves ripped out. But there were lots of guys in sleeveless tees who *loved* to shop.

She smiled brightly, warding off Jamie's stare. Hopefully, she looked as cool as a cup of lime sherbet, but inside she was soft serve, melting and running at the mere sight of him. It was almost inconceivable that she could long to be in his arms again, despite the embarrassing things she always did when she got there. *What was wrong with her?*

A sigh welled in her throat. It was probably a good thing she had an *L.A. Times* reporter in between her and that kitchen island, or she and Jamie would be having primal sex there, too. She had no control whatsoever. There should be rehab units for people like her.

"Loren," she said, "why don't you put the bags away and fix our guest some iced tea. Would you like that, Hud?"

He beamed. "I would love that. May I call you Jamie?"

"Excuse me?" the real Jamie cut in. "What about your flight, Ms. *Baird?* You're going to miss it. Shouldn't I be driving you to the airport?"

"No." She tapped her wristwatch. "Just our luck— that flight's been delayed. Hud and I should have plenty of time to rap."

*"Rap?"* Jamie glowered at her from the island countertop, where he set the packages. He raked a hand through his dark hair, messing it up in interesting ways, and then planted both hands on his hips.

Lorna's heart seemed to be running on the spot. She couldn't tell if he was angry because she was doing the interview or because of Hud's admiring glances, but one thing was clear. Mr. Baird was dangerously sexy when he was perturbed.

She was hopeless. Just wheel her in for a lobotomy. Immediately.

She dragged her attention back to the interview, which was exactly what Jamie didn't want her to do. The great room had a large leather couch near the fireplace. Beckoning the reporter over there with her, she said, "Hud, why don't we get started on those questions? Please, ask me anything."

The reporter rushed over, yanking his notebook from the pocket of his jacket as he sat down. "Rumor control, here," he said with a lopsided grin. "The grapevine has it that you don't just crunch numbers, Jamie, you design, as well. Was the breakaway underwear your idea?"

Lorna was startled by the question. She could see Jamie gesturing at her from the kitchen. He shook his head, waving at her so frantically she couldn't think straight. "Jamie, stop it."

"*He's* Jamie?" Hud looked puzzled. "I thought you were Jamie."

"Oh, I am," Lorna said quickly. "I was talking to myself, really. It's a bad habit. Sometimes I can go on and on, and that's how I stop myself. 'Stop it, Jamie!' See?"

Hud didn't seem to see at all, and Lorna had to act fast. She diverted him by going back to his question. "If by breakaway underwear, you mean StripLoc lingerie," she said, "let's say, just for the sake of argument, that I did come up with that concept. How do you like it?"

"Well, it's definitely a male fantasy. Is that what you had in mind when you designed it?"

Now Jamie was nodding and mouthing the word *yes*, which confused Lorna even more. He wanted her to say she designed it? Or that it was a male fantasy? Or what?

"Absolutely not," Lorna said.

Hud frowned. "You don't design women's lingerie with the idea of turning men on?"

"No, I design it for women to turn *themselves* on."

He leaned toward her. "So, then you *do* design? Tell me why, Jamie. Tell me more about that."

Lorna blithely ignored his eager questions. She also blithely ignored Jamie, who was still doing semaphore in the kitchen.

"VLL is a company run by women *for* women," she said, taking another tack. "Our customers are women of all shapes, sizes and ages, and we want them to feel sexy and good about themselves whether men are around or not. We believe it will translate into every area of their lives. Sensuality has an energy all its own, and it radiates confidence."

Now Jamie was rolling his eyes and making throat-cutting gestures.

But Lorna had more to say, and while she was at it, she wondered how Jamie Baird liked being brushed off as if he were a piece of lint. She doubted he'd had much experience with that. Welcome to my world, Jamie.

"Too many women suffer from insensitive treatment," she told Hud, "especially women of size, and we want them to feel good about themselves again. We believe our designs will help women see themselves as sexual and worthy whether or not a man sees them that way."

Hud seemed a little disappointed. "Is that why your designers are all women? You don't think a man can design for women who aren't supermodels?"

"Quite honestly, I think it might be difficult for *some* men to set their fantasies aside. I could see a man creating a gown simply because he'd like to take it off a woman, or…wear it himself, depending on the man."

She made a point of glancing at Jamie with the last

remark, and he turned pale again. She had him off balance, but she knew he was going to be breathing fire when he recovered...unless she could turn this interview around somehow, and *maybe* do something to boost the company's sales.

"Hud, can I show you what VLL has in the works?"

Lorna jumped up and grabbed Hud's hand, taking him with her to the kitchen, where Jamie stood, sullen and suspicious, his arms crossed.

"Loren," she said, trying to smooth things over, "why don't you get the sketch that goes with our special Christmas package? You know the one I mean, right? It's in my bedroom."

She glanced at the pole, signaling her intentions. Jamie had asked her to plug the pole-dancing package, and she was letting him know that she would. But he didn't seem all that excited about her idea. He probably could have melted the metal pole with his eyes.

She sprang into action as soon as Jamie left the room, getting Hud a soft drink from the refrigerator and then briefly explaining why there was a pole in the middle of the kitchen. She gave him a quick demo, swinging in a wide arc, then hooking her leg around the pole and spinning into it. She shook her head and let her hair fly, but that was all she could safely do with a dress on. Apparently, it was enough.

Hud's eyes nearly bugged out of their sockets. He was still applauding as Jamie strode back into the kitchen.

"You have a winner there," Hud told her. "I wouldn't mind having a pole in my own kitchen, just to remember you by." He winked at Lorna and pulled a business card from his pocket. "In case you want to give me another demo sometime. *Anytime*."

Jamie whipped the card out of Hud's hand, spun him

around and had him at the front door before Lorna could respond. Jamie was all very polite about it, but there was no mistaking the command in his voice as he told the reporter that Ms. Baird had to get to the airport, and the interview was over.

Nor did Lorna have time to brace herself before Jamie came back.

"Why didn't you show him the sketch?" she said, scrambling for anything that might put him back on the defensive. No such luck.

"You pole danced for that guy?" Jamie was clearly appalled. The disbelief in his voice was palpable.

"Not *for* him. It was a demonstration. I thought you wanted me to push the pole-dancing package."

He shook his head, apparently overcome with disgust. "I do not love to shop! Why did you say that?"

Obviously it was a delayed reaction. "What else could I say? You walked in carrying shopping bags."

"And why did you have to go and tell him that I design the stuff."

"I didn't mean to do that. You were confusing me."

"VLL has male customers, too, Lorna, lots of them, and yes, we do design with their fantasies in mind. They buy lingerie for their wives and girlfriends."

She lifted a shoulder. "Okay, but if a woman feels sensual, and if it comes from within, wouldn't men pick up on that? Wouldn't a sexy, confident woman be a male fantasy?"

He spun away from her and went to the refrigerator. When he came back he had a bottle of beer and an air of menace that made her think he was about to open it with his teeth.

"So, are you going to date this guy now?" he asked her. "Are you going to call Hud Campbell?"

Nervous laughter surged up, but Lorna didn't dare let it out. "Why are you so angry?" she asked. "I was trying to help. I could call Hud and tell him I've given his male fantasy question more thought, if that would help— No? Okay! I was only thinking about the article."

"I don't give a shit about the article."

"Then what's wrong?"

*"Nothing."*

He took the bags from the island, stuffed them under his arm and headed toward the back of the house. "I'm going to take a swim."

Lorna watched him stalk out of the room and a question popped into her head. He wasn't jealous, was he? Her throat burned with sudden heat. Had he risked his publicity campaign and eaten a business card because of *her?* No. No, she couldn't let herself go there. That was wishful thinking. Women who entertained such notions about rogues really did need lobotomies.

She hadn't accomplished any miracles. She hadn't reformed Jamie Baird, and she certainly hadn't made him fall in love with her. But at least she'd said a few things she wanted to say, even if only to a reporter with Jamie listening. She'd also made a new friend, the tough little cookie inside her that she no longer referred to as her inner *B* word.

Her sense of satisfaction couldn't sustain her, however. Sadness swept her. It settled into her chest like a weight as she looked around the room and saw her bags, packed and ready. Maybe it was time to go. There didn't seem to be much else to do around here.

JAMIE BURST THROUGH the surface of the water and swam to the edge of the pool. He'd almost expected to see Lorna standing there, and something clicked in his mind when he didn't. *She was gone.*

He could feel it.

He didn't bother with the ladder. He hoisted himself out of the pool with his arms and then he whipped the towel off the deck chair, where he'd left it. The house was eerily silent as he stormed through it, and the scent of strawberries that had hung in the air wherever she'd been was already gone.

A note lay on the dining-room table. He read it with a sense of dread. What had he done? What the hell had he done?

"Good luck with your fashion show—and your life."

She hadn't even signed it. Well, that was plain enough. It was a goodbye, if ever he'd seen one.

He toweled off his dripping hair and breathed a profane word. He could hardly fathom how anyone could have messed things up this badly. Unintentional or not, this was a disaster. He'd just thrown an *L.A. Times* reporter out of his house. He had jeopardized VLL's ad campaign, and all because of his silly scheme to keep the real Jamie Baird under wraps. He almost wished he could find it in himself to blame it on her. If she hadn't insisted on giving that interview none of this would have happened. Then again, the switch had been his idea. She wouldn't even have been here if not for him. And now she was gone.

The wet towel hit the floor with a splat.

She'd messed with his mind, his company, his life. And he should have been outraged. Why wasn't he outraged? Why did his sense of loss outweigh everything else? He had a fashion show and a company to salvage, and all he could think about was whether or not he'd ever see her again.

# CHAPTER EIGHT

SOMEONE WAS TAPPING on Jamie's shoulder. "Go away," Jamie mumbled into the sleeve of his shirt. The painful crick in his neck told him he'd fallen asleep with his head on his desk again.

"Aren't you ever going home, boss?"

"Probably not." Jamie opened one eye and saw Frank Natori, leaning on his trusty mop and frowning at him.

"You slept here last night, too," Natori observed. "Someone at home you're avoiding?"

Jamie sat up slowly and rolled his neck, absently aware of the cracking noises. He'd been camping out at the office the last couple days, going home only to shower and change. If he was avoiding anyone, it was Hud Campbell, who'd been dropping by to see "Jamie."

Jamie had used the excuse that Ms. Baird was traveling, and he was house-sitting, but by Campbell's third visit, Jamie had decided to vacate. Otherwise, a certain reporter was going to get his glasses wrapped around his bony throat. The guy was turning into a stalker.

"It's myself I'm avoiding," Jamie said at last.

"Ah!"

"No," Jamie cut in, "it's not a woman. It's my life. Everything's going to hell on me."

"Just as I thought. It's a woman."

Natori seemed pleased with himself, which brought

an exasperated snort from Jamie. He was about to argue the point when he realized the futility.

"Okay, it's a woman," he admitted with a sigh. "She's killing me, *and* she's killing this company."

Jamie fell back in his chair and pointed to the newspaper that lay open on his desk. His green banker's lamp was the room's only illumination, but it clearly lit the feature in the business section.

"What's this?" Natori pulled the paper around to look at it. "A newspaper article about your company? What does it say?"

Natori was the genius who'd told Jamie that women needed to hear certain things from a man, the right words. Jamie gave him a pained look. "All the wrong words."

LORNA WAS RIGHT BACK where she'd started, trying to make sense of her life. But now there was more frustration than hope. And maybe even some bitterness. *What the hell had happened in the last week?* This wasn't the new start she'd imagined just days ago, before Jamie Baird made his reappearance.

She couldn't seem to get started at all. Her humidifier sat unused, and the rituals that had brought her harmony seemed pointless now. Nothing made much of an impression on her, except the fact that the phone hadn't rung, and most of her energy was taken up in reflection, but not about herself.

She couldn't get her damn thoughts off Jamie. There'd been no word from him, not that she'd expected any, but it was becoming clear that she needed some kind of resolution in order to get on with things. The entire course of her life had been disrupted, but that wasn't what preoccupied her, either. She needed to know that he was all right, and that she hadn't disrupted *his* life, at least not too badly.

She opened her refrigerator door and peered inside at the emptiness. Breakfast anyone? There was a six-pack of cranberry-apple juice and a carton of eggs, probably months past their use date. She grabbed a can of juice, popped the top and took it with her to the knotty pine breakfast nook off the kitchen.

Her one-bedroom apartment was cramped, but cozy, and her favorite room was the nook. She'd once referred to the wood as "naughty pine" because the knots reminded her of men's testicles. Hmm, maybe not a good place for her to be this morning? Surrounded by testicles?

Absently, she fished a piece of paper from the pocket of her pajamas and realized it was a grocery list. She really was in a funk. She'd actually been too distracted to shop. Must be a sign of the apocalypse. Here she was back in her apartment, alone and on vacation but without the bare necessities of life. No comfort food?

The only thing comforting her this morning were her threadbare, cloud-print pj's. She'd even patched up the worn spots, determined not to give them up. They'd snuggled with her on Saturday night dates with the VCR and kept her company on sick days. When she was lonely and blue, they were almost as good as a security blanket.

She took the juice with her into the living room, where she'd opened the front door and windows to create a cross breeze. She had no air-conditioning, and it was still early enough in the day to be cool. When the breezes carried in the perfume from the neighborhood jasmine trees, you could almost imagine yourself being bathed by trade winds.

A week's worth of newspapers lay unopened on the floor. She'd been going to throw them out, but she had an entire weekend to kill before she went back to work, and she had to do something. She grabbed one at random and began to look through it. Maybe she would see an ad for a fabulous sale that would give her the will to shop.

Thirty minutes later, she was still sitting on the floor, leafing through newspapers at random, skimming page after page in search of something to occupy her mind. And finally she found it. On the front page of the business section of yesterday's paper was a headline about the Velvet, Leather, & Lace fashion show.

From the opening paragraph, Lorna knew it was going to be bad. Hud Campbell was implying that VLL engaged in sexism.

"The luscious Ms. Baird refuses to hire men as designers," Hud had written, "yet has her own male assistant."

Lorna read on reluctantly, wincing at several more implications about VLL's anti-men attitude. Halfway through, she stopped, unable to go on. She had never wanted to hurt Jamie's business. She'd only been trying to teach him a lesson, perhaps foolishly, she realized now. She'd had little personal experience with the media and hadn't foreseen how her statements could be misconstrued. Obviously, that's why Jamie had been gesticulating like a traffic cop during the interview. And that damn Hudley Campbell. It would be a cold day in hell before Lorna would ever demonstrate anything for him, except how to call an ambulance.

*Call Jamie and apologize. Ask him if there's anything you can do.*

Lorna had just decided to do that when a shadow fell over the newspaper. She glanced up to see the man himself standing in her doorway. She struggled to get up, catching her foot in the leg of her pajamas. A ripping sound told her she'd torn the thin material.

"Jamie? What happened?"

"Why?" His voice was hoarse, angry. "Do I look that bad?"

She didn't say it, but he looked as if he'd been living on the streets for a week. His clothes were rumpled, his dress shirttail hanging out of his slacks. His hair was messy, even for him, and his jaw was shadowed with stubble. But it was the blood that riveted Lorna's attention.

He rubbed his jaw and grimaced. "I guess I should have shaved, huh? Changed my clothes?"

"What's that cut on your lip?"

"I just came from a meeting with Hud Campbell at his office." He touched his lip, as if he hadn't realized the cut was there. "He looks worse."

"You fought with Hud? Oh, my God, Jamie, why? Think what he'll write now."

"I *know* what he'll write now. I told him what to write."

Lorna was almost afraid to ask. "What do you mean?"

She opened the screen door and let him in. Her apartment complex was smallish and wrapped around a swimming pool. The design made the courtyard an echo chamber, and she didn't want Jamie's business broadcast to the neighborhood, not that it wouldn't be broadcast everywhere else soon enough, once it hit tomorrow's edition of the *Times*.

Jamie came in at her urging, but he didn't take the chair she offered him. He hovered, hands fisted in his pockets, shoulders hunkered like a boxer in his corner of the ring. Lorna had never seen him so disheveled— or desirable. He could have been green and scaly, and he would have been desirable to her. *Oh, dear God, was she falling in love with this man? No, no, no. Please, no!*

"What did you do?" she prompted.

He was matter-of-fact. "I told Hud that VLL couldn't be anti-male, as he implied, because Jamie Baird is really a man, and not only does he run the business end of VLL, he's responsible for several of the designs, including StripLoc. And then I shook Hud's hand and introduced myself."

"He knows you're Jamie, and that I was impersonating you?"

Jamie nodded. "I laid it all out for him. I figured the anti-male publicity might do more harm than the truth, as long as it was clear the company didn't deliberately set out to deceive anyone. I told him the media, including his paper, had assumed I was a woman, and there hadn't been time to clear up that confusion before we got caught up in a major advertising campaign for the satellite fashion show."

"You explained that there wasn't *time* to clear things up?" she prompted.

"Not once the investors got involved. The ad campaign and satellite show were their idea, and they financed it with a huge infusion of cash—at which point, things took off at breakneck speed. Before that, I'd been happy to stay in the background. There hadn't been any pressing need to explain my presence at VLL because no one ever expected me to stay on and make a career of women's lingerie, least of all me. I was just doing some friends a favor."

"And Hud bought that?"

Jamie managed a grim smile. "Well, it is the truth. But I didn't pretend to be a victim of the media. I told him VLL's executive team was concerned that negative publicity before the fashion show could sink it and take the company down with it, so I'd planned to clear up the confusion after the show—by giving him an exclusive."

He shrugged. "VLL isn't blameless, and I couldn't pretend we were. Anyway, it's out there now, and we'll see what happens."

Lorna blurted, "I forced you into that, didn't I?"

"The only thing you did was force me out of hiding. It was time for me to step up to the plate and take responsibility."

Guilt made her rush right over what he'd said. "No, I was wrong, totally wrong. I should not have gone ahead with the interview after you'd cancelled it. Maybe you deserved it, but your company didn't."

"Thanks, I think."

She found a tissue in her pajama pocket and dabbed the blood from his lip, which made him wince, the big baby. She was just so glad to see him. She honestly was. "Do you think Hud will give you a break?"

"I thought so, right up until the end."

"What happened?"

"He asked me how to contact you."

Lorna's heart sank. "And you hit him?"

Jamie grinned. "I returned his business card in one of those fancy gift bags with tissue paper—and he hit me. Caught me as I turned to leave. *Bad* thing to do."

She shook her head, exasperated. Men, fists, testicles. Not a good mix. Somebody had messed up on that one. But she *loved* that he was jealous.

"So, how is it that Hud looks worse?" she asked.

"Well, I couldn't let him get away with that sucker punch, could I? Hud's editor pulled me off him," Jamie explained with more than a little male pride. "Afterward, we all had a good long talk, believe it or not. In a nutshell, the editor assured me that their follow-up article would clear up the gender confusion and the anti-male stuff. Plus, he would personally supervise Hud's writing of the story."

"So, that's good, right?"

"If the public thinks it's good, it's good. Remains to be seen." He rubbed his neck as if it were stiff, and while doing so, he got a look at her tattered pajamas. His eyebrows lifted. "Not VLL, I'm guessing?"

Lorna looked down and sighed. She was ragtag, torn, devoid of makeup and emotionally overdrawn at the bank. "Vintage Lorna," she said.

"Good year." In the next breath, he said, "You frighten me."

She held out her pajama pants, as if they were wings. "No surprise there."

"No, your pajamas are fine. They're exquisite. But *you*. You actually frighten me. Like a mouse frightens an elephant."

Lorna could summon up no objections to being the mouse in this case. She just wished the floor wasn't so far away. She was suddenly unsure of distances. Too far from the floor, too close to him, *too late to turn back.* Frightened? He didn't know the meaning of the word.

"Is this all part of revealing the real Jamie Baird?" she asked. "Like right now? With me?"

He locked into her gaze so deeply he could have picked her up and moved her telepathically. "Yeah," he said, "I think I am."

"Okay…good…don't let me stop you."

*Please, don't stop.*

But it felt as if she'd stepped back, as if she'd had to for protection. Her need to hear what he had to say was as crazy as her fear of it. What if she didn't get what she needed? What if she did?

*What did she need? Something so terrible it could just rip her apart? That's what it felt like.*

"Before you," he said, "I'd been going from woman to woman, always on the move, never with anyone long enough to get involved. I think I feared what I'd be giving up."

"And what was that?"

"The search." He drew in a breath. "The search for what was missing. But after you, I stalled out. I couldn't go anywhere, to anyone. There wasn't any way to escape the reality that what was missing was inside me, and that scared the hell out of me. I needed an excuse to swear off women altogether, so I buried myself in work."

"Are you saying—? What are you saying…that I ruined you for other women?"

The thought made her giddy. He couldn't have meant it, and now she was going to force him to say that he had.

He cocked his head, as if perhaps she'd gotten ahead of him. "Well, I haven't been with anyone since you, so yes, you could say that."

"And that's why you never called back? It wasn't about me? My size, my shape, my person?"

"Lorna, your shape is the stuff men's fantasies are made of. And your person—" His voice went oddly scratchy. "This is going to come off sounding like a bad Hallmark card, but your person is the mate my soul has been searching for."

Who said the mouse couldn't be scared to death of the elephant, especially an advancing bull? "So, what then…you love me…you want me…you can't live without me?"

*What was she trying to do, get him to say no?*

"That, too."

"There's something else?"

"I need you," he said softly. "I don't know about the rest of it. I just know I need you, and I've never let myself need anything before, not like this."

*Beyond giddy. Dizzy. Beyond afraid. Awed.*

Lorna could feel the trade winds and smell the jasmine. The scent was so sweet it made her light-headed. She didn't know what to say, but it was all right because he was managing quite well without her.

"I have a friend who swears that certain words are important to women," he went on. "I don't have a clue what those words are, but that *is* what I feel."

She shook her head at his unflinching honesty. Deep down in her gut, she didn't know if she could ever allow herself to be as vulnerable and exposed as he was at this moment. She wasn't that brave.

"Have I said too much?" he asked. "Should I go?"

"No, God, no." It was fear that had made her want to step away, but now she was held fast by the feeling that he could see her. That Lorna Sutton was being seen for the first time, rather than just weighed and measured.

"I love you, too."

The words rushed out of her, barely discernible. Tears welled, catching in her lashes when she blinked. She didn't know what he meant by the right words, but nothing had ever felt more right than the ones she'd just said. Still, the shock of it kept her where she was for a moment.

He didn't move, either. He seemed to sense that she'd just taken a huge leap of faith. But his face was etched and urgent.

The distance between them only intensified Lorna's

feelings. She wanted him. Every minute of every day, she wanted him. Even listening to the sound of his displeasure made her want him. It was bizarre, but he could have been rejecting her now, and it wouldn't have stemmed this wild exuberance inside her.

She was hooked on him, hopelessly. They should have rehab units for people like her, except that she was beyond rehab. She was a lost cause, and maybe her only salvation was surrendering to the truth. To him. To herself.

She pulled the thread on the waistband of her pajama bottoms and let them fall. She freed a button on her pajama top and worked her way down, freeing all the rest of them. Freeing herself. She had thought that would be enough of a signal, but he seemed to be waiting for something else.

She slipped two fingers in her mouth and whistled.

He cocked his head, intrigued.

"Don't you remember? That first night at the pool? You told me if I ever wanted anything, I should whistle."

"That's true, I did." He smiled. "What is it you want?"

"Not words this time."

He reached for her hand, he tugged her into his arms, and they swung around, falling over each other, into each other. He squeezed her so tightly she couldn't breathe. She feared he might even bruise some ribs before he was done with her, and she couldn't imagine anything more wonderful.

He sprinkled kisses over her eyes and her nose and her mouth, then pulled back to look at her, as if he were reveling in her glowing face, and waiting for her response.

"Why did you stop?" she asked.

"Women aren't the only ones who need words. Is this what you want?"

So that was it. He wanted to hear it.

Her face went hot and her voice sounded like steam from a kettle. "You and me in my knotty pine nook? And by the way, I'm spelling that n.a.u.g.h.t.y."

"That's a pretty good word, too," he said.

IT WAS THE SEXIEST ROOM Jamie had ever been in. The round knots in the wood were like something out of a Georgia O'Keeffe painting. Lorna had told him they reminded her of male genitalia. All he could see was the female variety. He was surrounded by it, but the only flower garden he cared about was hers.

She was sitting on one of the chairs, her legs open to him and her head thrown back in ecstasy. She wore only her unbuttoned pajama top, and it was an almost unbearably erotic sight. The lust that swelled up inside him confounded him. It was fed by love, and it made him want to ravish her in the most primitive of ways, yet cherish her tenderly at the same time. He *burned* with tenderness.

She tasted like strawberries.

Her quivers and gasps and sighs were music.

The fingers she'd tangled in his hair were his guide.

God, he loved her. Maybe the right words were the ones you felt and expressed. But it seemed impossible that one man could feel this much. The ache went so deep it filled him. She filled him. He had no need at this moment to do anything but please her. Whatever did that, pleased him.

She arched with an orgasm, crying out. She wanted him inside her. Those were the words she gasped, and they sent knives of desire slicing through him. He lifted her from the chair and wrapped her legs around him. He had it in mind to trade places with her. Him on the chair and her on his lap, flush up against his painfully stiff erection. He would let her decide when she wanted him, and how.

It was an easy choice for Lorna. The sight of his hardened flesh inflamed her. The pressure against her pubis set her to trembling. She reached for him and he was there, lifting her, gathering her into his arms. And the moment she was joined with him, sweetness flooded her. Relief flooded her. His body was her anchor. His arms her shelter. And she was complete.

## EPILOGUE

THREE SHOPPING BAGS sat in the middle of Lorna's living room when she walked in the door from work that night. Each had a small hand-printed sign propped against it, and the first one said: "This is for you." The second said: "This is for me, but you get to open it." And the third: "This is for us."

Wildly curious, Lorna set down her groceries and knelt to investigate. They looked suspiciously like the shopping bags Jamie had been carrying the day of the interview, but he'd only had two. She peeked inside the first one and sifted through the tissue paper. What she found was a five-by-seven white envelope. Inside was one first-class airline ticket to Tahiti and a week's accommodations at a five-star resort hotel.

Lorna sank to the floor, heedless of the damage to her favorite linen pantsuit. Laughing out loud, she pressed the ticket to her chest. Amazing! He was honoring their agreement, even though the interview had tanked, and mostly because of her.

A note from him was also tucked in the tissue paper. She opened it and read the short message: "Lorna, these trade winds are the real thing—and so are you. I love you." He'd signed his name and added a postscript: "If you'd like company, I'm available on a moment's notice. Just whistle."

Her smile was now out of control. She'd had several days of playing catch-up at work, and she'd come home exhausted, but this surprise had breathed new life into her.

She dived into the second package, the one he'd given her permission to open. It was a VLL pole-dancing package, including a red velvet leotard, which looked as if it might have been custom-made for her. The shockingly low-cut neckline sent a rush of heat to her cheeks. There was no note, but she knew exactly why this one was for him. One word summed it up. Foreplay.

The last package confused her. Inside the tissue paper, she found a computer printout with a list of names, all of them women, and one of them her. There were probably thirty names on the list, every one of them x-ed out except hers.

Avidly she read the notes by her name. Sex goddess? Really?

She'd just started checking out the rest of the list when she heard someone whistle. It came from the doorway behind her. She stumbled to her feet and turned, the printout in her hand.

Jamie sailed through the open door in a crisp summer suit, looking very businesslike, a newspaper in his hand. His dark hair and eyes made a fashion statement out of the tan jacket and slacks.

It took her all of thirty seconds to mess him up. "Thank you," she whispered against his lips. She'd thrown her arms around his neck and she was playing in his lovely dark hair.

"I *love* the presents," she said, "even the one for you." She untangled herself enough to show him the printout. "But what's this?"

He took her fingers and kissed them. "It's my electronic black book. You'll notice all the names have been deleted except yours."

"So, what does that mean? I *am* your black book?"

"It means, Lorna, that there are no women except you."

The printout floated to the floor as she pressed herself against him. Their kiss was long, lingering, sweet. She wanted to drag him to bed, or maybe back into the nook, which had become their favorite place, but he didn't seem to be finished with his surprises.

"You gave me a gift, too," he said, whispering in her ear.

"I know, the pole-dancing package."

"Well, yes, there's that. But I was thinking of this." He showed her the newspaper he'd brought in with him. It was folded open to the business section, and the first page had a follow-up article on VLL.

"Our friend, Hud, has cleared up the anti-male confusion *and* outed me as a designer, of course." The alarm must have shown on her face. "No, it's okay," he said. "The orders are pouring in for pole-dancing packages. They don't want to wait until Christmas. We have them back-ordered through next Valentine's Day."

"Wow, that's great."

"Yeah, Hud gave the packages another rave review, and I think we have you to thank for that. Also, it seems, the public's interest was piqued by the idea of a straight guy—a bean counter at that—designing women's lingerie."

Their bean counter, her *rogue,* she thought. She was relieved, and more pleased than she could express.

She tweaked his tie, flirting with the idea of untying it. "Just as soon as your fashion show is over, Mr. Baird, this sex goddess would like the pleasure of your company in Tahiti."

He pulled an envelope from inside his jacket that was clearly an airline ticket. "I was hoping you'd say that."

She laughed softly. "You're awfully good at making my fantasies come true, but just so you know, I'm *not* going to wear that Victorian nightgown on our wedding night."

He pulled back to look at her, a sexy sparkle in his eye. "Don't get ahead of yourself. I haven't asked you."

Suddenly her laugher was as bright as the peel of silvery bells. "I know...but you will."

# CALLING THE SHOTS
## Donna Kauffman

## CHAPTER ONE

"NO, NO, THAT WON'T DO. If you want to see your work beamed out to every major international market world-wide, then I need to see everything you have before I can make a decision." Samantha Wallace pressed the phone closer to her ear, while simultaneously click-ing her way through the endless incoming messages in her e-mail folder. A moment later she smiled and spun her chair around to face the picture window be-hind her desk. Another hot July night in Los Angeles flickered before her in an endless sea of twinkling lights, but she barely noticed. "Perfect. Fantastic. Fax them to my office by morning and I'll get back to you Monday."

She hung up and did a little dance with her feet as she gave her chair a victory spin. Another designer in the bag! "God, I'm good."

Her phone buzzed again and when she saw who it was, she snapped it up. "I'm kicking ass and taking names," she crowed.

"And this is supposed to be a surprise?" her partner, Mia, chuckled. "I take it you landed Matsuoki?"

"I sure did. And I've got two more lined up tonight. What's up with you?"

"Nothing much. Just pulling out what is left of my

hair, juggling a gazillion different details and in general having a nervous breakdown. You know, the usual."

Sam laughed in sympathy. "A few more weeks and it will all be over."

"That's what I'm freaking out about. I have at least a month's more work to do on the set design."

Sam spun around as her office door opened. "I hear you. Is there anything you need me to do?" She waved her assistant into the room.

"Nah, I just needed a good whine break. I'm over it." The beeping sound of Mia's pager blared over the phone line. "Finally!" she said with a sigh. "It's one of the suppliers. Who was supposed to call me back eight hours ago."

"Hey, considering it's past midnight, it's a miracle he's calling at all."

Now Mia chuckled. "You're not the only one who knows how to kick ass and take names." The beeping sound went off again. "I have to get this."

"No problem. Next time I'll call you when I need a nervous breakdown break."

"Deal," Mia said, then clicked off.

Sam smiled as she hung up the phone. As one of three partners in the lingerie catalog company Velvet, Leather & Lace, it was something of a relief to know that, if she was going to kill herself getting them ready for their first live, globally televised fashion show, she wasn't the only one knocking herself out and putting her ass on the line. Sifting through the growing stack of messages, she sighed and smiled wearily at her assistant. "Just don't tell me anything bad. I'm trying to take over the world here. I can't risk losing my kick-ass juju."

Marcy grinned. "Not to worry. Global domination is

still within your grasp." She handed Sam a stack of folders. "I've gone through these and everything looks in order, but I know you'll want to check them yourself. The Stenson collection prints are on my desk. I set up the two conference calls for you for later, and I'll have the latest batch of demos organized for you to look over Monday morning." She patted the thickly stuffed satchel hanging on her shoulder.

Sam nodded, pleased. "Thanks, Marcy. I really appreciate all the hard work."

Marcy gave her a sassy salute. "Apprentice ass kicker, reporting for duty, sir."

Sam laughed. "Well, get some rest this weekend, junior. We're going to need to be in prime kicking form for the duration."

"You're telling me. God, I can't believe the show is in two weeks."

"You're telling me," Sam repeated dryly. "Now get out of here while you still can, before some other crisis befalls us."

"Yes, boss." She paused by the door. "You pulling another all-nighter? Want me to have something delivered? I can call the twenty-four-hour Chinese place?"

Sam just pointed with her finger. "Home, slave."

Marcy's laughter echoed down the hall as she left. Moments later Sam heard the sound of the private elevator rising to their top-floor offices. She made a mental note to discuss with her partners the idea of giving her assistant—all of their assistants for that matter—a raise after this was over. If all went according to plan, they'd certainly be able to afford it.

She glanced up at the clock and groaned. It was well past midnight. Again. And she still faced those two international conference calls and a stack of pink message slips a mile deep. In spite of the pressure, she found herself smiling. Only weeks away from launching their biggest media blitz yet—a live fashion show, beamed via satellite to viewers all over the world—she was privately nervous as hell. But she was also excited.

She and her two partners, Mia Tennario and Jamie Baird, had worked like slaves themselves to get their latest brainchild up and running. But then they'd all been working like slaves ever since launching their lingerie catalog two years ago. And with Jamie's recent exposure as the designer behind VLL's most popular lingerie line, things had only gotten crazier.

Samantha was still stunned at how Jamie had managed to turn that potential fiasco around. Exposing the secret that a man was designing their "real women" line could have destroyed them. Instead, he'd managed to flip it to their advantage and, in the end, the whole thing had only amped up the media hype to new proportions. They couldn't have gotten better exposure if they'd planned it.

"Go Jamie," Sam murmured, lifting her mug of tepid coffee in the general direction of Jamie's dark offices. Used to be he'd be pulling later hours than she did, but since Lorna Sutton had strolled into his life, well, he'd suddenly found reasons to work away from the office.

Samantha's lips curved a little at that. She was still highly amused at the idea that playboy Jamie's heart had been snagged right out from under him. Not that he seemed to mind all that much. In fact, he'd been almost sickeningly happy about the whole thing. Her smile slipped a little as her thoughts naturally drifted to her own sex life. And the man she was currently involved with. There was no denying she enjoyed his company as they were both usually naked at the time, but it wasn't like her heart was in jeopardy. But then she never put that particular piece of real estate on the market.

She rubbed at the funny little twitch in her chest, telling herself it was too much caffeine and not enough sleep making her feel off-kilter. She turned her attention back to her desk and the pile of folders Marcy had left her. "What made us think we could pull this off, I have no idea."

She sipped at her coffee, made a face as the cold dregs washed over her tongue, then downed the rest of it anyway. What the hell, a boost was a boost at this point, right? She glanced at the red leather couch tucked against the opposite wall of her office and debated whether she could stand sleeping at work yet again.

Jamie and Mia had found a way to work away from the office, but Sam hadn't mastered that particular feat yet. Of course, they were both probably pulling all-nighters, too. She smiled. In Jamie's case, he probably wasn't pulling his alone. "Brat," she muttered. He was their money and finance guy, but as their newly revealed hot designer, he was just as frantic as the rest of them, getting everything ready in time to launch his new designs in the show.

Normally Mia's job was to design the layout, theme and "look" for each catalog. She was a genius at her job and made it almost easy for Samantha to fill those carefully designed pages with whatever new and daring pieces she decided to showcase in each issue.

At the moment, however, Mia's task was to oversee the endless details surrounding the actual construction and design of the stage and set for the show itself. Sam's job was to line up the lingerie designers, choose which pieces she wanted to showcase from each collection, then coordinate the models for each. All the VLL models were real women, with real bodies and real curves, which, along with Mia's innovative design, was what made their catalog stand out from the rest.

To further complicate matters, they were featuring designers, all women—except for Jamie, of course— from around the world, as well. Which meant handling details in every time zone on the planet. At the moment, Sam was due to call Auckland for an evening consultation, New Zealand time, then handle an early-morning conference call, Pacific Rim time, with a new Singapore designer she'd only just discovered.

She checked the clock and picked up the phone, but instead of dialing the international number Marcy had typed out for her, her fingers hovered over the speed-dial buttons. Specifically the second one from the bottom. The one she'd marked Cowboy. After all, if Jamie could combine work and pleasure, she should be able to.

"No. Thinking about Marshall Conley right now is absolutely, positively the last thing you need to do," she schooled herself. She wasn't good at mixing business with pleasure. In fact, she sucked at it. Business always won with her. Which was why Marsh had been the perfect companion. She'd met the horse trainer out at his Canyon Country ranch nine months ago when she'd decided after one too many rolls of antacids and far too many nights sleeping on her office couch that she needed something other than work to balance her life. One of her clients had recommended riding lessons and Samantha had been intrigued by the idea. Trotting around on a horse sounded a lot more relaxing than taking up tennis or golf.

Well, she'd found a distraction all right. Although in terms of exertion… She smiled to herself. Tennis might have been less strenuous.

At the moment, however, a distraction was something she could ill afford. Thinking about the man who'd started as her riding instructor, but had ended up becoming her lover, would definitely be counterproductive to the workload she faced in the oncoming early-morning hours. Of course, it did provide a nice bump in her pulse rate that the cold caffeine had failed to produce.

Thoughts of what else she'd like Marsh to bump up made her smile, even as she fought to shut that mental track down…and the vivid images those thoughts inspired. She wasn't entirely successful. And not sure she cared. Sighing in remembered pleasure from their last time together—which had been far too long ago—she reflexively sipped from her now empty mug, then rolled her eyes at her own silly mooning.

The great thing about Marshall was he was as busy and dedicated to his work as she was. The perfect lover really. Growing up as the only child of a single parent, Samantha had vowed early on that she would never end up like her mother. Her father had walked out on them when Sam was a toddler, stranding his poorly educated wife—who'd intended to spend her life being a housewife and mother—in a low-paying job with no hope for advancement, and no time to improve herself.

Samantha had only been nineteen when, after years of struggling just to put food in their mouths, her mom had been killed in a single-car accident; she'd fallen asleep behind the wheel after a week of pulling double shifts. But one thing Sam had gotten from her mother was her work ethic. She knew better than most that if you wanted something badly enough, you worked for it. For her mom, it had been putting a roof over their heads and clothes on their backs. For Sam it was the dream of a better life. Her mother's sudden death had only strengthened Samantha's resolve to never depend on anyone but herself. She'd already busted her ass all through school and landed herself a college scholarship. She went on to earn a degree in fashion marketing, and never looked back.

Sam had taken an early liking to power and control. In all areas of her life. Financial stability would give her both of those things. But that was only the beginning of her plans. After a few years of working hard to make other people successful, she realized the only way she was going to control her own destiny was to work for herself.

Realistically, she knew she needed help to make that vision come true, so she'd compromised. Her first call had been to her college buddy, Mia. Mia had the design smarts and Sam had the industry contacts. All they needed was money. Enter Jamie, financial wizard, and recent fling of Mia's. The fling didn't survive, but the friendship had. They'd ended up forming an equal partnership, and Velvet, Leather & Lace had been born. Sam was intensely protective of their baby, as were her partners, and they all worked just as doggedly to make their venture the success they knew it could be.

Sure, it got lonely on occasion. Having a career as your significant other was like that. But even with her thirtieth birthday mere months away, Sam had no regrets on how she ran her life. Besides, the occasional hot fling took the edge off and, more importantly, didn't slow her down.

Which was exactly what Sam thought when she first laid eyes on Marsh Conley. It had been late fall, and plans for their show were just heating up. They'd been so busy, it had been months since she'd squeezed in even an afternoon's worth of R & R. Or S & S as Samantha called it. Sex and Socialization. So she had been feeling a bit needy.

Watching this enigmatic cowboy tame half a ton of writhing horseflesh as easily as she handled nailing a six-figure deal for a new line of bras and panties had definitely gotten her mind off of business...and onto more personal matters. Like Marsh's rugged body...and how hard it would be to tame that.

She'd been intrigued, to put it mildly. Marsh was completely different from the men she usually dated. The epitome of the quiet cowboy. No flash, no cocky bravado. Just all man. And inside one hour she was dying to find out how fast she could get Marsh out of that saddle...and into hers.

As it turned out, Marsh wasn't all that impressed with her brand-new, formfitting riding pants. Nor did he seem to care all that much about power or success. Mostly he seemed disappointed in her woeful horse-woman skills. Not that he was overt about it; he wasn't overt about anything, but she sensed his growing impatience with her inability to sit on a horse properly, her lack of communication skills with the beast—it was just a horse for God's sake!—not to mention her less than graceful dismount technique.

Samantha smiled now, remembering just how arrogant she'd been that afternoon, convincing herself that, despite appearances, Marsh must be gay. After all, no man could resist Samantha Wallace when she put her mind to it. Well, Marsh had resisted her with no apparent problem.

Then she'd slid off the mountain of a horse she'd been attempting to ride and all but fallen butt first into the mud. Rather than let her fall—which she knew he would have relished watching, and which she admitted now was the least of what she'd deserved—he'd proven himself to be the gentleman he was, and had swung her clear of the mud and the snorting, stamping horse.

She sighed, remembering that first time he'd put his hands on her. He had plucked her off that horse as if she'd weighed nothing more than a feather. And at five foot nine, Samantha was no feather. He'd punched her pulse rate up a bit that day, too. Then he'd set her back on her feet and walked away as if he hadn't just set her entire body on high alert.

She'd followed him into the barn, not really thinking at all clearly. She'd forgotten all about seduction. Okay, so that was a lie. She wanted him more than ever at that point. But she was mostly intent on just figuring the man out. She'd assumed, with the arrogance of a woman who was willing to work for what she wanted—and was used to getting it—that the rest would simply follow. But Marsh wasn't most men. He didn't say much, and when he did, he chose his words carefully. He didn't reveal much about himself, but somehow she'd ended up revealing a great deal about herself that day.

She'd ended up leaving the ranch alone. But not before scheduling another riding session.

And then another.

Restless memories made focusing on the pending business calls all but impossible. She needed a fresh influx of caffeine, not more thoughts about the man she'd been seeing far too little of lately. She missed him. And that bothered her. Okay, it was more like it scared her. A lot. She didn't really *need* Marsh. Well, other than for the obvious reasons. But a lack of sex didn't quite explain why he popped into her thoughts far too often, and at the most inopportune moments. She was too busy to be mooning over a lover. Especially when she'd never been one to moon in her entire life.

Samantha shoved her chair back and went to put a fresh pot of coffee on. Fifteen minutes later she was gripping the warm mug like a lifeline and punching in the overseas number. She made both calls in record time and was even happy with the results, but rather than congratulate herself with a chocolate bar and the usual renewed zest for success, she found herself standing at her office window, frowning.

She wasn't looking out and absorbing the pulse and vibe of the city at night as she so often did. No, in her mind's eye, she was still seeing Marsh. As she had, all throughout the damn phone calls.

She shook her head, trying to free herself of the sensual spell, then resolutely turned her back to the window and resumed her place at her desk. She'd already given Marsh far too much of her time and thoughts. They both understood theirs wasn't a traditional relationship. It was a union of…convenience. One that would last as long as they were both getting something out of it—one that would end the moment either one decided it was time to move on.

And that's what unnerved her. Nine months later, and she wasn't ready to move on. Sometimes she kept him at arm's length, even when she didn't have to, just to test herself. She didn't do it on purpose; it was more like an instinctive measuring stick. If things were getting a bit too hot, a bit too…good, she purposely dived back into work and refused to come up for air—or Marsh—for as long as she thought she could get away with it.

And every time she saw him again, she'd end up holding her breath as she waited those endless seconds to see if he'd tell her not to bother this time, that he'd moved on. He hadn't.

Yet.

She blew out a long breath and leaned back in her chair, stretching the kinks from her lower back. With the show moving into the frantic final stages, she'd had little time to spare, even if she'd wanted to. Marsh never pushed when she begged off, but lately, rather than feel relieved, she'd found herself hoping he'd push for more, demand more of her.

Which made absolutely no sense. Her company was finally on the verge of making a global impact on the lingerie industry. It was the worst possible time for her to be thinking dangerous thoughts. Thoughts about wanting something more…permanent in her personal life. It would be the ultimate in stupidity on her part to risk what they did have. Especially when she was far from sure what she really wanted from him.

Besides, he hadn't given any indication he was unhappy with their arrangement. No, Marsh wasn't the whiny sort. She smiled, unable to imagine him pouting, much less throwing a temper tantrum. That wasn't Marsh's way. He was patient, quietly confident, observant. Much like he was with his horses. He was content to let his actions speak for him. She shuddered with remembered pleasure of just how…illuminating some of those actions could be.

The buzzer on her intercom went off right then, startling a surprised gasp out of her. She barely kept the coffee from sloshing out of the mug. Hand to her heart, she set the mug down. "No more coffee for you," she said, knowing damn well it wasn't caffeine overload making her nerve endings twitch. It was Marshall Conley withdrawal.

Sam shook her arms, rolled her shoulders. "Get back to business," she murmured. "Keep your eye on the ball." The buzzer went off again and she punched the button to the lobby desk. "Yes, Dave?" she asked the night guard.

"Your car is here, ma'am."

Samantha frowned. "My car?" She hadn't ordered a car.

"A limo. The driver has a personal delivery for you."

"I'm sorry, there must be some mistake."

There was a pause. "No, ma'am. No mistake."

"Who's the sender?"

There was a pause, then Dave said, "There is a card with the package. The driver says you'll understand when you open it. If it helps, I'm familiar with the limo service, Ms. Wallace, and I've scanned the package. Everything appears to be in order. Shall I send it up on your private elevator?"

Samantha smiled as she suddenly realized what was happening. It was probably one of the designers she'd yet to decide on, trying to impress her. After Jamie's big media splash, the hype around the show had mushroomed. Now instead of wooing the hottest designers, they were coming to her. Not usually in the middle of the night, but she was dealing with an international clientele at this point, so maybe they had crossed a time zone or three. Intrigued now, she pushed the button. "Send it up."

# CHAPTER TWO

SAMANTHA WALKED out of her office to VLL's private elevator. It had been one of the perks of securing the top-floor offices. When they'd first set out to open up shop, Jamie had insisted on the three of them getting as nice an office space as possible. "You have to look like a success to be a success," he'd told them. Mia and Sam had readily agreed but wondered how Jamie would pull it off with their limited capital. In the two years since, Sam had learned to never underestimate the creative money genius that was Jamie Baird.

She reached the doors as they slid open. "Wow." The box was huge. Flat and rectangular, it was wrapped in a red silk bow and filled her arms as she lifted it out of the elevator car and carried it to her desk. "I could fit our entire summer catalog of lingerie in this thing."

As promised, there was a cream-colored envelope tucked inside the ribbon. No name on the back. She pulled a thick vellum card from the envelope. Handwritten in black ink, in a decidedly masculine slash, the card read:

*Your chariot awaits, the driver discreet.*
*Come if you dare, a challenge you'll meet.*
*Open the box, wear only what you discover.*
*Life is more than just work, or being your lover.*

*What?* Her heart had begun pounding halfway through the note. This wasn't from a designer. So who the hell—? Then she reread the last line…and sank back against her desk, suddenly weak in the knees. Could it be? No. But she only had one lover. She read the note a third time.

*"Marsh?"* she whispered in stunned surprise. Marsh had sent this?

As the shock wore off, she realized she was both disconcerted…and intrigued. She was so used to calling the shots between them and him being fine with that, that this really threw her. "'Come if you dare, a challenge you'll meet,'" she read aloud. A shiver raced over her skin as she set the card aside and fingered the ribbon on the box. And only part of it was in trepidation. The other part was undeniably excitement. What was he up to?

There was only one way to find out, but she didn't immediately tear into the box. She was dying to know what was in it, as of course he'd known she would be, but still… Something about his assumption that she'd blindly follow his request—his command performance—annoyed her a little. Of course, he knew her well enough to know she'd probably react like that, too. "Come if you *dare*," she repeated. "Bastard," she said, but her lips were curving into a reluctant smile as she did. He did know her. Better than she'd realized.

She tugged off the ribbon, telling herself that just because she opened the box, didn't mean she had any intention of putting the contents on, much less hopping into a limo to be taken God knew where. She slid the lid off and pulled back the tissue paper. Her mouth dropped open. She'd expected—well, hell, she really had no idea. The box had been too big and weighty to contain lingerie or something slinky or sexy. Still, she hadn't expected anything like this.

She lifted out the folded pile of black leather and couldn't help but stroke it as she laid it across her lap. It was the softest thing she'd ever felt, so supple it pooled in her lap almost like heavy silk. She flipped back the edge to find it was, indeed, lined in lustrous champagne silk. As blankets went, it was beyond decadent. But hardly the sexy, naughty something she'd thought his note had implied.

Unless you were a cowboy.

Leather and silk. A combination of masculine and sexy that admittedly got her pulse rate pumping. Did he really expect her to strip down and wrap herself in this? She ignored completely the fact that her nipples were already hard at the idea of driving off into the hot summer night wrapped in nothing more than soft leather and icy silk. She also ignored the accompanying thought of what one could do in the back of a limo on a blanket like this…

Was that it? Was Marsh downstairs right now, in the back of that limo? She stood up abruptly, letting the blanket slide off her lap in a curtain of calfskin, torn between the immediate desire to race straight out to the curb to find out…and sending the empty box back downstairs with a note of her own, informing him she wasn't impressed with his high-handed tactics.

Admittedly, it was harder to fight against the former impulse than the latter. It was only when she scooped up the blanket again that she realized it wasn't a blanket at all. It was a cloak. A floor-length cloak, with a collar trimmed in black fur.

It was much harder to ignore her body's immediate

response to that new piece of information. Okay, impossible to ignore.

"Damn you, Marsh," she said, but only partly in irritation. Because she was already pulling it around her shoulders. *Wear only what you discover.*

She shivered in pleasure, imagining what the unbearably soft, silk-lined cloak would feel like sliding over her bare skin. Of course, there was no way she was doing such a thing. She quickly bundled it up and laid it back in the box. Before she changed her mind. "Get your mind back on business," she told herself. She had a million and one things that needed her attention. Marsh, leather temptation and all, would have to wait.

Just as he always did.

She frowned at that. *Life is more than just work, or being your lover.* He was pushing for more. And hadn't she just been wondering how to have the same thing? Jamie had found a way to do it. Maybe she could—no. No, she couldn't. She never had before. And she certainly couldn't afford to even think about it now. Not with the show only two weeks away. The timing couldn't be more horrible. Certainly he could wait another couple weeks. She chewed her lip as she paused in front of the open elevator doors. Couldn't he?

She had abruptly thrust the box down on the floor of the elevator, had even stabbed the lobby button and was prepared to step out…when she just as abruptly changed her mind. Not that she was going on any drive, dressed in that cloak or not. But she should return the box to the driver personally, shouldn't she? Ask him to deliver a message to the sender, whether he was presently parked outside or miles away. After all, Marsh had gone to a lot of trouble. It was the least she could do. And it might buy her some time with him. Which meant she had about thirty seconds to figure out what that message was going to be. She stepped out into the lobby, box in her arms, still not sure what to say.

The driver was a big, well-muscled man with skin the color of midnight. His smile was wide, his bow courteous. And she had no earthly clue who he was, much less whom he worked for. For a moment, her certainty that Marsh was responsible for this little game wavered.

"Ma'am," he said, gesturing through the glass doors to the mile-long white limo that purred at the curb.

Samantha had ridden in many a limo, so she wasn't easily seduced by the glamour of it. And yet something about envisioning herself in the black leather cloak, being tucked into that white gleaming ride… She shook the image free and turned a pleasant, professional smile to the driver, glad she could feel Dave's hovering presence just behind her.

"I'm sorry, but I—I don't think I'll be able to attend," she said haltingly, then drew in a breath and tried for her normally confident smile. "Please let your employer know I appreciated the effort." She held out the box. "And the gesture. It was very thoughtful, but—"

The driver took the box, his smile not wavering in the least. He slid another card from his suit jacket pocket. "I was told to give you this."

Very aware of the eyes on her, she slid the envelope open and pulled out another card, bearing another note in the same masculine slash.

*Chicken.*

A short laugh spluttered from her before she could stop it. *Chicken?* So now she'd been all but double dared. She eyed the box…and the driver's gleaming white smile.

"Will you please accompany me, Miss Wallace?" he asked courteously.

Samantha tapped the card on her finger. She couldn't deny the little thrill of adrenaline pulsing through her. It had to be Marsh. Not that she'd ever dreamed he could come up with something like this. But then, how well did she really truly know him? Outside of bed, that is? That made her shiver again…in pleasure, and yes, anticipation. She knew going out there would be a capitulation of sorts.

*Life is more than just work, or being your lover.*

Was he telling her he wanted to have something more? A real relationship? Was getting her to agree to this outrageous—but admittedly intriguing stunt—his way of coercing some kind of commitment from her?

Now it was her turn to smile. *Well,* she thought, *we'll just see about that.* She thought about the files that awaited her attention, the meetings she had to set up before Monday and all the other myriad details begging her to go back to work. But after this little surprise, she doubted seriously she'd be worth anything the rest of the night. She was admittedly distracted now. And after all, it was just one night, already half over. She still had the entire weekend to tackle her workload. She'd order in Chinese and pull a whole weekender. Surely she could give herself a few hours to see what Marsh had up his sleeve.

Despite the bad timing, with all the thoughts she'd been having about him lately, she knew she'd forever regret not following through on this. What was the worst that could happen? They'd argue and she'd come back to the office and bury herself in work as she always did.

*Yeah,* her little voice whispered, *but on the other hand, what's the best thing that could happen?*

She didn't let herself think about that. Didn't dare. That would mean admitting maybe she wanted what he appeared to want. She wasn't ready to go there. Yet.

Before she could change her mind, she shot the driver a quick, if somewhat nervous smile and said, "Apparently I'll be leaving with you after all." She took a quick look at Dave, took his amused nod in stride, then followed the driver out of the building before she could change her mind.

He tucked her safely inside the limo…then handed her the cloak box. With a knowing grin, he closed the door, then slid into the front seat, on the other side of a smoked partition. It wasn't until they were safely away that she realized she'd left her purse, her keys, basically everything she owned, back in her office.

She felt a moment's alarm, realizing she was heading off to God knew where, driven by God knew who…and just what if it wasn't Marsh waiting at the other end? She was reaching for the button to call the driver, who was hidden from her through a solid panel, when she spied the envelope tucked in the seat across from her.

She picked it up and pulled out another note. Same handwriting.

*Are you wearing it yet? Remember, nothing else.*
*Or the night will end early.*

She stiffened. How did he know she hadn't donned the cloak? A guess? Or was he—she rapped on the panel. It slid open, revealing only the driver. She sighed, disappointed to find Marsh wasn't a surprise passenger after all.

"Yes, ma'am?" the driver asked.

"How long a ride is it?"

"Just under an hour, ma'am."

"Thank you." The panel slid shut. An hour. About how long it would take to get to the ranch.

So this was definitely Marsh. He was her only lover, after all. And now he was demanding she come to him, dressed like some sort of sex slave or something. That made her shift in her seat. Well, she wasn't about to take off her clothes in the back of a limo and put on a cloak, no matter how decadent it was. Her gaze strayed to the box. What had caused him to dream up this little escapade anyway? Did he think their love life was getting boring? True, they didn't see each other nearly often enough, but when they did… She shook her head, not wanting to go there. She knew the sex between them was downright explosive. It was why they were together, was it not?

She found herself remembering the first time he'd put his hands on her…when it wasn't training related. It had been her fourth riding lesson in just over a month—a testament to her attraction right there, given her hectic schedule—and already a longer time frame than most of her relationships from beginning to end.

He'd been so damn patient with her but she still couldn't get the hang of things. Frustrated with her uncustomary ineptitude, not to mention his endlessly cool gaze and measured responses, she'd finally lost her temper and stomped off to the barn. Clearly the man was too much trouble, and she'd berated herself for giving him as much time as she had.

Marsh surprised her by stomping in right behind her, stopping at the door to the tack room and demanding to know what she thought she was doing, walking out in the middle of a lesson.

She'd tossed her hair back and said, "Leaving, what does it look like I'm doing?"

And then he'd gone and done it. He'd smiled. It had been the first she'd ever gotten from him. The transformation was stunning. She'd been attracted to his rugged good looks and enigmatic demeanor from the get-go. But when his eyes sparked and the hard line of his jaw softened as his once-shuttered features split into that wide, cocky grin…her attraction to him had gone into instant overdrive. He'd caught her so off guard, she'd forgotten her retort, forgotten to shove past him, forgotten to walk away.

Still smiling, he'd leaned oh, so casually against the frame of the open door, his body still radiating that controlled power that did something wicked to her insides. "You're going to leave now?" he said, in that laid-back, take-me-or-leave-me drawl of his. "When it's finally getting interesting?"

"Finally?" she'd spluttered. "I've been trying my damnedest to get your attention and now, when I'm a bitch, you notice? What's wrong with you?"

He'd laughed then. "I'm beginning to wonder about that myself." Then he'd cornered her in that room that smelled of tanned leather and sweaty flesh. He'd kicked the door shut, advanced on her. And suddenly it was as though none of this had been her idea at all. As if it had been his idea all along; the stalking, the planning…the seducing.

Samantha shifted her weight on the leather seat of the limo, pressing her thighs together as the memory stirred her. As thoughts of Marsh always did. She remembered how she'd quickly taken the upper hand in that tack room; her pride had demanded it. He had to know he wasn't going to control her, control them. But she hadn't forgotten, either, how he'd continued to smile as he'd allowed her that control. As if he'd planned that, too, all along.

The miles slid by as she wondered what else he had planned for her. What was in store for her out at the ranch tonight? And how would she control the situation? Control Marsh? "Since when have you ever lost control of anything?" she murmured, a slow smile playing at the corners of her mouth. The answer to that was never.

Feeling emboldened, she slid the lid off the box, pulled the supple leather out and let it lie across her lap…imagining just what might happen if she put it on. And what might not happen if she didn't.

And as the lights of L.A. winked out behind her and they wound their way into the hills, Samantha began to take her clothes off.

## CHAPTER THREE

THE LIMO SLID THROUGH the night, the windows so darkly tinted Samantha couldn't see much of anything beyond them. It was as if she were trapped in a cocoon, in her silk-lined chrysalis. She shifted slightly and the heavy cloak slid across her skin, making her shudder. Between the images of what she must look like—a leather-girded gift—and what was likely to happen to her when Marsh unwrapped her…well, she'd quickly learned to sit very still. The least bit of movement, the watery slide of silk over her bare skin, was almost unbearably arousing.

And then the smooth ride changed, grew more bumpy. Marsh's spread was up in the hills, but he wasn't hurting financially, quite the opposite. The roads leading to his house and main barns were all paved and well maintained, just like everything else he owned. So…where were they now?

She clutched at the cloak, pulling it closer, sucking in her breath as it slid over now highly sensitized skin. Had he planned on that, too? An hour of leather and silk-lined foreplay? She angled herself so she could peer more closely out the side window, but it was hopeless. She couldn't see a thing. For all she knew she was going to be dumped out in the middle of nowhere.

They turned, then the car rolled to a stop. Her heart began to race faster, her skin growing damp…admittedly with trepidation as well as arousal. She was suddenly overwhelmed with doubt.

*What in the hell had she been thinking?* What if someone else had written that note for nefarious reasons? Maybe they'd wanted her to think it was her lover. After all, this was so unlike anything Marsh would do. Wasn't it? Would Dave call someone if she wasn't at her desk first thing tomorrow morning? Except it was Friday night. A different guard was on weekend duty. She swallowed hard, a million thoughts racing through her mind as she waited for the door to be opened for her. For the driver to lead her into…God knew what. She began to panic, an emotion so foreign to her it was all but paralyzing. *Get a grip, Samantha. Think!* She forced in one deep breath, then another. She was just groping for the handle when the door swung open.

She snatched her hand back, clutched the cloak shut as the driver's smooth, calm face appeared. He nodded in approval over her attire. She glanced quickly to where she'd discarded her skirt and silk blouse. *Idiot, idiot, idiot.* For all she knew, she was about to be sold into some foreign potentate's harem! Okay, maybe that was a little far-fetched, but still, she was nervous. Just having that thought should have made her feel ridiculous, should have allowed her to put things in perspective. It didn't.

See, this was why she didn't try and mix business with pleasure. She knew better. She should have stayed at her desk, dammit. This was possibly the stupidest decision she'd ever made. She had too many things to do before the show to be fooling around like this. This was exactly why she always put work first. Succeeding in work was a clear and focused goal. When it came to her personal life, it was obvious her judgment became seriously suspect.

She was about to lunge for her clothes, when the driver extended his hand for hers. She looked at him, tried not to let him see the panic. Okay. If she was going to be in control of this situation, she couldn't let her feelings show. She'd brazened her way through many a power lunch, doing whatever it took to forge ahead with her business interests, at times gaining success by sheer will, and a refusal to accept defeat. She could certainly handle this.

*Of course, you weren't usually naked at the time.* Taking as deep a breath as she could manage and not be obvious, Samantha forced a calmness into her body she did not remotely feel, and reached for the driver's huge hand with a light smile.

"Thank you," she said, hoping he didn't hear the slight tremulous thread that was beyond her ability to control at the moment. But surely, once he'd taken her to…wherever it was she was going, she'd find her ground, find a way to assume control, take the upper hand, do whatever—

Her thoughts broke off as she looked at the scene before her. She wasn't at Marsh's ranch house. In fact, she'd never seen this place before in her life.

There was a pathway of stone steps leading up the side of the mountain, lit only by a row of small luminaries. Though it was the middle of summer, the air this high up was clear and chilly, causing her to gather the cloak more closely around her as she stared up the hillside to the house that sprawled along the peak. It was log and glass, the sides angled away from the edge of the precipice it sat out on, the center a soaring, two-story A-frame structure made almost entirely of glass. It wasn't ablaze with light. In fact, a dim glow from somewhere inside, along with a small curl of smoke rising from the chimney, were the only indications that anyone was at home. There was no car parked nearby and when she turned to look back in the direction they'd come from, the heavy stand of pines kept her from seeing more than a few dozen yards back down the winding gravel road.

"Miss?"

She jerked her attention to the driver, silently cursing herself for being so jumpy.

He smiled, gestured for her to go ahead of him.

She gathered the cloak so she wouldn't trip over it, glad she'd at least had the wherewithal to keep her heels on. For that matter, she'd kept her bra and panties on, too. Her one small act of defiance. Not that those flimsy garments felt like much of a shield at the moment, but it was a crucial difference between being stark naked, and one she clung to at the moment as she mounted the flat, stone steps.

She assumed the driver was still standing behind her, so she was startled to hear the crunch of tires on gravel. Whirling around, wobbling and almost falling in her haste, she watched as the limo pulled smoothly around the drive and headed back down the mountain. She opened her mouth to shout, to demand he stop, but the red taillights disappeared around the bend. And she was alone.

Shivering now, she slowly turned and looked back up the hill. Somehow, in the space of one hour, she'd gone from being Samantha Wallace, partner in her own company, confident and in control, sitting in her office like a queen sat on a throne…to Samantha Wallace, half-naked woman, all alone on a mountaintop. She shuddered. And was shocked to find that a tiny bit of that shivering sensation was due to anticipation. Someone—and it had better be Marsh, she thought, trembling—had gone to a lot of trouble to get her here. That same someone's goals were obviously sexual in nature. Another ripple skated over her skin…and an ache of awareness sprang to life between her legs.

*Okay,* she told herself, *this is just ridiculous.* She had no reason to be so afraid. Much less aroused. What she should be is furious, for being stupid enough to come here in the first place, for being manipulated by Marsh into playing this little charade. And just as soon as she got up these steps, she planned to deliver a stinging little set-down right before she demanded the return of that limo.

Grabbing that sliver of control, she moved up the stairs, head held high, shoulders back. She would not let him see how rattled she'd been. And she definitely wasn't going to reveal she'd been the least bit aroused by the situation that had been created exclusively for her.

When she got to the top landing, she stepped onto a small patio made out of a mosaic of round stones. A path to her right led to a small, softly lit in-ground pool. The luminaries, however, continued up the steps to her left. Steps that led to a wide veranda, at the top of which was a wide set of double doors, inlaid with stained glass. She looked up at the towering facade of glass, but could still only make out a dim, flickering glow. She realized now the glass was not clear, but smoked. Probably as a means to cut down on glare from the sun. At the moment, however, it only made the place seem more remote, more…dangerous.

Steeling herself with a deep breath, she debated whether to climb the stairs and knock…or wait for him to come to her. The latter would leverage control to her side. So she wandered down to the pool, walked along the edge, not allowing herself to glance up again at the front of the house. Was he watching her? Was he waiting? Was he scowling at her power-play tactics?

She fingered the fur-trimmed collar and allowed a small smile to surface. What would he do if she simply let it slide from her shoulders. If she slid off one heel, then the other, and dived cleanly into the water? Of course, unless the pool was heated, the water would be much too cold for that. She was half-tempted to do it for that reason alone. Would he rush to save her? The balance of power would shift and all his plans for the evening would be dashed with that one splash of cold water.

She pulled the cloak up, sank down just low enough to test the water with her fingertips. Frigid. Even the thrill of victory wasn't worth the risk of that icy a plunge. She turned, studiously avoiding the window. Had he suspected the direction of her thoughts? Was he even now chuckling over her inability to make the jump?

Probably, she thought, her smile fading. It was unnerving to realize how well he did know her. She wandered around the edge of the patio, but there were no other paths leading from it, other than the one that led to that wide staircase…to those double doors. Finally, she turned, looked up. Saw nothing…and yet felt… something.

"The hell with this," she said suddenly. Gripping the cloak so she didn't trip over it, she strode with full conviction toward the path, up the stairs, to the wide doors. No way was she knocking. Bidding an entrance. She'd been brought here, stranded here. As far as she was concerned, she'd earned herself the right to direct entry. She twisted the knob, shoved the door open and strode in. Only to come to an abrupt halt, her mouth dropping open once again.

The place was nothing more than shadow, lit only by a low fire in the massive stone fireplace that backed the far wall. But even hindered by lack of light, it was obviously stunning. The chimney rose to the top of the A-frame structure. A railing framed the second-floor loft, but it was too dark to see anything up there. Her gaze traveled back to the sunken living room, the leather furnishings that circled the great fireplace, then down to the thick piles of fur, leather and silk that lay tumbled in an undulating heap in front of it. Between the fireplace and the decadent orgy of leather and silk, there was a low glass-and-iron table, which bore a small round tray. On it sat a single champagne glass, half-filled with clear sparkling liquid. In the flickering light, she also saw the envelope propped against the slender glass stem.

She found herself swallowing against the sudden dryness of her throat. It was the only thing dry about her at that moment. And she was forced to admit that, in that one swift instant, arousal and curiosity suddenly outweighed fear or outrage. She longed for just one sip, something to soothe her jangled nerves, grasp back that elusive sliver of control. And yes, she wanted to know what was in the envelope. Dammit.

She glanced around, but couldn't make out anything else except the wide, open riser stairway that twisted up to the second-story loft. Was he up there? Or was he somewhere in the shadows beyond that pile of decadence in the living room?

She debated calling out, demanding he show himself. Instead, she opted to get the champagne first, fortify herself. She picked up the glass, letting the note fall flat on the tray. Twirling the contents, Samantha wondered just how much more at risk she'd be putting herself by tasting it. Was it drugged? What would happen to her then? It was alarming in the extreme that the thought only made her clench her thighs together as the ache deepened sharply.

But she'd stepped from reality into fantasy, and as the moments passed, it was harder and harder to think clearly, rationally. She sat the champagne down untouched, her thinking clouded enough, and picked up the note, sliding yet another card out of a weighty envelope.

*Control. Commitment.*
*Neither will you give.*
*After losing one and making the other,*
*You'll know what it is to live.*

Her body twitched hard at the threat...the promise, that she read between those lines. So that was his plan? She would be made to lose control, coerced into making a commitment. She shook her head. "No one can make me do anything I don't want to do."

"Exactly."

She inhaled a sharp gasp, and turned to find him standing halfway down the staircase. Cast in flickering shadow, he wore a loose white shirt, carelessly unbuttoned at cuff and neck. Below that he wore riding breeches, dark, smooth...fitting his thighs, his buttocks as if he'd been born to them. His boots didn't reflect any shine from the firelight, apparently as worn as the breeches, as natural to the wearer as his skin.

It was only when she drew her gaze to his face that her shallow, rapid breaths stopped completely. Dark tousled hair lent a reckless look to the dangerous glitter she saw in his eyes. His mouth was composed, neither fierce nor gentle, but the serious set to his jaw she recognized as determination, just as he'd have with a particularly recalcitrant horse.

Her breath caught in her throat when she spied the riding crop he flicked along his thigh. Was that how he'd come to see her? As some kind of filly that needed taming? And since when did he use any kind of force, much less pain, as coercion to gain the response he wanted?

No, the man she knew used softly spoken words, a gentle touch, a whisper in the ear, with females both four legged and two. But as she moved toward the base of the stairs, drawn there by a force she didn't quite understand, she understood one thing completely....

This was not the Marshall Conley she knew.

## CHAPTER FOUR

IT WAS ALL MARSH COULD DO to stand there, to remain still. He'd spent the past two hours prowling the house, wondering what the hell he thought he was doing, pushing her like this. Once his driver had called to say he was on the way back with Samantha, he'd only gotten more agitated. Now she was here, standing before him, perfection in her icy blond defiance.

*Please don't let this be a mistake,* he silently prayed.

The idea had started on a whim. Something that would challenge her into making more time for him. He wanted to see her. It was as simple…and complicated, as that. He understood she was busy with the upcoming show, but she was always busy. Her life was her work and he was only part of it because she needed occasional R & R breaks. His work demanded a lot of his time as well, so he'd been more than happy with that arrangement. Or he once had.

Somewhere during the past month or so, as they'd found less and less time for each other, he'd found himself missing her more and more. Not just for the sex and recreation, either. But her. Her laugh, her humor, the way she challenged him to think differently about things, to look at the world in a different way. He wanted to believe he challenged her the same way. He knew he'd been in her life longer than any man she'd ever been with. But that fact alone didn't instill him with confidence.

Samantha had a thing about control. He'd known that, from the very start. But he was a successful man, too. In large part due to his steady, unending reserve of patience. And frankly, as long as everyone was having a good time, he didn't feel threatened by her need to run things. In fact, it had been rather refreshing.

But as they continued to see one another, he learned that her need for control reached further than wanting to be on top, or to always want to direct their sex play. Afterward, they would usually lie in each other's arms and talk. At first they'd both keep it light, almost impersonal. But little by little, he'd urge her to open up, share more of herself with him, usually by sharing something of himself first. Even then she'd be reticent, and what she did share was almost all work related.

Still, slowly they'd begun to trust one another, or so he wanted to believe. And…somewhere during all that, he'd found himself falling in love with her. She might like to control things, but she was intensely giving, as well. She had no problem with working for what she wanted…in bed or out. He knew how hard she worked to make her business a success, and how dedicated she was to her partners. She felt a responsibility for their success, too. She just had a hard time, an almost impossible time for that matter, letting go of the reins. Given his life's calling, he understood that better than anyone.

Just as he understood the enormous reward there could be in developing a trust so strong, so complete, that giving over control was just as rewarding as wielding it.

So what had begun as a means of tempting her to

abandon work for a weekend with him—a weekend at his cabin where he hoped he could somehow get her to lower her walls a bit further, loosen that tightly held grip—had ended up developing into something far beyond that simple idea.

He understood animals instinctively, knew what made them skittish, knew how to earn their trust. Each and every relationship was different, but there was one constant he'd discovered in forging the bond that was so necessary to gaining that crucial trust. He simply needed to discover what his personal strength was in each particular relationship, then use it. Because that very strength in him was usually the greatest vulnerability in the other. So, relying on those same instincts, he knew that the only way to get Samantha to trust him enough to really give herself to him, was to make her realize she would always be safe with him. And the best pathway there was relying on their joint strength, their base connection and best source of communication.

Which, in their case, was explosive sex.

So he'd devised a plan that would incorporate the element of surprise, moving her out of her comfort zone…and into his. Even then, he'd been filled with doubt since sending out the note and the cloak hours earlier. He knew it was crunch time for her with the show on the horizon, but that had only decided him further. Her life was always frenzied like this. If she didn't use the show as an excuse, it would be something else.

But one thing he absolutely couldn't lose sight of, was that vulnerability went both ways.

Standing above her now, watching her, wrapped as he'd commanded in leather and silk, his body was rigidly, almost painfully hard. His heart was pounding so rapidly he could barely think straight. Could he do this? Could he carry through with his plan?

It felt like an all-or-nothing bargain now. He'd admitted to himself he wanted more now. Settling for less wasn't his way. Nor was it hers.

If he relented and let her take charge this time, let her dictate how things were going to be between them, he knew the relationship was doomed to end. He couldn't settle for a one-sided arrangement any longer. For either of them. And he didn't want her to settle anymore, either. He knew there could be more, so much more, with her. He hoped like hell she knew that about him, too. And wanted it badly enough to rearrange her priorities to include him. To include them both.

But getting her to even consider that there could be more between them wasn't so simple as just putting the question to her. Anymore than he would waltz into a ring with a skittish colt and attempt to throw a saddle on its back right off the bat. Samantha had spent a very long time exerting her need for control. She wasn't just going to give it up because he asked nicely.

Not that he wanted to tame her. Not at all. Nor did he want to break her. Most importantly, he didn't want her to relinquish her need for control entirely. What he wanted was to find some way to make her understand that sharing control could be far more rewarding than doing everything all on her own. And he wanted her to share it with him.

He wanted a true partnership.

Now all he had to do was pray like hell he knew what he was doing. Instinct had driven him this far, he had to hold on to that and hold hard, if he was going to carry through with his plans for this evening.

She'd donned the cloak, which meant she was at least curious enough to want to know what he had in store for her. But all he had to do was look at the defiant tilt to her chin, the icy glint in those arctic-blue eyes and the set of her shoulders to know that the battle was far from won. And hell, he thought, fighting a grudging smile, what fun would there be in that?

Holding her gaze, he descended the stairs, not stopping until he was less than a foot away from her.

SAMANTHA'S FINGERS sunk more deeply into the ermine collar as she forced herself to stand her ground and hold his unwavering dark gaze. Her knees shook slightly, the muscles in her thighs quivering as he stopped before her. And despite the myriad emotions coursing through her at the moment, there was no way to deny that one of them was arousal. Sharp, stinging, fiercely aching arousal.

If this was some kind of goddamn game, then she was forced to admit that maybe, just maybe, she wanted to play along. For a little while. She had given herself the rest of the night off after all. She could play his game. For now. Until she found a way to wrest control of it away from him and turn the tables. Yes, that would be her plan.

"I'm going to make one thing clear," she said quietly, if not as evenly as she'd have liked. She tilted her chin toward the crop. "I'm not into pain. At all. If you even think of using that on me, I'll—"

He lifted the slender wand then, holding her gaze as he did so, and ran the leather-looped tip along the side of her face, very, very softly. It made her gasp, both the act itself…and the touch of the worn leather, warm from his hands, on the delicate skin of her cheek.

"I would never hurt you. You know that." He waited, and she finally nodded.

She did know that much about him. Both with her, and in his work, he'd always been gentle.

"My goal is quite the opposite in fact," he said, his voice a deep rumble. "If at any time you're unwilling to do what I ask, then we stop. And I'll let you go."

*Let* her go?

She wanted to splutter in outrage. Wanted to turn and walk right out the door. *Let* her go, would he? Then she remembered; she had no way off this godforsaken mountain. Unless she planned to hike down in heels and a leather cloak. Or he provided her with a way out.

"Do you want to leave now?"

She was trying to regroup, find a new strategy. Clearly he wanted to keep her off balance. It was obvious that Marsh had spent some serious time thinking out his strategy. He was a quiet, observant man. Traits she'd admired, mostly because they made him an exquisite lover. No doubt he'd specifically waited until she was completely overwhelmed by the fashion show details to throw this little wrench into the works. She'd be more easily thrown off her stride. And he'd been right.

Still, she couldn't help but wonder why he'd decided to go about it this way. He wasn't an easy man to read, her lover. Although he'd never hesitated to answer her, only now did she realize how few questions she'd ever asked him. Yes, they'd talked shop, but she'd never probed much into the man himself.

Staring now into his enigmatic dark eyes, she realized why. Her self-preservation instincts were well established. She was drawn to him. Deeply so. In ways even she didn't understand. So she'd purposely, even subconsciously kept herself from finding out too much. She'd told herself she enjoyed the mystery, but she knew she was afraid she'd only come to want him more. And that would have put her at a distinct disadvantage in this relationship. A place she would never willingly put herself.

Until now. He was forcing her to decide what she wanted. Making her choose. She didn't know what she wanted…but she did know she wasn't ready to walk away. "No," she told him. "I don't want to leave. Yet." She hadn't meant to deliver that last part in such a taunting manner. She couldn't seem to help herself. That was her modus operandi, after all, wasn't it? Pushing him away when what she really wanted was to pull him closer?

He was a skilled lover, understood his body and hers, was unselfconscious about that and totally unselfish about pleasing her. She shuddered a little, remembering just how well he'd learned to please her. Looking at him now, she wondered where that patient, quiet lover had disappeared to. Maybe this power she spied in him had been there all along, and he'd simply thought he didn't need it with her. It might have been a relief to have someone else take charge for a change.

So, what had changed? Why did he think he needed it back now?

"Good," he told her, his eyes betraying his amusement. As if he knew she'd fight him every step of the way.

Another little shiver of awareness raced through her. The gleam in his eye was decidedly predatory…and emotional. Both revelations shook her. In that moment she understood that if this was a game, it was a decidedly serious one for him. He held all the cards. And if she didn't play what he dealt her, it was very likely she would never see him again.

It shouldn't have bothered her. In fact, it should have incensed her, that he thought he had to do this. Instead, her stomach fluttered at the thought of losing him. Her heart tripped, them stumbled…just a little. Which meant…what?

"Mar—" That was as far as she got before he slid the end of the crop to her chin and tipped her mouth closed.

"There will be time for talk later."

She arched one brow, prepared to deliver a sharp rebuke, but when he drew the crop tip down along the side of her neck, her shivery sigh belied any real irritation his heavy-handedness had stirred in her. He made her gasp when he suddenly, and quite expertly flipped the edge of her cloak open.

There was a pause, then maybe the slightest quirk to the corner of his mouth as he spied the edges of her lacy bra. She wanted to smile at him, gloat a bit over keeping some command of the situation. Only when his lips smoothed, and his gaze flickered back up to hers, did she feel a twinge of embarrassment. She'd disappointed him. By doing exactly what he'd apparently known she'd do.

Did she do that to him often? She hadn't thought so, but going back over some of their interludes, perhaps she had been a bit more controlling than even she'd realized. Her rationale was that she was merely protecting herself, both of them really, from getting hurt. And besides, it wasn't as though he hadn't always had a good time. It was her experience that most men didn't really care who called the shots as long as everyone got theirs. And Marsh always got his…and then some.

Now she realized that maybe what he'd gotten hadn't been all he'd wanted. Or needed. The idea confused her, had her guard wavering. And it was obvious a moment later that he'd noticed it, because he took full advantage. With a flick of his wrist he twisted the loops on the crop so they snagged the heavy bow, tied at her throat. Before she could react, the cloak had slithered off and lay in a pool of leather and silk at her feet.

She'd pictured doing exactly this, putting herself on display for him, out by the pool. Only now that he'd chosen the moment, that he'd done the disrobing, she didn't feel remotely as though she was in the superior position. Normally she'd have squared her shoulders, dared him with a direct look that demanded to know if he liked what he saw. She might have even turned around, arms held out, taunted him a little.

Her inability to let go bothered her. He'd wanted to do something exciting, and she couldn't even let herself play along.

Her gaze shot to his. His expression was unreadable, but he held her gaze definitively. And didn't look at all at her body. Whatever power, whatever control she had over this situation, over him, was rapidly deserting her. She didn't understand any of this. And, oddly enough, she wasn't wanting to wrest control back from him. Not right that second anyway. Her curiosity was too strong now. Both to discover what it was he wanted from her…and whether or not she'd be able to give it to him.

And for the first time in her adult life, Samantha Wallace worried that she might fail at something.

## CHAPTER FIVE

"TAKE THEM OFF," Marsh commanded softly, fighting to keep the edge from his voice.

He couldn't waver in this. He had to trust his instincts, follow through with his plan. He'd expected her to taunt him again, to try and wrest control of the situation away from him. Instead, the look in her eyes had revealed she was somewhat shaken, almost abashed. It was a reaction so foreign to the woman he knew, that, despite the fact that it was exactly what he'd wanted, it made him that much more aware of just how dangerous this little game could be. He didn't want to hurt her. In any way.

Then her shoulders squared a little, and that flash sprang back to life in her eyes. "I beg your pardon?"

Once again he had to fight the urge to smile. He shouldn't be so relieved. He needed her to let her guard down as she had moments ago. But this was also the Samantha he loved. He wanted both. Needed to know she could give all the parts of herself to him.

"I hadn't intended to make you beg for anything," he replied and saw her body quiver, felt his own body leap to life. He'd never considered whether he even could make her beg. She certainly had that power over him. But he had no desire to push her in that way. This was about willingly giving control over to someone you trust. Nothing more. But absolutely nothing less.

Yet, he saw in her eyes that she was realizing he might, in fact, have that kind of power over her. If he wasn't mistaken—and he could clearly see through the thin silk of her bra that he wasn't—she was aroused by the idea. Very much so, in fact.

As, it turned out, was he.

Control, he was swiftly coming to realize, was going to be a double-edged sword this evening. He'd have to be quite careful not to slice himself on it.

He watched as she grappled with this most recent revelation. As expected, she slowly stood straighter, held his gaze levelly. She wasn't going to give an inch to him. Not until he made her want to.

"What happens if I don't take them off?" she taunted, jutting her chin toward the crop he still held in his hand. "You'll whip me?"

She was so stunningly beautiful in her imperiousness, clearly certain he would never do such a thing to her. And she was right about that. But as long as she held herself so tightly in control, she'd never unbend enough to let him in. Not to all the innermost places he most desired. To the center of her heart.

To get there, he had to keep her off balance. He didn't want her to be so certain of him. "Are you pushing me?" he asked, letting his mouth curve in a deep, knowing smile. "To see how far I'm willing to go to get what I want?"

Her eyes flared, but not in anger. His response had shaken her. "Why are you doing this?" she asked, real confusion clear in her voice.

His fingers tightened on the crop as he resisted the urge to throw it down and pull her into his arms. He didn't like seeing her shaken and confused. His instincts warred with one another. To push forward, get past this to what lay ahead? Or give up, console her, let her return to her comfort zone, let her take control again.

He knew the answer. And it wasn't an easy one. He had to exploit the chinks in her armor when they appeared. There were so few. So rather than answer her oh-so-vulnerably asked question, he drew the tip of the crop along the swell of her breasts, then traced the lacy edge to her bra. "I want you to take this off."

She jerked in awareness at the caress of soft leather on even softer skin, her chest rising and falling more rapidly as he drew the crop down along her bare midsection…then traced it along the whisper-thin, lacy edging of her panties.

"These, too." His own heart pounding, he struggled to flick his gaze casually up to hers, as easily, as smoothly as he flicked the tip of that crop oh, so lightly across one nipple. "Now," he commanded softly.

She gasped, her body jerked and he knew damn well it was in pleasure. Desire punched her pupils wide, and he could see her body quivering. But she immediately lifted her chin. "Or else what? I know you won't use that on me."

He flicked the tip again, eliciting a soft, surprised moan from her.

She fought to regain her composure, but her voice was huskier when she spoke. "I meant you wouldn't—"

"I know what you meant. There are other ways of getting you to give me what I want that have nothing to do with pain."

He watched her fight to regroup, to regain her control. She didn't argue the point, because they both knew he was right. When she finally lifted her gaze to his, her eyes were slightly less focused. The desire he saw there was palpable. She could try and brazen her way through it, but she couldn't hide it. "So if I refuse…then what?"

"Are you saying you're unwilling to go further?"

"So the night would be over then?" she countered. "We're over?"

Just hearing her say that made his heart tighten. "We can't go back now, Sam," he said quietly. "We can only go on."

He watched as a myriad of emotions played across her face, but she doggedly continued. "You picked a hell of a time to push me like this. I—"

"When would there be a better time?" he queried softly.

She held his gaze, but in the end, she only said, "So, to go on means I have to—"

He flicked the crop to her chin, just enough that she snapped her mouth shut to avoid feeling it land on her skin. It did anyway…but he knew the touch was soft, gentle. She'd never feel anything else from him. If she didn't know that by now, trust him in that way now, she would before leaving here. "Do as I request," he finished.

"You mean command," she said shakily, if still defiantly.

"Would it be so awful? To give me whatever I want?" He stepped closer, ran the crop along her jaw, down her neck, across her collarbone. "Have I ever given you reason to think I'd hurt you, or any living thing?"

She shook her head.

"Then trust that I know what I'm doing now." He let the leather loops drop into the soft crevasse between her breasts. "You do trust me, don't you, Samantha?"

He was so close now, he could smell her. Both the spicy scent she dabbed on her pulse points…and the scent that was pure Sam. His ache for her grew, if that were possible, forcing him to lock the muscles in his thighs to keep steady.

In her heels, she held his gaze squarely, but said nothing.

So he pushed. Slowly, he drew the loop over one nipple, peaking hard through the satin cup of her bra. It made her jerk again, made her gasp.

"Do you trust me, Samantha?" He flicked the loop to her other nipple, which hardened instantly. Her breath came out in a shuddering sigh. He knew exactly what he was doing. "Answer me."

He saw the war waging behind those beautiful blue eyes of hers. He hoped she was coming to realize that he could have an even greater power over her than this physical, sexual one. That she could come to care for him in ways that left her unable to protect herself, to protect her heart.

She'd already done that to him. And it was exactly that risk he was pushing her to take. "You understand what it is you really fear, don't you," he murmured. "Trust me with that, too."

Her chin wavered as his meaning sank in. He drew the crop down her belly, then lower, down the front panel of her panties. She moaned softly, her breath coming in quick pants now. His heart was thundering and the fact that the silk panel clung to her told him how wet she was, how aroused she was. In fact, all he had to do was slide it down another inch and— He jerked his gaze back to hers. "Tell me, Samantha." He slid the loop a tiny bit farther between her legs, fighting to keep his own legs from shaking.

She could have rocked herself forward, taken what she wanted from him, proven to him that she would never willingly let him rule the situation in any way. Instead she squeezed her eyes shut and stood perfectly still. It was a telling moment. And yet she still gave nothing. She simply couldn't make herself completely capitulate.

He leaned closer, careful to keep his only contact to the tip of his crop, pressing into the increasingly damp silk panel of her panties. "Tell me what you're afraid of," he whispered next to her ear.

Her eyes blinked open. And for an excruciatingly taut moment, he thought she was going to tell him. But at the last possible second, she shifted her body forward, deciding to take what she wanted after all. Rather than risk giving anything of herself—her real self—to him.

Disappointed but not surprised, he snapped the crop away. Patience was his strong suit, but even he was aware how close he was treading to the edge of his control. Rather than risk her discovering any vulnerability on his part, he turned abruptly, headed for the stairs.

"Wait," she blurted, more plea than command in her voice this time.

He paused, one foot on the first riser, but didn't dare look back at her. When she didn't say anything else, he began to climb the stairs.

"Damn you, Marshall Conley."

He kept climbing.

"Fine," she called out. "Go ahead and go. I don't need this ridiculous…test, or whatever the hell you think this is. I've got a lot of people counting on me. I shouldn't even be here. I sure as hell don't need you."

He paused at the top stair and looked back down at her.

She was something, his Nordic blond temptress. Only she wasn't his. And he wondered now if she ever would be. "Did it ever occur to you that you could count on someone? I thought we needed each other. My mistake."

His heart felt like a burning knot in his chest. It had been stupid to think he could push her like this, that this was the way to get past her defense to what lay inside her heart. But what choice did he have? Somehow, going the conventional route, sharing a bottle of wine and some serious conversation over dinner, just wasn't a realistic alternative. Not with Samantha. She'd simply reel off a list of reasons as long as those fabulous legs of hers as to why a real, committed relationship would never work between them. Then seduce him back into bed. Nothing would change between them. She'd never risk it.

No, for her to really understand what she could have, what they could have together…he had to make her vulnerable enough that she'd finally let herself expose that need, her own need for more. And he only knew one way to do that, to get her there, and that way was positive and good and pleasurable.

So, if this wasn't going to work, then he didn't know what would.

Hell, maybe he'd read her all wrong and she really didn't want anything more than the physical relationship they shared. He was about to apologize, to offer to call her a car and whatever else she wanted, when she opened her mouth, and said, "Okay."

She'd said it very quietly, so quietly he wasn't sure he'd heard her, or if it had just been wishful thinking. "Okay, what?" he asked.

Still holding his gaze, she reached for her bra strap.

His pulse rocketed up so fast he felt light-headed. "Slowly," he choked out, scraping together every last ounce of control he had.

Her gaze narrowed slightly, but it was all-or-nothing time now. He knew that. He had to be a worthy match for her. He knew that now, too. Capitulation on his part wouldn't serve either one of them.

She held his gaze defiantly…then she did as he asked.

Watching as she slid those silk cups down and over her nipples had him gripping the banister so hard his knuckles ached. It was the least he deserved in this. It shouldn't, after all, be easy on either of them. His body twitched and twitched hard as she slowly pushed her panties down her thighs and calves, then kicked them away, before looking back up at him, bared to him completely.

He began to descend the stairs then. And it took considerably more control than he expected to keep from grabbing her and pulling her to him. Or under him. He'd seen her naked, seen every inch of her in fact, many times over. And yet this was so entirely different.

His gaze roamed her body, from head to toe, and it was more electric, more intimate, than any of the hundreds of times he'd touched her before.

Her breathing grew shallower as he stopped just a foot away. Her body quivered when his lips twitched, then spread. The smile he finally bestowed on her was nothing like any he'd ever given her before. But then, she'd never given him this much of herself.

"Now," he said softly, his voice rough with emotion, "we can begin."

# CHAPTER SIX

SAMANTHA WAITED...for what she wasn't entirely sure. His next request? She wasn't used to waiting on someone else to decide the next course of action. Professionally, or personally. Which Marsh apparently knew, as he let the silence between them spin out.

*Damn, but he was beautiful,* she couldn't help but thinking. Had always thought so. Dark good looks, quietly deliberate in word and deed, like some kind of mysterious fallen angel.

But the most shocking discovery of all, as she stood and simply held his gaze, neither regally, nor with any submission at all, was that rather than feel subjugated in any way, she felt...free. Complete, unfettered freedom. It wasn't about power, or who had control. It was simply about...being.

As he walked past her, then around behind her, she stood as casually still as possible. And yet she found it impossible. She didn't have the urge to preen, or show off, or even entice. Her entire body responded to his drawn-out appraisal. Her skin grew warmer, her thighs trembled. She realized, when he didn't come around in front of her again, that she wanted to see his face, interpret his expression. She wanted to see...what? If he approved? She knew damn well he approved of her body.

Which meant this was about something else entirely. And while the drama he directed—stripping her naked…or, more specifically, having her strip naked for him—was affecting her sexually, intensely so, she understood his intention went far beyond that of titillation. Hers…or his. This was about baring far more than her body.

*Did it ever occur to you that you could count on someone?*

Only now was she beginning to realize what he was really asking of her.

*I thought we needed each other.*

She could feel his presence behind her as intensely as she felt her next breath. *You want me stripped totally bare before you,* she thought. *Naked down to my soul.* It was a feat no one had ever achieved with her. But then no one had ever been tempted to try. Until now. God help her.

"All or nothing," he said, his mouth directly behind her ear.

She startled, unaware he'd moved in so closely.

"We both win…or we both lose," he went on, before finally moving in front of her. He held her gaze steadily. His was still unreadable. "Gather your cloak."

She was so caught up in the spell he was weaving that she did as he asked without thinking. An act that surprised them both. It was the first emotion she'd seen him reflect, other than palpable desire.

As she straightened with the cloak in her arms, he shocked her by flicking out the crop and lightly caressing her bare nipples with the leather loop. "I like keeping you aroused. Do you like it when I do this?" He caressed both nipples again, then dipped the tip to trace a circle around her navel.

The muscles between her thighs clenched so tightly it was almost painful. Yes, dammit, she liked it. But when she opened her mouth, the word that came out was, "No." She'd stated the bald-faced lie evenly, not sure why she was irritated again. He was only giving her pleasure. Perhaps because he was so expertly toying with her…and there was seemingly nothing she could do about it. Except respond.

His eyes flared at her response. "Why is it so hard, Samantha? To let someone else direct the course of your pleasure?"

She opened her mouth, the denial automatic, but she stopped, closed her mouth again. He knew damn well how hard this was for her.

His lips twitched again. "Go over by the fire. Make yourself comfortable."

She gathered the cloak in her arms, as if it would provide some kind of shield. But when he looked at her, it was as though he were seeing far past her bare, highly sensitized skin. The soft ermine trim that lined the edges of the cloak brushed against her skin as she walked over toward the fire, eliciting a soft moan as it tickled the highly aroused tips of her breasts. She glanced back to see if he'd noticed, only to find herself alone once again.

"Marsh?" She hadn't intended to call out. Much less with that thread of…what? Worry? Vulnerability? Maybe it was the fear that if he left her for too long, this cocoon he was weaving about them would dissolve, robbing her of what little chance she might have for succeeding in this quest to give herself willingly to him. All of herself. She shuddered then, unsure how much was in fear of what it would be like…and how much was in expectation of what it would feel like if she succeeded. A big *if* at the moment.

He didn't respond to her call, nor did he return after another full minute ticked by. She turned back to the fire, and wondered exactly what he expected to find when he returned. Her, splayed and waiting for him amidst that huge pile of ridiculously decadent pillows?

She stepped closer, slid her heels off and waded into the sea of silk and leather. Just the feel of the slippery fabrics on the soles of her feet, both cool and warm, softly thick and whisper thin, brought her to another level of awareness. She moved closer to the fire, letting its warmth seep into her, praying it would relax the array of muscles that were so tight and twitchy. Hoping that with a moment's relaxation would come a chance to regroup, think, analyze…plan.

God, she was doing it again. Plotting to take control. But dammit, she couldn't help it.

"Are you comfortable standing?"

Startled by his return, she turned to find him bearing a covered tray. She shivered a little at what might lie beneath that swath of cloth. And it wasn't a shiver of fear. Far from it, in fact.

He gestured with his chin. "Sit. Relax."

She wasn't sure which was stronger: the urge to laugh at the suggestion that she could relax under the circumstances…or scream with the frustration of being held so long on the edge. *Just do me and get it over with,* she wanted to shout. The twitch of his lips was enough to keep her silent. Fuming, but silent. Smug bastard.

She turned abruptly and scanned the pillows and spreads arrayed at her feet, deciding which way would best torture him. Anticipation, hell. If he was determined to play her out, then play her he would, she decided. She could hold out longer than he could. By the time she finally allowed him—yes, allowed him—to bring her off, he'd be begging to join her. If he hadn't already gone over the edge himself.

She swung the cloak in front of her, silk side out, and let it fall atop a nest of pillows, then knelt on it, her back to him. Oh, they'd both win all right. Well aware the firelight was burnishing her skin like molten copper, she shook her hair so it brushed the center of her back, then looked at him over her shoulder. She'd expected to see naked hunger in his eyes. At the very least.

Her mouth dropped open at what she did find. He wasn't even looking at her. In fact, his back was to her as he placed the tray at the edge of the sea of silk, popping four short legs from each corner, so it sat just above the pile, within easy reach. "Lie back," he told her, still not paying the least bit of attention to her.

Tempted to snap something at him, she bit the comment off. He was pushing back a corner of the cloth, and despite her growing frustration, she couldn't deny she wanted to know what lay beneath it. To get a heads-up on what he had in store for her. So she could thwart it, she thought waspishly. Then immediately decided that would only be denying herself. No, she wanted to see what was on that tray…so she could figure out how to best use it to her own advantage. To their own advantage. When it was over, he wouldn't be complaining. Of that she would make very sure.

He glanced up just then, caught her staring. With nothing more than a look, he made it clear he understood exactly the direction her thoughts had taken once again.

With what she hoped was an insouciant mien, not a care in the world, she reached forward until she was on her hands and knees, facing away from him, then slowly moved down until her elbows rested on the silk, before swiftly rolling to her back, knees together and slanted to one side. She held his gaze with a half smile of her own. No way had that little show left him unaffected. Hell, it hadn't left *her* unaffected.

And yet, blast the man, he let nothing show. Except for that damnable ghost of a smile. As if she'd once again been predictable. She silently snarled, wanting to pound her fists into the silk. He was being insufferable. *Much as you are with him when you call the shots,* her little voice supplied.

She had to force herself not to slump in defeat. It was just all so damn confusing. She wanted to give him what he wanted. She knew he wasn't asking for more of her than she had of him countless times. Only she also understood this was about so much more than who was on top.

He came to stand over her, still fully dressed, the worn toes of his black leather riding boots mere inches away from her hip. "You make everything so difficult on yourself." He said it softly, sincerely, without any smugness or pity. "Not everything has to be a contest, something to win. Not every interaction has to end in conquest or defeat."

"Did I say—"

He flicked the ever-present riding crop up and she fell instantly silent, even though it came nowhere near her. She wasn't sure which made her angrier, that he already had her conditioned to it…or that the reaction he'd conditioned her to feel was a hot, pulsing pleasure.

"Lie back," he said softly.

She held his gaze, wanting like hell not to be predictable this time. Wishing like hell that meant anything other than doing as he asked without comment or complaint. Slowly, she let her elbows slide across the silk, until the softness caressed the entire length of her spine. He continued to stare at her for long, silent moments. She wanted to close her eyes, relax and simply feel, let her mind drift to what was to come, to where she could let this be all about sex.

And not about him wanting her emotionally vulnerable to him.

But his direct gaze wouldn't allow her even that simple retreat. Those dark eyes of his all but challenged her to continue the direct, intimate contact between them. Even as his focus finally shifted, drifting down over her body, she kept her eyes on him. His riding breeches did fit him like a second skin. Most often he wore jeans around the barn. On only one other occasion had she seen him dressed in English riding gear. He'd been astride a huge buckskin mare, taking jumps in a ring out behind the main barn. She'd been transfixed, watching him control such power, with little more than the pressure of his thighs. And she knew exactly how powerful those thighs were.

She skimmed her gaze along the tight curve of his hamstrings, over the snug cup of his buttocks. She wished he would turn, even a fraction of an inch, toward her. Then she'd have a clear indication of just how much she was affecting him. And given Marshall's very generous proportions, the clinging fit of the pants would hide nothing. She rubbed her thighs together. Just the image of what he'd look like if she were to peel those pants down his thighs, how thick and hard—

She bit back a small moan when he shifted and gave her the view she wanted. Dear God, she silently breathed. He was definitely not unaffected by this little game. She grew wetter yet, and was unable to pull her gaze away.

He turned and lowered himself to his knees in front of the tray.

"Close your eyes," he asked quietly.

Damn him for knowing how hard it was for her to give up every tiny shred of control. Moments ago she'd wanted to drift away. Now, she could barely stand the idea of losing even the small edge that open eyes gave her.

He glanced over his shoulder, the low glow of the embers casting his face in contrasts of red-gold and shadow. His cheekbones and jaw stood out in sharp relief…his lips looked both chiseled and somehow softer in the golden light. "Trust me. Let me take you."

"You've taken me before."

He shook his head. "You've given yourself to me. Parts of yourself. An entirely different thing. And I've let you, reveled in it even. But it's no longer enough for me, Samantha. I want all of you." He turned, rose to his knees over her, his hand and whatever was in it hidden from view. "Let me have you now. However I want."

She trembled. "You want more from me than I can give."

"I don't think so. You still have the power here, Samantha. The power to deny me…or to give me what I desire."

"You desire more than I want to give."

"Want to give? Really? Or *can* give? Because I think you do want. You just don't know how to go about doing it."

"So sure of yourself," she said, striving to sound unaffected. Knowing she was far from it. Also knowing he was right. Again.

"Not true," he said, his tone not changing. "In fact, I've never been so unsure of myself." He flicked his wrist and the soft edge of a peacock feather flicked down along her thighs, the silky fronded ends brushed between her legs.

She sucked in a breath, her back arching convulsively, as a spasm of pleasure speared into her. Her breath came in little pants. "You could have fooled me."

His lips twitched then, but he sobered quickly. "I know you want more, because you always want more. In everything you do. And I'm betting everything that you're only still here right now because you want more with me, too. But this is one arena where you've never been persuaded to give what it takes to get what you so badly need."

"What I need?" Dammit, why did she keep pushing him? "So you say."

He flicked the frond between her legs again. She moaned instantly.

"So I know."

She struggled to get her quivering legs under control. "Sexual need isn't what you're talking about."

"Yes, but it's what you understand. So we'll start there."

"And from this, you can persuade me to need more, to want more, of you?"

He flicked the feather again. Then again. "That is what I plan to find out."

Back. Forth. Stroke after feather-light stroke. She didn't even try to avoid them. A series of soft groans were ripped from her, the pleasure almost painful the way it made her clench so tightly with need.

Her body thrummed, ached for release. It took considerable will to focus on talking, when what she wanted to do was grab him and demand he finish what he'd so thoroughly started. "You think this proves you own some part of me?" she said, her voice rough and shaky. "That you control me?"

"I want us both to own something of the other. And yes, a part of me needs to know I can take control of this power we have between us, if I wish to. You know already that you have that power over me."

"You're not talking about sex."

"No."

That one quietly spoken word stunned her into silence. He was all but telling her she had laid claim to more than his body. His heart? And that he wanted as much in return from her.

She began to tremble, this time in fear. Fear, because he was right. If she didn't want him, all of him, she'd have hiked down the mountain naked to get away from here. She did want more from him than this. It was something she'd been fighting against for some time now.

She grew more terrified still as she was forced to accept that he was also right in knowing she might not be capable of breaching her own defenses to let him inside that part of her that no one had ever touched.

But he was willing to try. Willing to risk what they did have to find out if there could be more. She'd never thought herself a coward, but she realized he was the brave one here, not her.

She had to decide if she trusted him enough to follow his lead. Let him control her body…in hopes that she would be too defenseless then to keep him from sneaking into her heart.

# CHAPTER SEVEN

MARSH SAW THE PLAY of emotions flicker across her face. The one he most easily recognized was fear. Because he felt it so keenly himself.

He leaned down then, needing her to know she wasn't alone in this. He brushed his lips next to her ear. "The need I have to give myself completely over to you scares the living hell out of me, too."

She jerked her gaze to him, obviously stunned by his quietly offered confession. "Marsh." She reached for him then, but he moved away, shook his head once.

It cost him dearly, but he had to keep things on track. "Keep your hands by your head," he said, his voice strained.

She scowled in frustration. "Why not tie me up then? Just do what you will?"

"Because that's the easy way out. For both of us. We both know I can pleasure you. I don't want you to have no say. I don't want to rob you of anything, or take anything from you. I want you to willingly hand me control. Like I do with you." He leaned over her again, brushed his lips along her jaw, pausing beside her ear. "I want you to all but demand me to take it. To take you. Because you want me to. Because you need me to."

She held his gaze, turbulent emotions clearly ablaze

in her bright blue eyes. But she said nothing. Gave nothing.

His entire body vibrated with need as he shifted away from her, turning back to his tray. "Close your eyes," he instructed again, his tone less congenial. *Patience, man, patience,* he schooled himself. He routinely took weeks, months, to bring a new charge around to his way of thinking. This shouldn't be so difficult for him. But it was. Because the stakes were higher than they'd ever been in his life.

"Marsh," she said from behind him, her voice taut, yet gentle, "I know you give yourself to me. I want you to know...I don't take that for granted."

He didn't turn to look at her. Nor did the tension lessen one iota; in fact, it all but crackled in the air between them. "I give part of myself to you," Marsh said after a long moment. "Every time we're together. I would give you more, if you'd ask. If I didn't think it would threaten you."

"Is it so bad?" she asked quietly. "What we have now?"

He turned then, sat back in the pile of silk, arms resting on bended knees. He twirled a small paintbrush in his hands. Her gaze flicked between his face...and that twirling little brush.

"It's more than I hoped for," he said, rolling the brush to his fingertips, then back. "Much, much more. And maybe for that reason alone, it's not enough."

She did look at him then, and spoke honestly. "What if I can't give more? You aren't willing to accept what I can give?"

He held her gaze for a long time, then slowly shook his head.

Shocked, he watched tears spring to her eyes. He steeled himself against reaching for her, pulling her to him and telling her he'd take whatever she had to give and just forget this stupid idea he'd had to push her for more. He didn't want to make her cry. He wanted to give her pleasure, to make her want more. To make her want him. All of him.

But if he capitulated now, it would end between them. He'd forever altered their relationship by putting his heart on the line.

She blinked several times to keep her tears at bay. "Why not?" she asked, her voice hoarse with emotion.

"I've let you call the shots, because that's what keeps you in my life. I haven't shared more of myself than I know you can accept. Too much and you'll bolt. I thought I could live with that. But I can't. In fact, I don't want to hold anything back from you any longer," he told her, moving the brush up…then down his long fingers, then up again. "And I don't think I can accept the fact that you would hold anything back from me."

He looked at her and saw the battle she was waging, knew she understood the real undercurrents happening here.

"You never complained about me taking charge before." She tried to pull out one of her very effective knowing smiles, but it was thwarted by the very real confusion in her eyes.

"And I won't now. Or in the future. What I want is equal time. I want us to share each other. A real relationship, a real partnership is give and take. In all areas."

She looked a little affronted. "I think I'm pretty giving."

"You are that. To a fault." He leaned in closer, spoke more softly. "It's one of the many reasons I'm so hooked on you."

Her eyes widened a little, her pupils shot wide.

"But you need to learn to take, too. To be the recipient. To let someone give to you."

"I don't think I ever complained about being satisfied."

His lips twitched. She was so stubborn. But while he knew it was one of the reasons she was so successful, he also knew it was the same trait she hid behind in order not to risk being vulnerable. "Thank you," he said, quite sincerely. "But I want to give you more than a response or reaction to what you're giving me. You might be surprised at what more there can be when it's truly equal. When you don't pick and choose what you get and when."

She didn't say anything for a moment, and he wondered if he was getting through to her. "You make it sound like I'm not a team player, like I don't understand partnership. My business—"

He cut her off. "Is different. Yes, you have partners. But you each perform very different tasks to make your business run." He searched for a way to make her understand. "I know you work very hard for what you have, and that you apply that same ethic to your personal life. It's another thing I admire about you. You don't expect anything for nothing. But life doesn't have to be hard work all the time. And you don't have to do all the work all the time to deserve the rewards."

He shifted back, let his words sink in.

After a long moment, she sighed a little, and looked at him. "And you think doing this—" she motioned to the pile of silk and the paintbrush he still held in his hand "—will change things between us? In and out of bed?"

"I hope so. This is where we started. This is where we are at our most comfortable with one another. It's what we know best of each other. But we could be more intimate. In bed…and out. I want that, I want to find out if we can have that."

He waited for what seemed like an eternity for her response. "To be honest…I—I've been thinking about that, too," she finally said, her voice barely more than a whisper.

His entire body at once both relaxed in almost abject relief…and tightened in anxiety and anticipation. "Then trust me, Samantha. Enough to explore this, to let me try this. If we can't find a way to share equally here, give and take equally, where it should be easy, all about pleasure, then I can't see how we'll be able to do it where it's difficult, and most important."

"I just don't know—"

He moved then, unable to keep his distance from her a moment longer. He leaned over her, bracing himself on his hands and knees, so he was situated at her feet, one palm planted beside her ankle, the other holding the brush. "Then why don't we find out?"

She watched him, and he still saw the fear and confusion tangling with need and emotion. He felt so sure of this…but what if she wasn't ready? Then he'd have to persuade her, he thought immediately. He moved the tip of the brush then and ran it over the very tips of her toes.

She gasped, and the need surged past the fear in her eyes, just before she squeezed them shut. "Marsh—"

He skimmed the tip of the brush over the front of her toes, then along the top of her foot. "Look at me."

She opened her eyes, and he found himself wanting badly to make this easier for her.

"Trust me, Samantha," he said. "You could find something more powerful than you've ever known." He reined in the urge to throw the stupid brush across the room and pull her into his arms. It would solve nothing. But resisting cost him all the same.

She glanced away, and he hated that he had to push her like this. After a long moment, she looked back at him. "I don't handle failure well," she said, her attempt at a smile miserably unsuccessful.

"Then don't fail," he told her, his tone more direct, more insistent, than he'd been yet that night. He leaned over her then, his control slipping badly. He tossed the brush aside and planted his palms on either side of her as he lowered his body close, but not close enough to touch. He lowered his face so near that all she had to do was lift her head, lift her mouth—

God he wanted her, more desperately than he wanted his next breath. What the hell was he doing, risking losing even this much of her? He tried to imagine her not being there for him like this, to never again feel this closeness.

"I—I was raised by a woman trapped in a life she didn't want because she'd trusted a man to take care of her," she began, her voice trembling, rough. "And he just up and left us. I trusted her to take care of me…and she left me, too. Not by her own decision, but it didn't make being left behind any easier. I—I want to be capable of unconditional love. I do. But the only thing I can trust in, that I've ever been able to completely trust in, is myself." She was shaking now, barely able to speak. "I don't want to cut myself off emotionally." Her eyes were so bleak, so scared. "But I don't know how not to. I've protected myself that way for so long." She let the sentence waver in the air as her throat worked. "Intimacy and trust…the kind of complete surrender you're talking about…I—I don't know how to do that."

"Am I worth the risk of trying?" he asked, knowing his expression was likely too fierce, but beyond being able to control it. "You fight for what matters to you in every other thing you do. So fight for me. Fight for what you'll be giving yourself. I know you don't accept defeat well…so don't lose." He pulled away, knowing if he didn't do so now, he'd never regain control and all this would have been for nothing. He rolled back on his heels, but continued to hold her gaze. "Don't lose me."

# CHAPTER EIGHT

SAMANTHA ALMOST cried out when he pulled away. She'd had no idea the true depths of his wants, of his need…for her. And she couldn't fault him for wanting what they had between them to be shared equally, fully. It wasn't fair to let him be the only one to put it all on the line. To risk his heart.

Hers began to race as panic swelled somewhere deep inside her. What he was offering was a precious, precious gift. One she realized in that moment, without any doubt, she wanted to keep. Desperately. Endlessly.

Normally, when Samantha determined she wanted something, she went about getting it. But she'd never gone after something so worthy, something with such potential for devastation if she failed. And she wouldn't just be hurting herself if that happened.

She realized now how lucky she was that he'd cared enough to go to all this trouble, cared enough to figure out exactly what it was going to take to break through that final barrier…make her want to break it down herself. Walk through it, to him. Willingly.

He'd already walked through that fire. He'd given himself to her in more ways than she'd realized, allowing her to have her precious control if that was what made her happy. And now he was handing the rest of himself to her. Handing her his heart. She'd never felt so unworthy of a gift in her entire life.

She turned her head, relieved to find him still there, crouched at her feet, his gaze burning twin holes in her, as if he could will her to give him what he'd himself just laid at her feet.

He'd proven what he was capable of giving…and taking. He rightly demanded that she come to him equally, or not at all. She wouldn't have respected him…couldn't have loved him if he didn't value himself that much. So caught up in the swirl of emotions roiling inside her, she didn't even realize the admission she'd just allowed to slip through.

"I want—" She broke off. Even this much, this first capitulation, was hard for her. How in the hell was she going to manage the rest?

"What do you want, Samantha?" His own voice was nothing more than a hoarse rasp. "Tell me."

"You," she whispered, then her breath caught in her throat, a silent sob rising at the sudden depth of emotion she saw baldly cross his face. "I'm afraid I won't be able to do it. Give you what you need from me." She broke off, swearing beneath her breath even as tears of fear and frustration pooled at the corners of her eyes.

The raw emotion that flicked over his handsome face almost undid her completely. His own eyes, so fierce, so full of emotion, grew glassy. "Trust me," he all but begged. "Trust me to take care of you. To never hurt you. To never leave you." He reached for her, then curled his fingers in tightly and pulled back.

She felt that retreat as keenly as if he had abandoned her. And realized then what it would be like to have him retreat from her completely. Devastating. But to get…she had to give.

"Trust me to have you," he demanded. "All of you." He waved his hand at the house that rose above them. "You've been to the ranch house, but this is my real home, my private retreat. I don't bring anyone here. Have never wanted to before. And yet I feel like I'm prowling in a locked cage when I come up here now. Picturing you in every corner, wanting to hear your laughter fill these rooms. I want to create memories here with you, memories we'll look back on, share with a smile. I want to start now. Tonight. Wake up tomorrow morning with you next to me."

He abruptly pushed to a stand. "Maybe I made a mistake bringing you up here before I tried this." He paced away. "Now that I know what it is to have you here…it will make it a hundred times worse when you le—"

"Don't say that. I'm not going anywhere."

He strode to her then and she had to dig her fingers into the silk pillows to keep from shrinking back from the ferocity tightening every muscle in his face. "Then do as I ask." He was no longer begging. He was all but ordering her to let him in. "Yes. Or no." When she didn't answer instantly, he abruptly turned away.

"Marshall—!"

He stopped just as abruptly, but didn't turn to face her. Hands on his hips, she saw his back rise and fall as he fought to harness his emotions. His own fear? The very idea that he could be as terrified of her failing as she was brought her new understanding of his sudden change in demeanor. He was instinctively trying to protect himself, as well.

"Choose one," he bit out. "Or shall I call my driver?"

The time for discussion, for revelation…for drawing things out until she could find some way to deal with them, was over. And yet she couldn't form the words, couldn't get them past the knot in her throat.

He turned back then, walked to her—stalked was more like it—held his hand out for her. It was the first direct touch he'd offered since she'd walked in.

She wanted to reach for that hand more than she'd ever wanted to reach for anything in her life, for all that taking hold of it would imply. Would reaching for his hand be enough? Would he know that by taking what he offered, she was choosing to try? Choosing him? She hadn't expected him to make it easy on her. Slowly, she lifted one, trembling hand.

He stared down at her, his dark eyes glittering with need, with desire, but mostly with determination. "For everyone else," he said, so softly she had to strain to hear him, "I want you to be Samantha Wallace, femme fatale, corporate powerhouse." He reached past her outstretched hand and took her wrist, taking the other one, as well, as he hauled her to her feet. He tugged her close, holding her wrists together between them. "But for me, and me only, I want you to be all of those things…and one thing more. Mine. Totally, completely, unwaveringly…mine." He began backing her up.

She had no idea what was behind her, if she'd trip, fall, bang into something. But she couldn't look away. She had to trust him to guide her. Now. Right now.

"I want to know that I can have you whenever I want, wherever I want, however I want." A pulse leaped in his temple, his jaw twitched it was clenched so tightly shut. "Just as already you know you can have me, in those very same ways."

Her heels hit the riser and she stumbled out of the pit that formed the sunken living room. But rather than direct her toward the stairs, he directed her toward the front door. She glanced over her shoulder. Surely he wasn't about to put her out? She gasped when the bare skin of her back met the icy cold ridges of the stained glass. She held his gaze for what seemed an eternity. And an eternity didn't seem long enough. She knew what was in her heart, what she wanted, despite the terror, despite the overwhelming wrenching sensation in her gut.

"So stop imagining failure," he told her. "And start picturing what victory could be like."

She couldn't. Not because she didn't want to. But because she literally couldn't picture it, the scope of it, the reality of it.

His grip tightened. "Choose now."

She was beyond trembling now, and it had nothing to do with being cold. She should have realized it wouldn't be as easy as making the physical gesture of reaching for him. He needed to hear her say it. He needed her to be able to say it. She shook, from her fingers to her toes. She bored her gaze into his, looking beyond the ferocity, seeing past the primal desire to what lay beneath. And what she found there literally blew her away.

He was already hers. All hers. And all she had to do was say… "Yes," she managed, more terrified than she'd ever been in her life. She forced herself to repeat it. "Yes. I want to try. I want to succeed. I want everything you have to give me. I want to give you everything in return."

His pupils shot so wide they swallowed the irises

whole. But if she'd expected him to yank her into his arms, kiss her deeply, soundly…reassuringly, well, she'd never been so wrong.

He released her abruptly and turned away. The only sign of his reaction to her capitulation the fast rise and fall of his chest. "Thank God," she thought she heard him whisper beneath his breath.

A modicum of relief seeped into her own lungs, allowing her to find her breath. But that was short-lived.

"Follow me," he said, walking to the stairs without looking back.

She opened her mouth, then closed it again as she realized this wasn't the end. Far from it. It was only the beginning. She'd given him permission now. Agreed to give herself to him, to do whatever he commanded her to do. To trust him completely.

She followed him, pausing at the foot of the stairs to look up to where he'd already climbed, to the loft above. Then, with a deliberate sense of purpose she could only pray stayed with her, she took hold of the railing, and on trembling legs, began to climb.

"In here." His voice echoed from a shadowy place down a narrow hallway.

At the top of the stairs, she turned away from the railed, open part of the loft that ultimately led to a closed door, presumably to his bedroom. Whatever was behind that door took up the lion's share of the second floor.

Instead, she turned left, and entered a small, darkly paneled room. She quivered as she stepped inside and didn't see him. Three of the walls were lined with dark mahogany wainscoting on the bottom half. The top of all three were inset bookcases, all packed full of neatly lined volumes. The fourth wall was dominated by a stone fireplace, dormant at the moment. He spoke before she could focus on anything else.

"Close the door behind you."

If she did, there would be no light at all. She'd be cast into complete darkness. But she'd given her word. With a trembling hand, she pushed the door shut, tried to quell her racing pulse as she was indeed plunged into complete darkness.

"Come to the center of the room."

She shuffled slowly, reaching her hands out. For all that the room appeared to be a small library or reading room, there hadn't been any furniture, nor any rug on the hardwood floor that she'd noticed.

"Stop."

She did so abruptly. He was close now. His voice had been just to the right of her.

Then he was behind her, and she trembled.

"Keep your hands to your side."

She was shaking now. In fear…although not so much of him, as of her lack of control. Something smooth and soft fluttered at her throat as he pushed her hair aside with his fingertips. She shivered at even this much of a touch.

Then she felt the soft strip fasten around her throat. She started to speak, to ask him what the hell he was doing, but managed at the last second to stop. At some point, she was sure she'd lose it, but dammit, surely she could last longer than this.

"This strip of velvet is a tangible reminder, but a reminder only, that while you are here with me, you belong to me." He moved in front of her then, and she strained mightily to see him, but failed. Then she felt a tug at the base of her throat. Had he—? No, no he wouldn't possibly think he could get away with—

But a short tug told her in fact he most certainly had. He'd essentially put a collar on her. A velvet one, but a collar nonetheless. She struggled mightily to keep from clawing it off and throwing it in his face. Wherever the hell that was. Then she realized that whatever he'd attached to the velvet strip had no weight to it.

She reached for her throat and felt the cool silk of a slender ribbon flutter across her skin, caress her stomach.

"Symbolic," he repeated. "That you're giving yourself over to my care. For tonight."

"Is that really necessary," she ground out, fighting to keep her temper in check.

"You tell me."

Did he really think he had to keep a constant reminder of her capitulation literally attached to her? As if she was going to forget why she was still here?

She felt the whisper of her fingers brush the skin below her breasts, then the very slightest of tugs on the ribbon. "Even now you're struggling to fight against me." He tugged ever so lightly again. "Against what this means." He leaned so close she could feel his breath against her cheek. "I think you do need a reminder, something to stay focused on."

She shifted away from him, only slightly, but very tellingly. The ribbon dropped back against her skin and she felt him move away from her. Dammit!

"Every time you want to rebel, imagine that the feel of that soft velvet at your throat, the satin caressing your skin, is my touch. My hand, guiding you. And let me. Let me."

She hated to admit he might be right. She didn't want

to think of it that way, like a constant presence, holding her, binding her to him. What she wanted was to demand he just get on with it. But the timing, along with everything else, was up to him. Damn, damn, damn. She'd never last.

But oh, the ache burning between her legs begged her to try. Never would she have thought that giving herself like this…to him…would excite her to such a degree. But he'd known. Of that she was sure.

Is this how he'd felt when she'd pinned him to the bed? When she'd taken him however, whenever and wherever she'd wanted? She'd never thought about it that way. Of course, he'd willingly given himself over to her, so this type of intense foreplay, along with constant reminders and repeated requests, had never been necessary. But he'd always enjoyed wherever she'd taken him—something she needed to keep first and foremost in her mind as she now allowed him the same privilege.

"Kneel."

The command startled her. Rattled her. "I—"

There was a slight tug on the silk ribbon. She bristled. Wasn't it enough that she was tolerating this much?

"Samantha."

There was neither warning nor plea in his tone. Just expectation.

So, what did she expect? Of him? Of herself? *Do you want to stop?* her little voice asked. *Or do you want to find out what he has in store for you?*

She wasn't sure who was more shocked when, thighs trembling, she slowly lowered herself. Dear God, what was she doing?

*Finding out.*

She braced for the bite of the hard wood into her knees, but something soft had been put on the floor in front of her.

"Don't move."

She said nothing to that command, but he couldn't rein in her thoughts. She might be a willing participant here, but there was no stopping her instinctive reaction. Of exactly how, precisely how in fact, she would exact her revenge when it was once again her turn to be in charge. Of course…he might not object to anything she could dream up. And that very idea only served to incite her further. She'd never felt so on edge, so electrically aware, in her entire life.

"Busy plotting, my darling?"

She swore beneath her breath, but realized that a part of her was pleased that he knew her so well. He knew her, and he still wanted more. There would be no secrets between them, no need to ever pull back, to pretend to be anything less than what she was.

"I hope you are," he said, his tone just a bit rough. "In fact, I can't wait to find out what you have in store for me."

His confession elicited another strong response in her. So, she knew him well, too. Which was just as gratifying. Surprisingly so.

She felt the air move behind her and stiffened.

"But for now, it's my turn."

Then she felt him nudge the toe of his boot between her feet, to her knees, forcing them gently apart.

"A bit more," he said, removing his boot and leaving her to move them apart herself. For him. She stifled the automatic urge to do the exact opposite. Grinding her teeth, she slid them an inch farther.

"More."

How could he tell? It was so damn dark. Still, she slid another inch, then another.

Suddenly she felt his body heat behind her, close behind her. She gasped when she felt him press his lips on her shoulder. He was kneeling, too. Right behind her. Equals.

But before she could decide how to react to that idea, he was taking both of her wrists in his hands, and pulling them behind her. Her fingertips brushed the soft cloth of his shirt as he pressed her hands together until she clasped her fingers.

"Keep them just like that," he whispered.

Instead of being incensed, or angry, her entire body shuddered in renewed need. She wasn't to be shackled. No, that would be too easy. He expected her to keep them there of her own free will. Symbolizing to him that she wouldn't interfere, wouldn't take over. Giving him that much more control over the situation, over her. He knew exactly what buttons to push. What shocked her was that they weren't so much buttons of irritation any longer.

Then she felt the floor shift as he stood and moved away from her. She wondered at the picture she made, then remembered he couldn't see her. So, it wasn't about the pose itself. Because he had no need to see it, she realized. That's not what this was about. So why the darkness?

She thought about that as she waited, every nerve ending in her body almost brutally sensitized, for whatever he would do next. The deprivation of sight served two purposes, she realized. One, it kept her focus on the action itself, not how she looked doing it, or how he might react seeing her like this. Secondly, it served to heighten her awareness of herself, and of him, while still retaining her pride.

The air shifted then, and the ribbon hanging from her throat shifted with it. Then it kept moving. Back and forth, as it brushed across the sensitive skin of her breasts, her stomach...and between her thighs. She had to stifle a moan as the pleasure both tortured her and brought her to a greater, fevered pitch. Her fingers tightened in their hold on one another.

She grew aware that he was right in front of her, that she could reach for him, drag him to her, beg him to finish what he'd so expertly begun. But her hands were behind her back. And there they had to stay until he wanted them otherwise.

Bastard, she thought...and yet again, it wasn't irritation over his methods, more like frustration because he was making her wait to find out what was going to happen next.

*Let me take you however I want.*

*Trust me. I'll never hurt you.*

His words echoed through her mind. She was definitely feeling only pleasure. Excruciating pleasure.

The ribbon fluttered more wildly then, as if caught on a hidden breeze. It shifted slowly until it caught beneath the edge of one distended nipple. She gasped, unable not to, then moaned as he flicked it expertly across the engorged point.

He didn't stop there. He drew the flat of it across the surface of that tingling, tight point of need. Back and forth. She had to work to steady her breath, half afraid she'd hyperventilate as he made her wait interminably long to discover if her other now-achingly hard nipple was to get the same treatment.

The ribbon once again brushed against her stomach, tickled her between her thighs. Her sigh of disappointment swiftly turned into a choking gasp of pleasure as something wet and warm flicked across the other nipple. Once, then again. Until a deep, growling moan was finally wrenched from her when the sweet torture of his warm tongue ceased.

"More?" he asked, so close, yet so totally out of her reach.

She nodded, forgetting he couldn't see her.

"No?" She felt the floor shift with his weight.

"Yes!" she blurted, then damned herself for the need she heard in her own voice, the desperation. How had he brought her to this? It was a shock to learn how little she cared at this point.

Suddenly something feather light tickled the inside of her thighs, making her gasp again, and twitch hard. Then it was gone. And she'd have done almost anything to assuage the ripping need that one little caress created. Just one touch, one little rub and she'd—

Another caress, higher up on the inside of her thigh, just below where she so badly needed it. She reflexively shifted her body, trying to move down onto whatever it was he was tormenting her with, but her spread knees made that impossible. Double damn him!

Another flick, this one whisper soft…right where she wanted it, but too brief to be fulfilling. Another brush, another convulsive clutch of those muscles. She cried out. So close. "Please," she said, not even realizing she'd spoken.

But nothing happened. She strained to hear him breathing, trying to place where he was, where he'd touch her next. Then there was a scrape that sounded like a match…and a small flickering glow filled the room. She blinked a couple of times, her pupils taking a moment to adjust. Marsh stood several feet away, his back to her as he lit the multiple wicks protruding from the thick, cream-colored candle that sat in the hearth of the fireplace.

Then he turned to her, the light casting his face in shadow, but she knew it bathed her perfectly. And suddenly, sight took on a whole new level of awareness. She was now intensely aware of the picture she presented. She knelt before him like a present to be unwrapped at his leisure. A toy to be played with as he wished. She knelt there at his complete and total mercy.

But now, she was so on edge with need for him, that rather than make her angry, it made her hungry. For more. More of whatever he would give her. She lifted her gaze to his and found she could hold it easily.

He smiled, slowly, yet fully. Animal, predator, hunter. Lover. Man. Hers.

And that was when she knew. Knew it was going to be okay. More than okay. He was going to make it perfect.

Because she knew then that she trusted him. Trusted he would finish what he'd begun. And that she'd enjoy every scintillating second of it. And that knowledge made her feel both immensely powerful…and completely humbled. She had this man—this man, who knew her needs better than she, who'd pushed her to reach out and take what she'd never dared hope she could have. Take, by being willing to be taken. And, before the night was over he was going to take her.

She would be his. Mind, body, soul.

Her only remaining fear was how to make sure, when it was done, that he would keep her. Forever.

# CHAPTER NINE

THEIR GAZES LOCKED, clashed. Marsh watched as her expression softened. Her lips curved slightly, but not in the knowing smile he'd come to love. This was a smile so tender, so loving, it took his breath away. Slowly, she nodded.

Something inside of Marsh settled then, and exploded at the same time. There, in her eyes, he saw everything he needed to see. He saw her want, her desire and, finally, her acceptance. But most of all, he saw trust. Complete and unconditional. She truly understood. *Thank God,* he thought, all but trembling with the relief of it. She wanted to give herself to him as he had to her. Now it was simply a matter of taking her there.

He only prayed he had the self-control to finish what they'd so dangerously begun.

His body twitched and twitched hard at the mere thought of what was to come. He lit a slender taper and picked it up, then walked toward her. With a hand still shaking from the revelations she'd made, the gift she'd already pledged to him, he reached for her ribbon.

He saw the slight widening of her eyes. He'd surprised her. She'd thought, perhaps, that he was going to reach for her, to pull her into his arms. There was nothing he wanted to do more. But being willing to submit her control to him was one thing. Doing it another.

At least now he knew she'd fight for it as hard as he was.

They walked side by side, along the loft hallway toward his bedroom. As they passed the railed balcony, he saw that the embers of the fire had burnt out below, leaving the main room somewhat chilly and dark. She shivered beside him, but kept her steps measured to his.

He was as aware of her body, the grace with which she walked, as he was of his own. He felt every flex and pull of the muscles in his legs, thighs. His shoulders felt tight after what felt like aeons resisting the natural urge to pull her close, warm her bare skin with the warmth of his body. He kept his hold on the ribbon a loose one, so the satin strip skated across her stomach and hip.

He wondered if she realized how badly he wanted to turn her to him, sink to his knees in front of her. He'd been granted access to every inch of her during their time together, but only as she permitted. Now, tonight, he'd indulge himself in her however he wanted. He could only hope she found it as enthralling an experience as he had when he'd allowed her such freedom with his own body.

Once inside his bedroom, warmed by a low fire that burned in a grate at the base of yet another stone fireplace, he put the taper on a small dresser beside the door, then made her jump when he suddenly kicked the door shut behind her.

"There," he said, pointing to the massive four-post bed that he'd built himself. The ceiling slanted here, making the room seem cozier, more intimate despite the fact that it took up most of the second floor.

He dropped the ribbon, letting the satin strip swirl

across her breasts before dangling between them, stopping just at the juncture of her thighs. She shivered, but he knew from the way her eyes all but glittered in the firelight, that it was in pleasure.

She wasn't looking at him. Her entire focus was transfixed on the very dominant bed that occupied the center of the room, positioned there because the tall, thick posts prevented it from being shoved back against the lower wall.

She walked to the side of the bed, stopping beside a small footstool that was half tucked beneath it. The mattress was so high, she'd need it if she hoped to get on the bed with any semblance of dignity. He had no intention of robbing her of even the tiniest shred of that. That was not his intention here.

"Stay there," he said quietly, hearing the strain in his own voice.

She turned to face him, hands clasped loosely behind her back, and held his gaze. Her expression was unreadable. Except for the flare of desire. And need. He had no idea what she was thinking, or how much of a struggle it was for her to let him take control so completely.

"You're unbelievably beautiful, do you know that?" The words just slipped out. He wasn't even looking at her body as he said them. Then before he risked giving her any more of an edge than he had, he broke eye contact and bent down. With one grunting tug, pulled one boot off, then the other, tossing both aside. Straightening, he walked to her, feet bared, silently convincing himself he could do this without wavering.

She watched him, gaze fixed, as he stopped just before her.

He reached out, so desperately wanting, needing to

touch her. "Do you have any idea the ways I've dreamed of taking you?" he said roughly.

Her eyes widened and she trembled slightly. His body jerked in response. He curled his own trembling fingers inward to keep from touching her. *Slowly,* he schooled himself. *Deliberate, not rash.* She was giving him an enormous gift here and it was costing her. He wanted to make sure she knew her trust in him was well earned.

"Show me." Her voice was a tight whisper, barely audible.

But it snapped at every single nerve ending in his entire body. It was a big capitulation on her part. He saw in her gaze that, though she was undeniably nervous, she was also highly aroused. He wasn't the only one being deliberate here.

Fingers still tightly clenched, he said, "Unbutton my pants. See for yourself what you do to me."

He had no idea if he'd survive it, and found himself wondering just who was learning more about themselves here, Samantha, or himself? With shaky fingers she fumbled at the hooks that held the waistband tight. Just her fingers grazing the skin of his taut belly made his breath shudder to a stop and his throat go dry.

One hook, then another. Each one made more difficult by the length and breadth of his erection, which strained the front of his formfitting pants almost beyond their ability to contain him. Dear God, he prayed, fighting to stand perfectly still. It took all his willpower. His breath whooshed out in a groan of relief as the last hook sprang free.

On legs that were far from steady, he turned so his back was to her. "Take them off," he told her, the words coming out as more growl than anything. But he was beyond doing anything about it.

He felt her right behind him, as if there was an electric field bouncing between them. His awareness of her was almost painful. He wanted to tear his shirt off, would have paid large sums of money to feel her hands snake around his waist, run her palms across his belly, up to his chest and across the light swirl of hair there. To feel her skate her perfectly manicured nails across the tiny hard nubs his nipples had long since become.

She'd taken him many times just like that. Asked him to disrobe as she walked around him, admiring his body as one might admire a newly acquired possession. He'd never minded putting on a display for her, in fact he'd always found it highly arousing. He wondered if she'd feel the same with the tables turned.

Her fingertips skittered along his waist just then, making him bite back a groan, but instead of taking the waistband edges and tugging them down his hips, she let her palms slide upward instead. As if she'd read his mind. To fully reach around him, she had to move close, which, he knew allowed the billowing white shirt he wore to caress her sorely unattended nipples.

They both gasped at the same time as her body brushed against his. He stilled; she froze. Then she slowly continued to move her hands upward.

He drew in one shuddering breath, then exhaled slowly. He had to stop her. It seemed innocent enough, but he knew her too well. She was too used to taking over. One slip was all it would take….

Her fingertips had barely brushed across his nipples when his control snapped. A second later she was flat on her back, in the midst of a soft down comforter.

Marsh stood beside the bed, eyes gleaming. "Enjoy your little adventure?" He could only pray she had no idea what this was costing him.

She paused before answering. Probably debating on what answer would make things easier on her. Her lips curved slightly. "Very much."

"Good," he said, very pleased she'd opted for the truth. Truth had to match trust. "Now, I plan to enjoy mine."

She watched him as he walked to the foot of the bed, then felt beneath the edge of the comforter before drawing out a long, soft piece of black silk cord. He tugged it lightly, so she could plainly see it was tied to the post of the bed.

"You said tying me up was cheating," she choked out, her voice stuttering a bit.

He also noticed she pressed her thighs together, and he didn't think it was a protective response. Her nipples were so hard…he could only imagine what awaited him between her thighs.

"And yet, you cheated on your first opportunity," he told her.

Her cheeks grew pink, but she said nothing.

"So, consider this a little assistance." He looped the cord around one of her ankles, then gently pulled it just snug enough so that her ankle slid halfway across the bed. He moved to the other post. "To keep you on the straight and narrow."

"I wasn't planning to resist," she said, the words sounding all but torn from her as he reached for her other ankle.

"Good intentions. Now you won't have to worry whether you can or not." He glanced at her, grinning. "For now, anyway."

"Doesn't that defeat the purpose?"

He paused. "Not if you're willing to allow me this freedom. It's still up to you. Are you worried about giving me this kind of complete control?"

She held his gaze for a very long time.

He slipped another soft cord free and tapped it against his palm. "What do you think I'm going to do to you, Samantha?" he asked softly.

She said nothing, but her body shifted, her hips moved slightly, belying what this was really doing to her.

He looped it around her other ankle, pleased when she didn't yank it away. "If you know you can't resist, then you can just give yourself over to it. To me."

He strode to the head of the bed, reached for her wrist, his expression all but daring her to pull it away. She didn't. But neither did she offer it to him. Once again, he'd exposed a weakness. And a need.

"So," she said, jaw clenched, but against what he wasn't entirely sure. She wasn't upset so much as…wound tight. He couldn't wait for the whiplash that would occur when she let go. "You're doing me a favor, are you? Making this easier?"

He took her wrist gently, pulled it over her head, secured her to the headboard. "You can think of it that way." He kneeled on the bed, reached across her to untangle the other rope. He paused, his face inches above hers. "It's all up to you either way. Willing. I want you willing to give yourself to me. Even like this." He brushed his lips across hers, making her moan, making him swallow one of his own. *Careful, careful.* "But only this first time. Next time you won't think twice. You'll grip that headboard and hold on until I tell you to let go because you'll want to. You won't even think about wanting anything else."

She quivered. Muscles twitching. And didn't even try to move her hand as he pushed it closer to the bedpost.

"Or I can stop this right now," he said, levering himself up again. "I could untie you. Would you rather hold on to the cords instead…test yourself?"

Her eyes were like twin flames, lasering him.

He bent down again, lasering his gaze right back at her. "Or would you rather me show you first? Show you what it can be like to let go. Having already given up control to me." He moved closer still, until his mouth was almost brushing hers. "Just how much do you trust me?"

# CHAPTER TEN

SHE HADN'T BEEN prepared for this sudden turn in events. Hell, who was she kidding? She hadn't been prepared for any of this. Which was precisely why he was doing it.

Part of her wanted to make him untie her. Prove to herself and him that she could do as he asked.

But there was an undeniable thrill coursing through her at the very idea of giving up all control to him now. Giving herself to him, all of her trust, all at once.

"What is it going to be, Samantha?" he asked, then skated his lips across hers, before dropping down and shocking her by lightly nipping her chin.

She moaned, her hips bucked. But she couldn't make herself say the words, giving him the ultimate control over her.

Then he abruptly got off the bed. And the words were wrenched from her before she could chicken out and take them back.

"Tie me."

Marsh's dark eyes gleamed in satisfaction as he looped the last cord over her wrist, and pulled it gently away from the side of her head. There was no missing how his body was responding to this, which only served to jack her up even higher. There was enough slack in the satin ropes to allow her to move and she squirmed in need as he walked to the foot of the bed. He'd robbed her of every pretense. And there was no denying she was aching for whatever was to happen to her next.

Still, she watched him warily as he moved the footstool in front of him, then stepped up on it. Now he was in full view from midthigh up over the high footboard of the bed. His breeches hung open, his shirt hung loose. He looked like some kind of decadent pirate. Which left her playing the role of some dockside wench he'd dragged on board ship to keep at his very personal beck and call.

Instead of making her laugh, the very image made her moan a little, and squirm in her soft restraints. She didn't miss the jerk and twitch at the front of his breeches as he watched her struggle. Rather than put her off, the overt dominance of it only served to inflame her more. The old Samantha would have worked his reaction to her advantage. She would have done whatever it took to get him to shove her over the merciless edge he'd kept her on now for what felt like hours.

The new Samantha held her tongue. And waited. Partly because she had no real advantage this time. Anything she did, or tried to do, would only delay the conclusion she so badly wanted to reach. But mostly she fought to keep still because she'd finally come to understand—in a way only Marsh could have known she'd understand—that it would be better, and that they'd both enjoy it more, if she did.

She hid a private smile. Would wonders never cease?

She expected him to strip, and waited with almost greedy anticipation for the show. Instead he surprised her yet again. She watched him reach down and lift up a small glass bottle. Her curiosity was immediately piqued. As was her anxiety over once again confronting the unknown. Acknowledging that she trusted him didn't stop her from trembling as he drew closer. Only Marsh knew what the plan was. The not knowing was killing her and he knew it. But she bit the inside of her lip to keep from asking him what he was going to do to her. Because asking would only delay her finding out.

And God help her, she wanted to find out. Badly.

The quivering began in her legs, spreading to her midsection, then to her arms and her hands, which clenched in their soft bindings as he slid a long glass applicator from the bottle. Something thick and clear dripped off the end.

He moved onto the bed, the mattress so thick and heavy it barely dipped beneath his weight. He moved between her widespread legs, still not looking at what he'd so neatly caused her to display. She was grateful for that, not sure she could withstand the sensations that his hot, lethal gaze would give her, just with a glance.

Holding her gaze, he took the glass wand and dipped the bulbous tip into her navel. She gasped. It was warm, almost hot. Heat radiated from that point outward. He swirled it a little, making her twitch. Then he dipped it back in the small, potlike vial, pulled it out again.

"What is that?" she choked out, as he lifted the dripping wand back out, letting the clear oil drizzle up her midsection.

"Almond oil, ginger. A few other things." He bent over her and she watched, trembling harder now as he waved the wand closer to her breasts. "Does it tingle?" he asked, his voice almost as heated as the oil.

She managed a nod, then arched almost violently as he rolled the glass tip around one nipple. Her gasp was harsh, deep, then repeated when he dipped the wand directly on the tip of her other nipple. "Ahh," she breathed. The ache between her legs grew to untenable proportions, so much so she was quite willing to beg him to put an end to this and take her. Now. Repeatedly.

But her gaze was riveted on that damn glass wand as he dipped it once again, then trailed it beneath both breasts, then along her midsection. He traveled slowly around her navel, and she let her head drop back, drawing in a deep breath as he moved lower. She was panting by the time he tickled the edges of the curls so tightly thatched between her legs.

He withdrew the tip. She held her breath. Waiting. Waiting for him to dip it back in the vial, then dip it—finally, blessedly—into her. The moment spun out so long, her body grew so taut with anticipation, she thought she'd scream.

"Watch me," he said on a heated whisper.

She thrashed her head, bucked her hips.

He shifted his weight off her, and she stilled instantly, not wanting to do anything that would make him stop.

"Watch," he instructed her again.

She lifted her head, snared immediately in his gaze. He held the wand just over her, each drip falling into her curls, soaking through until she could feel the warmth on her skin, running downward. She twitched, moved a little, wanting, needing to do anything to get that trickle of heat to run right where she so badly—

"Still," he commanded. "Hold yourself perfectly still. And watch me."

She was riveted now. She couldn't control him—a reality that was becoming increasingly intoxicating to her—but she could control herself.

Still, it took every last ounce of it she had not to twitch with need as he very methodically slid the wand into the bottle. He dipped once, then twice, until a moan was torn from her. Just the very motion, the same motion she so badly needed herself, was enough to wrench her up another notch.

He tore his gaze from hers, apparently satisfied now that she wouldn't—couldn't—look away. He moved the rounded glass tip closer…then closer still. Her gasp caught in her throat as one hot bead of oil dropped, rolled between lips so sensitized now that the mere way his breath stirred the air across her skin down there was almost unbearably pleasurable. Another drop…and then another. He glanced up at her, the tension spiked as her skin grew more heated as more oil dripped and glided across her oh-so-sensitive skin. Then finally he lowered the wand. A growl of pleasure was ripped from her as he finally pressed glass tip to skin. Soft, hot, oiled skin. Lower. Lower. He slid the wand until it parted her lips. So close, so damn close.

"Don't move," he reminded her, at the very split second she was about to jerk her hips up so he could slide that damn thing—

"Oh!" she gasped, then a long groan was torn from her as he slid a finger deeply inside of her at the very same moment he let that glass tip roll over her throbbing flesh. She started to wrench upward as he slid deeper, right on the edge of a climax more powerful than she'd ever experienced. But at the last possible second, she held herself still.

"Yes," he whispered, his own voice hoarse, almost tortured. He rolled the glass tip over her again.

She began to keen. A low moan, both of pleasure and of frustration at not being allowed to move, to take what she so badly needed. It was so alien to her, being forced to take like this, without controlling the situation, without being the one in position to give permission, dictate the course. It was with stunning awareness that she realized he could, and likely would, prolong this almost excruciating pleasure for however long it suited him.

All she had to do was accept and enjoy the increasingly intense sensations rocketing through her. It shouldn't be so damn hard, she thought, struggling mightily not to buck up and take what was so, so close to being hers.

But she knew, deep down knew, in a way only he could have proven to her, that where before today she'd have taken her pleasure and been done with it…he was taking her higher, further, far past whatever boundaries she'd thought it possible to reach.

And then the glass wand was gone. The sweet pressure of his finger inside of her…gone. Her eyes flew open, making her realize she'd stopped watching at some point. Her gaze flew to his. He watched her intently, the bottle gone. His shirt gone. His breeches—

She moaned without constraint as he slowly rolled back to the stool, then skimmed his pants down, and off. He was perfect.

And he was hers. All hers.

She hoped he understood now how completely she was his.

She opened her mouth, to tell him she realized, then closed it again.

"What?" he asked, the single word belying the constraint his own control was under.

Instead of making her feel victorious, it simply made her feel…joined. Now they both understood the power of true sharing, of complete trust. She shook her head.

"Tell me what you want, Samantha."

"You," she choked out.

"How?"

"Any way you wish."

His eyes sparkled. "Are you sure?"

She nodded with absolute certainty, her chest rising and falling rapidly in anticipation as he lowered his weight to the bed, began to climb over her.

He moved so that no part of him touched her, and yet every part of him was so close, so perfectly, frustratingly close. She knew he was steely hard, fuller than she'd ever seen him before…and yet, despite how badly she wanted to touch him, taste him, have him, every inch of him, she couldn't look away from his eyes.

"Very sure," she said, then groaned as his thigh brushed hers.

"You realize this is only the beginning. That there is so much more for us to learn. About each other."

She nodded, knowing just how right he was. She felt as if she'd exploded into a whole new world in the past couple of hours, a world she hadn't known existed. A world she entered via intense sexual pleasure, but actually had to do with so much more.

"It will take years to learn all there is to know of what we can do with one another, to one another," he said, moving his mouth closer to her neck, but touching her only with his breath. "A lifetime, in fact."

He blew across her oiled nipples, making her twitch, but otherwise she fought to keep still. So perfectly still.

He would make it worth her while. She knew that he always would.

"I want those years," he murmured, moving his lips to the outer shell of her ear, blowing a soft breath along the rim. "If you give them to me, I will promise to do my best to make every single day worthwhile." He dropped his mouth to where it barely brushed hers.

She moaned somewhere deep inside her chest. "Yes," she managed.

"To find every way in which you can share yourself with me," he said, brushing his lips over hers again. "Discover all the ways in which I can share myself with you."

She twitched hard, fighting more than ever to hold still. Thinking about what it would be like to switch places, to do this to him, with him, almost undoing her entirely.

He grinned then and it took what was left of her breath away. "You like that idea, don't you. Making me helpless for want of you. Taking me. Like this. Like I'm about to take you." He speared her mouth with his tongue, so suddenly, so completely, she gasped and bucked. He used his body to press hers back into the mattress. She cried deeply in her throat at the sweet pressure of his body on hers, the insistent, rock-hard erection so teasingly close, yet pressed against her belly.

The instant she was still, he lifted up on his hands and knees.

"No," she cried.

"Don't get ahead of yourself. We still have all night. And you're the one tied to the bed." His grin returned. "For now anyway."

She shuddered at the very images that swamped her brain. Oh, they were going to enjoy each other a great deal. It helped her to keep from begging him now. Barely.

As if he saw the war she was waging with herself, his smile turned a shade cocky. "Shall I get the brush back? The feather? Or perhaps you'd like to see what else I have on that tray downstairs?"

Just his words, and the images they painted, were almost too unbearably stimulating. And yet what she said was, "Yes. Yes, I want all of that. I want—"

"What?" He teased her again, brushed the inside of her thighs, her oh-so-vulnerably parted thighs.

She growled, swore beneath her breath and fought to keep perfectly still. "Damn you," she muttered, jerking her head to the side, mostly so he wouldn't see she was fighting a smile. A smile of anticipation of what he would do next, of realizing that the unknown didn't have to be a scary, terrifying thing. That sometimes, giving up control was remarkably freeing, especially when you were with someone you trusted. Someone you loved.

She turned to him, held his gaze. And saw beneath the desire, past the raw heat, to the absolute knowledge. That he was made for her. And she for him. All she had to do was tell him.

"I want this," she said, the words coming surprisingly easily. Her final capitulation wasn't one of weakness, but a move toward a newfound strength and power. The power of two.

"This," he repeated.

"Yes. This," she breathed. "I want you to make me want. I want you to want me to do the exact same thing to you."

His eyes gleamed with an almost unholy light. "Tell me more," he demanded, his voice nothing more than a rasp.

"I want you," she said. "And I want us. Always."

He plunged into her then, arms still braced above her. The shock of it, the sweet, amazingly wonderful invasion of him into her, locking them together in ways far more profound than she'd known was possible. He made her scream. With pleasure, with joy, with exultation.

He withdrew as suddenly as he'd come into her.

"Marsh," she cried. He couldn't stop now, not when it would have been perfect.

"No," he said, shaking himself as he rolled back to his heels. "Not like this. Not this time. I need more." He all but ripped the cord off of one ankle, then the other. He moved between her legs, gripped her hips and dragged her up over his thighs, until he could watch her as he slowly, torturously slowly, pushed back inside of her.

"You are mine," he said, so fierce, so primal in his claiming of her, she had already started to shudder uncontrollably.

And then he pushed all the way in, held her tightly to him, so she had all of him. So deeply. Far more deeply than merely a body joined to a body.

She shook hard as he moved his hand between their bodies. Stroked her slowly, up then down, with his finger. "Mine to take." He stroked her, with his finger, with himself. Up. Down. In. Out.

She cried out as he ripped her along that fine edge, dancing, dancing. Then finally wrenching her completely over. She thrashed, she bucked, wildly, uncontrollably. She begged, she shouted, she screamed. And she came. Over. And over. It washed over her in deep, undulating waves, engulfed her, drowned her, in sensation after sensation.

Still shuddering, still shaken, still overwhelmed, she

watched him lower himself over her. So hard, so thick, she'd never felt so filled by him. Aftershocks shook her with each long, slow stroke. The thundering beat of his heart belied the steady control he seemed to so easily possess.

He pressed more deeply into her as he laid his body over hers, pressed every inch of himself to her. He laid his legs on hers, he reached his hands up to cover hers, pressed his mouth next to her ear as he began to move, slowly, deeply. His body matching her position from fingertips to toes. "Mine to be taken by," he finished.

Tears burned behind her eyes and she longed to hold him, to wrap her arms and legs around him. But he kept them that way as he continued to move, showing her, proving to her that he was as committed as she. "Thank you," she whispered.

He shifted his head, looked down into her eyes. "For?"

She held his gaze. "Loving me."

Emotion so deep she couldn't put words to it exploded across his face. "I'm glad you realize that. Because I do. Profoundly. I just wanted—needed—to find a way to make you understand. What we have. What we can have."

"I'm beginning to. I want to know more."

He ripped the cords then, from the upper bedposts, twined his fingers through hers as he pulled her arms down. "You will. We will." He kissed her, deeply, and with such emotion and honest need and affection she felt the tears trickle from the corners of her eyes as she kissed him back, pouring everything into it that she couldn't find the words for, hoping it was enough. Wanting it to be enough. For him. For them.

"I do love you," he whispered.

"Oh, Marsh." She arched into him, gasping. Crying. Knowing he'd help her be enough, take her when she needed taking, give himself when she needed to have him. It was more than she could have ever hoped for. And she was determined to do whatever it took to keep it. To keep him.

"I love you, too," she whispered back, voice thick with tears. Tears of unbelievable joy.

And then they were lost in each other. Moving, lifting, sliding. Bodies joined. Hands joined. Hearts entwined.

## EPILOGUE

"I'VE GOT ONE WEEK to showtime and your trunks aren't here." Samantha tapped her pen against her keyboard as she listened. Her other hand drifted to her throat, as it often had over the past week. She fingered the small gold heart that now dangled from the velvet strip she still wore. Marsh had given her the heart that night. Not that she needed a tangible reminder of what had transpired, or their commitment, but she just enjoyed the feel of it there. It made her smile, knowing she'd be seeing Marsh at the end of each day. No matter if her day ended at midnight or three in the morning.

"Tomorrow?" She blew out a long sigh. "Fine, fine. I'll be in touch." She disconnected, then jammed the pen behind her ear and swiveled her chair so she could reach a stack of files. There was so much left to do and so very little time left to do it. "Marcy!" she called out. "Follow up on Matsuoki. Send shipping labels, hire a driver to get the damn trunk to the airport if you have to, whatever it takes. Just make sure it gets here." She didn't wait for an answer, she was already punching another blinking light on her phone pad. "Yes, Serena, I'm still here," she said to one of her more skittish buyers. "Trust me, you'll love Jamie's new line." Sam didn't have to feign her sincerity or enthusiasm. She'd been in a meeting with him yesterday and gotten a firsthand look at the final lineup. It was going to blow everyone away. She grinned. "Bring your checkbook. You won't be sorry."

Sam disconnected, blew her hair off her forehead and debated on whether to tackle her mountainous message pile, or go track down Jamie and catch up on the five million details they still had to go over. Speaking of details, she'd had a call from Mia earlier that she'd never gotten around to returning. "Dammit," she swore under her breath. "Marcy!" she shouted. "Get Mia on the cell, will ya? Page her, whatever."

Her stomach was jumpy with both nerves and anticipation. She hadn't eaten yet today, but she had managed to down a pot of coffee. *Food, she needed food.* But instead of picking up the phone to call down to the deli, she found herself fingering the heart again. And smiling. Normally she'd be in a frenzied, ulcer-inducing panic at this point. And she was, but only part of the time. All she had to do was think about a certain cowboy, and her nerves settled a bit. Well, the bad ones anyway.

She took a moment to take a deep breath, and thought about Marsh, how much he calmed her, how just knowing he was there for her helped to center her. It should scare her how much she looked forward to having him be the end of her day, how much she'd already come to need him, to step away from the insanity, even if it was just for a few minutes, and look outside herself, outside her work. And look into the face of what was really important.

She'd been afraid her new relationship with him would prevent her from focusing on what had to be done, not just during this intensely important time in the growth of her company, but during all that would come afterward, too. Instead, it had given her the exact opposite. A place to escape to every night, where she could get completely away, indulge herself in something besides work. Indulge herself in the man she loved, in her own needs, needs that had nothing to do with her career. It felt so satisfying, decadent even.

Even if it was only a quick dinner and holding hands while they talked over the day. Her smile broadened just thinking about it. No matter the duration, she'd always returned to work refreshed and clearheaded. She only wondered now what it was she'd been so afraid of.

*Life is more than just work, or being your lover.*

"When the man is right, the man is right," she murmured with a smile.

Just then, Marcy popped her head in her office door. "Hey, boss."

"Did you get Mia?" Sam asked.

"Working on it. And the Matsuoki thing. In the meantime, delivery for you."

"Whatever it is, just put it in the office down the hall with the rest of the trunks," Sam said, flipping open the top folder. She still had to coordinate the different pieces she'd chosen into groups for the runway lineup. Then she had to match a model to each piece. Which would be a hell of a lot easier if all the trunks from each designer were already here. International shipping was her current worst nightmare.

"I think you're going to want this delivery in here," Marcy said.

Samantha barely remarked on the coy note in Marcy's voice. She raked her hand through her hair and spared a quick glance at her assistant. Whatever command she'd been about to give died unspoken, however, as Marcy edged into the room with a flat white box, tied in a huge red bow.

With a mischievous smile and a wiggle of eyebrows, her assistant handed it across Sam's desk. "Here you go, boss."

Sam would have tossed back some wry comment, but her heart was suddenly pounding too hard. She took the box and started to rip it open, only remembering at the last second she wasn't alone. She looked at Marcy. "Is there anything else?"

Marcy's shoulders fell. "I slave away my life for you—"

"For which you'll be amply rewarded," Samantha reminded her, lips curving in a knowing smile. She'd already decided to personally groom Marcy to take on more responsibility. Her assistant was young, hungry, and most importantly, she could handle it. And that would free Samantha up to spend less time at the office…and more time having a life. A life with Marsh.

"Sure, okay, don't share," Marcy teased.

Sam's fingers itched to tear open the box. "Not this time."

Marcy playfully stuck her tongue out, but dutifully backed out of the room.

The door hadn't even clicked shut when Sam was tearing open the box. A card lay on top of the tissue paper. She opened it and laughed at herself for having such trembling hands. The note was short, in Marsh's masculine slash.

*Your turn.*

Grinning, even as her pulse sped up, she peeled back the tissue paper. Nestled inside were four very familiar lengths of black satin rope.

"Think you might find a use for those?"

She jerked her head up. Marsh stood in the doorway. He was in jeans, Western boots and a denim work shirt that was a little worse for wear after spending the afternoon teaching inner-city kids what it felt like to climb on the back of a horse. Gathered in the hallway, Sam could see the entire office staff unabashedly ogling him. Marcy shot her two thumbs-ups from just behind Marsh's shoulder, along with a wide grin.

Sam started to order Marsh to get inside and close the door before she had to explain him to everyone…then stopped herself. *Oh yeah,* she thought, *I don't have to explain anything, anymore.* That warm spot that had sprung to life in her heart the moment she'd spied him in the doorway, expanded until she felt consumed by it.

She got up and walked to the door, very deliberately lifted up on her toes and kissed him soundly on the mouth. "Hey, cowboy."

"Hey, yourself," he said, then took her into his arms and pushed her back against the door and laid claim to her mouth.

Sam wasn't one for public displays, but she'd fast come to realize that where Marsh was concerned, she was discovering she enjoyed all kinds of new things. Breathless when he finally let her go, she could only grin stupidly up into his handsome face.

With what little aplomb she could muster, she shifted her gaze to the now openly gawking group. "Everyone, Marsh. Marsh, everyone." She glanced back at the man she loved, and her smile was slow and so very satisfied. "He's all mine. Eat your heart out."

With cheers, catcalls and hearty applause echoing off the walls, Marsh walked her back into her office.

"Marcy, hold my calls," Sam managed to call out, just before Marsh kicked the door shut.

"I know you're busy," Marsh murmured against her neck.

"The world won't end if I take a short break." Samantha fumbled to lock it behind them, then laughed. "But I might be a little later getting home tonight."

"I'll send a limo," Marsh told her.

"Be in the backseat, and you have a deal."

"You drive a hard bargain, Ms. Wallace."

Marsh dragged his hips against hers. "Speaking of hard…where are those ropes?"

A real partnership, Sam was fast discovering, was indeed a wonderful thing.

# BARING IT ALL
## Jill Shalvis

# CHAPTER ONE

NORMALLY MIA TENNARIO felt cool as rain, poised under pressure and endlessly calm, but today she was a Tums-popping, head-spinning maniac who was about to chew some serious ass. "What do you mean, *you quit?*" she asked Todd O'Ryan, aka contractor from hell. "You can't quit."

"Watch me." On the stage of the outdoor Greek Theater, with the July Los Angeles sunshine beating down on them, Todd bent over to pick up his tool belt, showing Mia far more than a two-hundred-pound, five-foot-five, hot and sweaty man should show.

She scrunched her eyes shut but it was too late, the image of his work pants sliding southward, past the Continental Divide, had imprinted on her brain.

Straightening, he glared at her. "Look, you're asking for a miracle, all right? And your secretary is a raving lunatic. She said I had two weeks."

"One."

He laughed. "Yeah. Good luck on that."

In Mia's pocket, her cell began to vibrate, probably the "raving lunatic" assistant herself, Jane Jennings. They were both crazed. Glancing down at the cell, she groaned. Thirty-six missed calls, a new record. And her must-do list was so long she threatened national forests every time she printed it off her Palm Pilot. This latest glitch in her day wasn't a bigger problem than any of the rest but it *was* the last straw. "You signed a contract," she said in the most tranquil voice she could muster. *Catch the bee with honey,* she reminded herself, and added the friendliest smile she could muster as she tapped the rolled set of blueprints tucked beneath her arm. "The plans are done. They're right here. Certainly if you added a few men—"

"No." Todd gestured around him on the stage he had yet to begin to transform. His crew of exactly one young kid stood around looking about as useful as Todd's own belt. "*Nobody's* going to be able to pull this stuff off for you," he said. "Not the catwalk or the archway on the stage—"

"Ancient wonder."

"Huh?"

"It's a replica of one of the seven ancient wonders, not just an archway."

"Yeah, yeah, whatever. No one's going to be able to do it in the time you have."

She understood it was complicated. There were mountains of wood and metal scaffolding already scattered across the wooden floor of the stage, ready to go. The plans in her hands would transform those materials and the stage into an exotic, sophisticated, ancient wonder for her company's live global satellite lingerie fashion show one week from today. They'd put everything into this show, calling it *Sizzling Nights* for the hot and wild designs they'd be showcasing, and it needed to go off without a hitch.

But at the moment it all looked grim.

"You're going to have to delay your panty show," Todd said, shaking his head. "You know it and I know it."

"It's not a panty—" *Argh!* She was wasting her breath with this idiot. Unfortunately, she understood men like him all too well—her mother had been fond of just such jackasses, and as a result, she knew how to deal with them, which was to grab them by the proverbial balls and squeeze. "Let me repeat. You signed a contract."

"Yeah, well, you and your panty people can sue me. I'm outta here."

Panty people. What he so eloquently referred to was Velvet, Leather & Lace, the lingerie catalog company she ran with her two partners, Jamie and Samantha. Mia was a graphic designer by trade; as a partner, her job was to design the cutting-edge layout of the catalog itself and, more currently, the set of the upcoming fashion show. She loved her job, every important and critical aspect of it, since for the first time in her life she felt indispensable.

It'd been a long haul. Still reeling from the tough two years they'd all put into VLL, they were shocked and thrilled by the designer roster they'd attracted for the show, a virtual who's who of designers from all over the globe. Thanks to celebrity endorsements and the fact that they catered to "real size" women, there was a huge buzz around them at the moment, but as the latest "it" company, one who'd suddenly taken off like a twin-engine jet, they were now trying to capitalize on their moment in the spotlight.

It all centered around this fashion show. In seven short days, the simple but beautifully stark stage needed to be transformed into a showcase fit for fashion royalty from all over the world. They'd go live, featuring the latest and greatest, and potentially boost VLL beyond the thing of the moment and into a full-fledged booming success.

Just the thought made Mia's head spin. And now Todd was packing up his tools, whistling toward the kid, who'd stopped even pretending to look busy.

"No," she said. "No, no, no. Don't go. We can work this out—"

"The only way we're going to work this out is if you delay the show and give me more time, or cut back on the details you've added, or—" he let out an obnoxious smirk "—add in a hefty bonus so that I can entice my crew to work nights."

Mia put her hands on her hips, another long-ago learned trick that always seemed to give her five-foot-three frame the necessary authority required to demand respect. "You can't ask for a bonus after you've agreed to the job."

Unimpressed, Todd shrugged and gestured toward the kid, who followed him stage left. *Damn it.* "How much of a bonus?" she called out to him.

Todd turned and gave her a lecherous once-over. "What are you offering?"

*Eeew.* Her stomach twisted. "Get out."

He did, leaving her completely alone on the vast stage. With a heavy heart, she sat on the sun-warmed wooden floor, risking sunburn and freckles, surrounded by towering stacks of expensive materials, hugging her blueprints. Looking out, she faced the orchestra pit and the 5,700 empty seats, which would soon be filled with the fashion world.

Oh God. At least the theater was gorgeous, nestled as it was on a lush hill in the picturesque tree-enclosed setting of Griffith Park. No doubt she couldn't have dreamed up a better setting. It was a historic venue, as well, where some of the biggest names in entertainment had been hosted over the years, and they'd been damned lucky to get it.

Still, she was screwed. Completely screwed. Pulling out her cell phone, she dialed the office to check in and make sure this was the only fire.

Jane answered after half a ring. That was the beauty of having an assistant even more anal than herself.

"Tell me it's going good," Jane said in lieu of a greeting.

Mia hesitated. She loved Jane but didn't want to deal with the ensuing panic of informing her they no longer had a contractor. "It's going."

"Oh God."

"Don't panic." Hopefully *no one* would. "Everything okay there?"

"Oh, sure. I'm just sitting here watching *Oprah* and eating a box of chocolates. No sweat."

Mia managed to laugh at the sarcasm. "Good. I'll get back to you in a little while." She hung up and allowed herself a three-minute pity party while she chewed half a dozen antacids. Then she brushed herself off and moved offstage, her heels clicking as fast as the wheels in her overtaxed brain.

It took her only twenty minutes northbound on Highway 5 to Glendale, but once on her cozy little cul-de-sac, with the neat row of houses from the 1920s, most of them restored several times over, she sat in her car for another few minutes, staring at the blue Tundra in front of her. She was about to do something she hated—ask for help.

With a deep breath, she walked past her house and knocked on the door just to the right of hers.

No answer.

Oh God. She glanced at her watch. Noon on a Saturday. He could be anywhere, doing anything, but his truck was there—

"Hey, Mia."

At the low, husky voice, she whipped around and faced the tall, broad-shouldered man making his way up the walk.

At just the sight of him, with his fawn-colored hair perpetually rumpled and his light green, see-all eyes sharp and crinkled with good humor, Mia took her first gulp of relief. Jake Holbrook, neighbor and friend.

*He would help her.*

He wore running shorts, a damp T-shirt plastered to his chest and athletic shoes, and would have looked perfectly at home on a Nike ad, all rough-and-tumble tough and leanly muscled. Obviously, he'd just come from a run. He probably had plans for the afternoon, plans she hoped desperately to alter.

He was smiling at her. Jane had once said he had the smile of a man thinking naughty things which he'd probably be willing to share, if only asked.

Mia had never thought to ask.

Not that she didn't like men—she *loved* men: tall ones, thin ones, built ones, cute ones… She wasn't picky, not when it didn't really matter since she never really *kept* a man. She didn't know exactly why that was, but it was a fact. Men came and went.

But Jake was different; he was a friend, and a friend only and she liked it that way. They ate together at least once a week, they saw movies, they had game nights— Monopoly, cards, whatever—he was great company. Great "friend" company. She'd kept things that way on purpose for reasons too complicated to think about at the moment.

In any case, Mia's favorite part of Jake was something far more intangible than just his sense of humor, tough good looks and poker talent.

He could always be counted on.

And that, in Mia's book, made him worth his weight in gold. In truth, at just the sight of him, she nearly threw herself in his arms for a hug, but something held her back.

Jake swiped an arm over his forehead and hunkered down to pull a key out of his shoe. The shoes had seen better days, and so had his threadbare Lakers T-shirt. His tanned skin shone with sweat. Good Lord, where had all that sleek sinew and smooth flesh come from? The man was a walking fantasy, but she tore her eyes off him and concentrated on the here and now. If she could get him to the Greek Theater today, now even, he'd still have a full week left to help her. "Jake, I've never been so happy to see you."

"Is that right?" Rising with his key in his hand, uncoiling that long body as he did, he looked down at her with amusement. "Never?"

"I mean, of course I'm *always* happy to see you," she corrected with a little laugh. "But…" she trailed off. Funny how smooth she could be when it came to running a company, or even seducing a man, but with Jake today, finesse flew out the window.

"How was work?" he asked.

He always asked. He always listened to her answers, too, and was one of the few people in her life who'd resisted making a crack about the fact that she sold underwear for a living. "Work was—*is*," she corrected, "hell."

"Sorry."

"But I think I can turn this whole disaster around if you'll—" She broke off and hesitated, having never asked him for help before. "Listen, I'm bad at this, so how about I just get right to it."

"Sure."

"How swamped is your calendar?"

He looked intrigued. "For what specifically…?"

"Work."

"Ah."

Was that…*disappointment* flickering across his rugged features?

He fit his key into the lock of his front door. "You live and breathe your work, Mia. You know what they say about all work and no play."

"That's not true, I do other stuff. I think of other stuff."

Again he shot her an amused glance. "Really? Name one."

"Well…" Okay, so nothing was coming to her right at the moment. And fine, so she was a workaholic. So what? She rolled her eyes at his soft laugh. "All I want to know is how fast can you get ready to come."

He arched a brow, and Mia felt her face flame as she realized how *that* had sounded, at how he'd clearly taken the unintended meaning. "Okay, back up. That came out incredibly…wrong."

His voice seemed lower now, rougher. "And here I thought maybe you meant—"

"No!"

"Oh, well." He was still amused, but also something else now, too, something deeper and darker.

*Arousal,* she thought in shock.

Jake wanted her.

She looked away. She didn't have time to think about this, not now, not with her life unraveling, and she stumbled over her words. "I didn't mean—damn it, Jake. You're twisting me all around."

"Fair's fair. You've been twisting me around for years."

"What?

"Nothing. Forget it." He let out a low laugh, then opened his door, gesturing her in ahead of him. "How about this? You sit down and have a drink of something cold while I take a shower, and then we'll start over."

"I don't have time to sit, and you don't have time to shower." She led the way to his kitchen and spread the blueprints across his kitchen table.

He came up behind her, looking at the plans over her shoulder, smelling shockingly good for a man who'd just gone running. But she had no business taking another surreptitious sniff, no business at all.

"What's all this?" His chest brushed her shoulder as he leaned in closer.

"My butt on the line. Look, can you build it?"

Craning his neck, he looked at her for a long moment. "I don't know. It's a pretty fine butt just the way it is."

"*Jake.*" She tapped the drawing of the stage, the pit, the seating, all superimposed with the proposed catwalk and ancient-wonder-type archway and set. "What I need to know is, can you build *this* in six days?"

He took a long look at the plans, his sea-green eyes scanning, taking it all in.

He was a general contractor. Granted he worked in residential, building one spec home at a time because he liked a small crew and liked even more to get his own hands involved in the day-to-day work, but surely what she needed here would be a piece of cake compared to a whole house.

It was the timeline that proposed the biggest problem. "So?" she pressed. "What do you think? Are you swamped? Do you have time for a job like this? *Can* you do a job like this?"

His eyes cut to hers again, and some of the amusement was back. His shirt was still damp and stuck to his hard, sleek torso like a second skin. Most women would be drooling standing this close to such a masculine, virile man, but Mia kept her eyes on his and her libido firmly in check.

"Yes to all of the above," he said. "The question is, *will* I?"

"Oh, Jake. Please? I'm so out of my league on this. The materials came late, the specs keep changing as we feel our way through our first live show and the contractor just quit on me. He said he didn't bid enough and he's willing to risk a lawsuit to get out."

"Hmm."

Hmm? What did *that* mean?

"Sounds like you're in quite a bind," he said.

"You have no idea. Just put me out of my misery, Jake. Say you'll do it."

He looked over the plans again, though she had the oddest feeling it wasn't the drawings that he saw. She held her breath and waited, and finally he turned his head, once again aiming those mesmerizing eyes of his her way. "Why?"

*Why?* "Top-dollar payment," she said. "We can even go time and materials instead of a fixed bid, which would save you a day of paperwork, right?"

"Yes, but I meant why *me?*"

"Because you're all I've got," she admitted. "I'll owe you for coming through for me," she promised rashly. "Big-time."

"Big-time, huh?" He tucked a stray strand of her hair behind her ear and let out a sound that might have been a laugh if his mouth hadn't been twisted in a grimace. "What's big-time mean?"

"You name it," she said, knowing that with him on her side, this whole thing would go off perfectly. "I'll watch football with you for a month."

He arched a brow. She had him—she just knew it. "I'll do your laundry, wash your car. *Anything.*"

At that, his expression distinctly changed, deepened, intensified. And for the first time, she hesitated. "Jake?"

"I'll do it," he said very quietly, watching her very keenly. "In fact, I'm all yours.

## CHAPTER TWO

JAKE GOT TO THE THEATER by one-thirty that afternoon, ready to begin the task of completing Mia's miracle. He'd rearranged his schedule—no easy task at the last minute—and had lined up a crew of three—half the size he needed, but Tom and his brothers were close friends of Jake's, and they'd do the job right.

Which meant Mia Tennario, owner of eyes the color of mocha and a smile destined to melt the coldest of hearts, not to mention a hot little bod that made his twitch, would owe Jake.

Oh yeah, now *that* wasn't a hardship at all, having her owe him one.

Now all he had to do was actually get the set and cat-walk built.

Truth be told, he'd had the odds against him before, many times. For one, he'd grown up in the gutter and had scraped his way out of it, clawing and fighting all the way. It'd taken him most of his school years to realize that brawn was one thing, but that brains were actually far more effective.

Following that epiphany, which had come to him while in the hospital after a beating he'd taken from refusing to join a gang in the mean streets of downtown L.A., life had become easier, even enjoyable. Even through the tough, lean years of building his own business, of counting every single penny until he had enough to scrape together dimes instead, then actual dollars, he'd still managed to get a thrill out of life at every turn.

These days things were even better. His construction company had been operating in the black all year, he had a bunch of jobs lined up behind this one, and best of all…his neighbor and close friend—the hot, sexy, funny, sharp Mia Tennario—now owed him a favor he most definitely intended to collect.

Between the sheets.

Not that Mia knew it. She thought of him as a friend, and that friendship was good. It was real and based on a mutual fondness that had begun the day she'd moved in, when she'd marched up to his front door and calmly asked him to get rid of the family of mice living in her pantry. To her credit, she'd kept her cool until he'd handled the chore, and only then had fallen apart, admitting that the mice reminded her of some of the places she'd lived with her mother, most of which hadn't been any better than where he'd lived. It had given them an unexpected bond.

And he'd admired her composure, and had especially loved hugging her until she'd stopped shaking. In return, she'd brought him home expensive men's lingerie from her company's catalog. He'd taken the gift, never mentioning that he didn't wear a robe. Or sleepwear.

It'd actually taken him a while to realize she hadn't been hitting on him then. That she simply, truly, only wanted friendship.

And try as he might, he'd never been able to break that barrier. There was attraction. Hell, the air crackled between them, always had. But she resisted with maddening stubbornness, saying only that she wasn't into sex.

*Who wasn't into sex?*

Sometimes at night he'd hear her coming home late from the job she put everything into, hear her letting herself into her empty house, just as he sat in his, and something deep within him would yearn and burn. It was elusive, intangible, and yet he couldn't seem to put it aside.

It was that indefinable thing he felt for her that had him dropping everything to jump to her aid today, simply because she'd looked at him with those melting chocolate eyes and said *please* in that voice that he wanted to hear panting his name in ecstasy.

There it was. His fantasy. Mia naked and beneath him. And over him. And beside him...

He had to laugh at himself. Mia didn't have any such fantasies about him, and though he thought maybe he understood why, it didn't mean he couldn't change her mind with the right sort of coaxing.

In the middle of the impressive but empty stage of the outdoor Greek Theater, he stopped and looked out at the large venue sprawled in front of him. He'd been here once. Dragged here actually, by a date who'd had tickets to the symphony. It'd been several years ago, when he'd had to work tirelessly seven days a week to make ends meet. At the time, he'd just finished a long stretch of seventeen-hour days and had been beyond exhausted. Halfway through the first act he'd fallen deeply asleep and his date had been so insulted he'd never seen her again.

Walking the length of the stage now, with no symphony in sight, thank God, the hot sun beat down on him, heating the afternoon into a hell-like status. Materials were stacked against the wings, and he could already see they were short on some things, while others wouldn't work at all.

No doubt *Sizzling Nights* needed help.

He pulled out his measuring tape and eyed the center stage, from where the catwalk would jut out over the pit. The plans he'd studied last night played in his head as he checked measurements. He got up on an extension ladder to take a good look at the scaffolding across the top of the stage, checking what the height would be on the archway, and also what they would have to do in order to suspend lights and cameras from above.

Truthfully, he didn't see any fatal obstacles.

"Jake?"

He craned his neck and looked down. The height was dizzying. Or maybe that was the view of the woman standing in the pit looking up at him.

"You're already here," she said with obvious relief.

He tried to figure out what it was about her that grabbed him by the throat and held on. It might have been her short red skirt and sleeveless silky tank that hugged her small but lush body. Or the open-toed high-heeled sandals that showed off her bare, toned legs in a way that could stop traffic. Or how she looked right into his eyes, quietly direct, no evasion, no hidden meanings to anything.

She probably had no idea how refreshing that was, that she said her mind and didn't hold anything back, that there would be no mind games. What you saw was what you got with Mia, and for that alone, he'd have wanted her.

Or maybe it was just the sheer wattage of her relieved smile. Yeah, that was it, the way she looked at him, as if maybe she hadn't really expected him to do this, but here he was and he'd made her day while he was at it.

Her hero.

That worked for him. "I told you I would be."

"Yes, I know, but…" She lifted a narrow shoulder as if to say "stuff happens." Not too trusting, his Mia, but he understood that, too.

She didn't trust many. He knew this was because she'd been raised by her wild-child mother, who'd paraded men through their lives like candy, leaving Mia unimpressed at the caliber of the male species in general.

A damn shame for the male species.

"So what do you think?" she asked, clasping her hands together in a telltale sign of nerves that he was sure she wasn't even aware of.

He tucked his notepad into his back pocket, his pen behind his ear, and climbed down the ladder. She took the stairs from the pit and met him on the stage.

"What do I think?" he asked. "That red is most definitely your color."

She rolled her eyes. "What do you think of the *project?*"

"It's a great venue for what you've planned."

She nodded, her long bangs nearly in her eyes, the rest of her dark hair layered and artfully framing her face. "I know."

"I need to revise the material list, though, you don't have enough."

"Okay."

"It's going to be expensive to get it all here quickly," he warned.

"I understand."

"I'm going to keep trying to get more men to work, but that'll be expensive, too."

"Of course." She still had her smile on her face but he knew her, and could see the worry in her eyes. He'd seen the expression before, several times. Once when she'd gotten stuck in the tree in the middle of her yard during a thunder and lightning storm trying to rescue a damn cat. Another when their neighbor across the street, Mr. Porter, had fallen down his steps. He remembered how Mia had sat with him until the paramedics had arrived, telling stories, stroking the older man's hand, only allowing her fear to show when she'd seen Jake.

Whenever she looked at him like that, he wanted to beat his chest like a Neanderthal and save the day, as he'd done when she'd blown out her knee last year. For a few weeks he'd cooked her dinner. And when she'd slipped in the kitchen one night, he'd carried her to bed. Setting her down on her mattress, he'd looked into her eyes and had thought, *God, I want you.*

That's when she'd given him the four little words he hadn't been able to get out of his mind.

"I'm not into sex."

For the thousandth time he wondered, how could someone not like sex? Especially someone as naturally sensual and earthy and *real* as Mia, someone who understood enough about human sexual nature to make a living selling sexy lingerie. He had no idea, but he'd wanted to change her opinion on the matter then, and still wanted to.

"What else?" she asked, looking out at the empty theater.

"On the schedule it calls for us to be done the day before the show to allow for rehearsals. That's six days from now. Five if we don't start until tomorrow." He shook his head. "I can't promise you that last full day."

She nodded. "We'll adjust. Anything else?"

"Not at the moment."

"Okay." She sighed. "I guess I just really wanted to hear 'I can do it, Mia.'"

"I can do it, Mia," he said obediently, and made her laugh. He'd always loved her laugh, and though he'd rather she throw herself at him, he'd take it.

"You, Jake Holbrook," she said with a full smile, "have just made my day."

"Yeah? You make mine, too. Every time you smile at me like that."

Her smile faltered. "Jake."

They'd been through this before. Him trying to talk her into taking their relationship to the next level. Her resisting.

Oddly enough, along with her "not into sex" declaration, they'd never both really been available at the same time. When she'd first moved in, he'd wanted to go out with her, but he'd been seeing someone.

Then when he'd been free, she'd been the one to be occupied.

Not the case now. There was nothing standing in their way but her own inner struggle. Taking a chance, he stepped closer, then closer still when she didn't back away. Reaching out, he playfully tugged on a strand of her silky hair. It was the kind of touch she allowed, a touch that kept them on the "friends" level.

Being friends was nice, and that she trusted him that much meant a lot.

But he wanted more. He wanted her to understand she could trust him with anything, including a physical relationship. And that she *would* like that physical relationship, very much. "How about dinner tonight?" he asked, and when she cocked her head and studied him, he smiled. "Yes."

"Yes what?"

"You're standing there wondering if I have ulterior motives. Sexual ones. I do."

She gaped.

And he had to laugh. "But I'll control myself. Come on, Mia. We have dinner all the time, why the hesitation now?"

"It feels different," she admitted.

"Because I'm going to do some work for you?"

"Because you're looking at me differently today."

"I always look at you like this. You've just not been paying attention."

"I'm paying attention now," she whispered.

"Good. So a little food, maybe a glass of wine. A round of poker. Maybe I can make back some of the twenty bucks you won off me last week. What's it going to hurt?"

"I have work."

"We'll add work into the mix. Say yes."

She stared at him, both of them knowing she had a weakness for food, especially food she didn't have to put together herself. "Pizza?"

"We had pizza last week."

"I love pizza."

"You love anything you don't have to cook."

"Pepperoni," she said stubbornly. "And I'm in bed by ten. *Alone,*" she added quickly at the look on his face.

*Not for long,* he thought.

# CHAPTER THREE

THEY WENT OUT. Mia knew Jake would have cooked them homemade pizza but she decided having dinner at the pizza joint on the corner was the wisest move. She was not a dating virgin, not a virgin of any kind and hadn't been for a long time. She knew the ropes. *Don't be home alone with a man who has sex on the brain.* And for whatever reason, Jake *so* had sex on his brain tonight.

Her mother had always had a revolving door approach to men. With her dad gone, no explanation, just gone, and no siblings, Mia had had only her mother's example to grow up on.

Men, she'd learned, were slaves to their penises.

Knowing this, Mia herself had chosen the men in her life carefully, picking the opposite of what had drawn her mother. Mia dated highly educated, quiet, calm men. *Betas,* all of them. The kind of man who didn't press for too much, who eventually faded away without complaint or a backward glance.

Jake wasn't that kind of man. She'd known it from the beginning. If he had a feeling, he shared it. Every emotion and thought flickered across his face and out of his mouth. Subterfuge was beyond him, and so was holding back. He wasn't necessarily quiet. And he sure as hell wasn't beta.

But even if he had been, he'd had a girlfriend when she'd first moved in. And then when he hadn't, she'd been dating someone. And then he'd spent a summer in the middle of the country somewhere working for one of those charity organizations that build houses for the needy, and she'd spent last summer in Europe working in fashion cataloging gaining more knowledge for VLL, and…

And it'd never been the right time.

Mostly because she'd never made it the right time, she could admit now.

At the pizza place he sat on her side of the booth, his big body taking up more than his fair share of space, apparently not bothered at all by the fact that he spilled into hers. Legs spread beneath the table, a powerful, warm thigh brushing hers, as well as a bicep. She couldn't have avoided contact if she'd tried.

And in fact, she didn't want to avoid it at all. It was an easy excuse to get close to him without leading him on in any way, allowing herself to enjoy the hard strength of him, his overtly guy scent, everything. In fact, he smelled so good, she kept trying to give her nose better access. Once, he leaned across the table to reach for a napkin and she leaned in, nearly pressing her nose against his back to inhale deeply.

Only he sat back suddenly, nearly squishing her head between his spine and the booth, all because she wanted to press her face to his body.

And the look on his face told her he knew it. *Ooops.*

"You've been working night and day," he said, leaning forward again to reach for the platter of pizza from the waitress, his great abs rippling beneath his white T-shirt as he offered Mia the first slice.

"Thanks," she murmured, thinking, *Jeez, cool it,*

you've seen him without a shirt. When he'd washed his car, when he'd watered his front yard… Yes, she had reason to know he had a stomach of steel, so what. In fact, his entire body was amazing, with wide shoulders, a sinfully sculptured chest and powerful legs. But his abs, with those ropy muscles defining a six-pack that led straight to his groin, were to simply die for. His last girl-friend had once admitted to Mia that she'd only dated him to get to touch his belly.

Mia understood the sentiment, and had been tempted, especially knowing that Jake was the whole package, not just a pretty body, but she'd always come to her senses. Dating Jake would be a huge mistake. He meant too much to her as a friend to lose him when their de-sires waned.

And they would wane; they always did.

Still, knowing he'd happily strip them both down to skin and then proceed to touch her with his mouth and fingers, all while driving into her with that body, made her a little breathless, but she shrugged it off. "Maybe I've been a little consumed by work," she admitted. "But once the fashion show's over, I can take a break."

"You won't." He loaded two pieces of pizza onto his plate and dug in. "You're a workaholic and you know it. The last guy you were seeing, what was his name, Chad? Brad? Tad?"

She rolled her eyes. "Ted."

"Yeah, Ted. You had to schedule his phone calls in your Palm Pilot."

"So? The last woman *you* were seeing left you dirty messages in her lipstick on your windshield."

He grinned. "So?"

At the time it'd seemed so tacky, so visible. Annoyingly…arousing. What was it like? she wondered, to let go so much that you could do or say or think anything, and have it accepted? No self-editor, no holding back, no overthinking. Just doing. God, the freedom of that.

"I'll have you know I really am going to take a vacation when this is over."

"Where?"

"A beach somewhere, I think."

"Tahiti? The Bahamas? Maui?"

"I was thinking Malibu," she admitted, and bore his laughter. "It's not a crime to like my work, you know."

"You need to like *life*."

"I do!"

"Uh-huh." He took another bite, chewed while looking at her, a knowing smile touching his face. "Let's see about that. What do you do besides work, besides worrying about your work?"

"I—" she shot him a dry look "—find other stuff to worry about."

"That's because you're a little uptight, which given what you do for a living, is amusing all in itself. I can teach you how to relax, you know."

She eyed him, all big and cocky. "Maybe I don't think I need to relax."

"Oh, baby, do you ever. But don't worry, all is not lost." He tipped his bottle of beer to hers in a toast. "Here's what we do. Together, we start a new thing."

"We already do stuff. Dinner. Games—"

"I'm talking beyond dinner. Beyond a board game. A night where we go do something, anything, the only rules being it can't involve work in any way, and you have to enjoy yourself."

Oh boy. Trouble with a capital *T,* because she already knew how much she enjoyed him, and how much harder it would be to resist if he really turned up the charm meter. "I don't know—"

He arched a brow. "Chicken?"

*Yes.* "Of course not."

"Cuz it looks to me like maybe you are."

"I'm not," she said through her teeth. *Did he see right through her?* "I just want to make sure this is still on the level of friends."

"Because heaven forbid it go deeper, right?"

"I don't like deeper." At that fib, she had to lose eye contact, and toyed with the cheese on her crust, pulling it until it popped free, then sucking it off her finger.

At that, a sound escaped him, a low muttered groan, a curse, and she looked up.

Jake's eyes, locked on her mouth, had gone opaque with heat. "I'm your friend, Mia. Always. I care about you and I think you know it." His voice was silky soft. "But keep sucking on that finger and saying the word *deeper,* and I'm going to have trouble remembering that friendship is all you want."

"What about you?" she whispered. "And what you want?"

"I can wait. Until we both want it."

She couldn't tear her gaze off his as she thought about her serious resistance to him. It was her biggest fear, that they'd have to stop being friends. "What if I never want it?"

"Don't jinx me. More pizza?"

"Um, yes, thanks." She blinked at how quickly he could turn her around and mix her up. He ordered her another beer, too, and before she knew it she'd consumed four slices of pizza and her skirt was too snug, and yet somehow she let him talk her into sharing brownies for dessert while they watched an exhibition Lakers game on the big screen.

"So." Jake's strong white teeth flashed when he shot her a grin an hour later. "Not so bad, right?"

"The pizza was excellent."

"Uh-huh. What about the rest?"

"Beer's not bad." She took a sip of hers to hide her smile when he laughed knowingly, low and husky.

Damn, he was cute. She knew she was crazy to call him cute. It was like thinking a lion was cute, or a leopard, or any wild cat, really, all coiled to pounce on his prey.

So *not* cute.

"The pizza *was* excellent," he agreed. "And the beer. And so is the company."

She looked into his eyes, prepared to roll hers at his obvious line, but his eyes were nothing but genuine. Reaching out, he wrapped his finger in a lock of her hair, tugging very lightly, reeling her in enough to bring her face extremely close to his. His eyes glimmered. "Let's do it again when you can manage," he said softly. "Another evening of no work and fun."

"What exactly did you have in mind?"

"I'll think of something. Or you can. Date?"

She stared at him for a long moment, at the strand of hair eternally falling over his forehead and into his eyes, at the mischievous sparkle in his eyes, at the day's rough growth on his jaw. Damn, he had a quality of irresistibility. "I don't know—"

"Just say 'yes, Jake.'"

"It's not that simple."

Very quietly he made the sound of a chicken, and she

had to laugh. "Fine," she said, caving. "But it's your fault then if…"

"If what? What's the worst thing that could happen? I fall for you? *Done.* You fall for me? I can only hope."

Before she could say a word to that—and good God, what could she say!—he stood and pulled her up, too.

She stared up at him, into his eyes, at his mouth. She realized he was looking at her mouth, too, and something deep inside tingled. Surely he wasn't thinking about kissing her… No.

But *she* was thinking about it, all the way home.

And then proving her wrong at her front door, he brushed his lips to hers in a short, quick kiss that was over so fast she blinked in confusion—even as she wanted more.

He'd not only thought about it, he'd done it!

"Night," he said with an expression that said he knew she wanted another kiss, an expression that said "gotcha, you're already mine."

And standing there, lips tingling, she knew it, too.

# CHAPTER FOUR

MIA STAYED UP way too late sitting at her kitchen table, talking on the phone to her partners at VLL, Samantha and Jamie, each of them frantically working on the million little details that putting on a global satellite show entailed, each of them wondering why they were doing this.

After that she spread out some style sheets for the next catalog and stared at them until her eyes blurred. Finally, still at the table, she fell asleep.

Only to jerk awake at the sound of her cell phone going off. She sat straight up, papers stuck to her face as she groped for the phone.

"Mia," Jane said. "I have a bunch of stuff to go over with you."

Bleary-eyed, Mia looked at her watch. Six. *In the morning?* "Are you in the office already?"

"Yes." Jane sounded suspicious. "You didn't oversleep, did you?"

She rubbed her face. "Of course not."

"You're on your way? Oh, God, don't tell me you haven't left yet. Not with only six days until showtime. If *I'm* eating, breathing, sleeping this thing, then so are you."

"Relax. I'm on my way." Sort of. She winced at the dawn light streaming through her kitchen window, and clicking off the cell, staggered toward the bathroom and her shower, stripping as she went.

She loved her job, loved immersing herself in it, but clearly this 24/7 stuff was beginning to get to her. Soon as the show was over, she really would take a weekend at the beach, she promised herself. All she needed was a towel, some sunscreen and the pounding surf for music.

No cell, no pager. No Palm Pilot.

Twenty minutes later she was in her car. Jake's truck was already gone and she only hoped that meant good things for the stage and catwalk. On Highway 5 South, she headed toward downtown, and VLL's offices. She wanted, badly, to detour to the Greek Theater and take a peek, but she also wanted to give Jake some time to get started without her breathing down his neck.

Once in her office, things got crazy. Six days and counting until the show, and everything was a blur. Samantha was handling the designers, and Jamie the money end—though he was also a designer—and both would be stopping by the theater later, as well, to see how the stage was coming along.

Mia just hoped it *was* coming along.

She spent hours on their next mail-order catalog, which was due into production, and then more hours on the fabrics and lighting order for the show, and then a frantic few minutes trying to locate some missing shipments. Before she could blink, it was late afternoon. Back in her car, she cranked the air-conditioning in defense against the one-hundred-degree temp, and headed toward Griffin Park and the Greek Theater. On the way there her cell phone rang nonstop, and her pager went off so many times she could have used it as a vibrator.

Not that she had the time for orgasms. Not these

days. Maybe on her beach weekend. What it meant that she had to schedule her orgasms, she didn't know. She could just imagine what Jake would say about that.

And the sexy look on his face as he said it.

In the parking lot of the theater, she got out of her nice, cool Honda and stepped into the muggy L.A. summer heat that felt like a live, breathing presence. Tossing back the hair she suddenly wished she'd put up, she entered the theater and came up the center aisle the way their guests would in six days.

Yesterday she'd seen only an empty stage. A beautiful stage, but empty.

Today, projecting over the orchestra pit and directly down the center, was the frame for what would be the structure of the ancient wonder, a sort of hanging garden with an archway for the models to come through. Far above it, the roofing scaffolding had been extended, so that at dusk they'd flip on the lighting to give the proper mood to the setting. That combined with the lush plants and Greek statues being delivered in three days, and all the miles and miles of black velvet for a backdrop…her heart started pounding. *Yes.* She came to a stop about ten feet from where the catwalk would be built, wanting to take it all in. She could just see it now—the stars above, the hot night air, the *Sizzling Nights*.

"What do you think?"

She nearly jumped out of her skin at the soft, deep voice in her ear. Jake, of course. Only Jake's voice could hatch butterflies in her tummy and make her skin tingle without so much as a single touch. She shook her head and clasped her hands tight to prevent herself from whipping around and throwing herself at him in gratitude.

"Mia?" His warm breath fanned at her temple, and though he still didn't touch her, she felt surrounded by him, by the heat of him, the strength of him, not at all a suffocating feeling but the very opposite.

Then she felt his hand on her arm, and he turned her to face him. "Well?"

"My God, Jake. It's…amazing."

He looked at her for a long moment, then let out a breath. "Yeah. It's coming along."

"More than. It's perfect." *You're perfect.* "Jake, I can't believe it, but this is really going to happen."

"I told you it would."

"Yes, but…"

Another smile. "Have some faith, woman."

The sun had kissed him all day long, leaving him deeply tanned. He wore a blue polo shirt with a rip on one sleeve and a streak of dirt across a pec, jeans that had faded at the stress spots—of which there were an impressive amount—and work boots he hadn't bothered to lace all the way up. His arms were bare and sinewy, his hands ropy with strength. His jaw had a day's growth and another streak of dirt. Fine laugh lines fanned out from the corners of his mouth and eyes, giving him a mischievous, disreputable, almost cocky air, and yet he was looking at her with those see-all eyes filled with a startling clarity and depth.

Not cocky. Just confident and easygoing enough not to care what anyone thought of him.

A shockingly arousing trait.

"Jake!" One of his men stood on the stage, gesturing him over.

"Go ahead," she told him, shading her eyes from the brutal sun beaming down on them, watching as he easily leaped up onto the back of a seat, effortlessly vaulting to the stage. Once there, he spoke to the man who'd called him over, and then turned and directed another crew member, while simultaneously speaking into his walkie-talkie to someone suspended high above the stage working on lighting supports.

Mesmerized by the goings-on, and sapped by the sun, she sank to a seat and took a few minutes to take it all in. Still, her eyes kept drifting back to the tall, energetic authority figure center stage.

Jake.

Kneeling now, by a pile of tools, he eased out a cord. Rising again, he uncoiled the cord, plugged it into what must have been an electrical source and then tossed the other end to the guy up on the ladder. Then Jake moved back to the pile of tools, lifting some sort of electrical saw, just hoisting the big thing into his arms, carrying it across the stage to yet another member of his crew. He spoke for a moment, then went back for a nail gun, which he took to a stack of lumber. There he began shifting the wood around before finally hunkering down and putting the nail gun to work.

His back was to her now, the material of his shirt stretched taut across his shoulders and back. His jeans were low-slung but unlike the obnoxious Todd, Jake did not expose any unnecessary body parts.

Not that she'd have minded.

"Stop it," she told herself firmly. The man was working, and working hard. Sheesh. Surreptitiously, she swiped at her hot, damp forehead. The heat was killing her. She could only imagine how hot the guys were, working in this weather all day long.

And indeed, Jake stretched out an arm, reaching for his water bottle. Tossing back his head, he took a long pull, then swiped his mouth with the back of his hand. She sensed his sigh when his thirst was quenched, but rather than setting the bottle down, he tipped it over his head. Water ran down his hair, his face and onto his chest and shoulders, soaking into his shirt. Tossing the now empty water bottle aside, he went back to work.

Mia let out a long breath, suddenly even hotter than she'd been a moment before. She fanned her face, then went utterly still when Jake craned his neck and unerringly found her gaze. Time seemed to stop, which was ridiculous in Mia's opinion. She'd stared at him hundreds of times. Thousands. So why today it felt…different, she had no idea.

Jake rose to his full height, and with his gaze still locked on hers, made his way to the edge of the stage, then expertly balanced across the wall of the orchestra pit and hopped down.

About ten feet in front of her.

She imagined him taking those last few steps, imagined him kissing her, a thought that brought her out of her trance and made her want to thunk her head against something hard to shake it off.

"Mia?"

"I've…got to run. Yeah. I've got to…" *What?* She had to what? Every single rational thought had vanished right out of her head.

Jake just looked at her from eyes that were male and very aware.

"Work," she managed to say. "I've got to get home and do some more…"

"Work." He let out a slow smile that upped her body

temperature even more. "Are you sure? Was there something you needed first?"

"Um…" She racked her brain for what she could possibly need besides his body over hers. "What are they doing?" She hitched her chin toward the two guys on ladders stage left, trying to be cool, trying to distract him.

"Setting framework for the hanging plants."

"And for the lighting? We're all worried about how that's going to work."

"Don't worry, I've solved all your problems," he promised, his eyes still on hers. "You were looking at me, Mia, like you wanted to gobble me up."

So much for playing it cool. "I was?"

"Oh, yeah." His eyes were full of a sexual hunger that would have buckled her knees if she'd been standing.

She firmly ignored that and the flutter in her belly. "Are you going to be ready for the prop delivery tomorrow?"

"We're starting at 5:00 a.m., so yes. We'll be ready."

"So early?"

He lifted a shoulder. "Nothing keeping me in bed."

The air seemed to hum around them as he held her gaze for a long beat. "You sure there wasn't anything else?" he asked softly. Edgily.

"No. Nothing."

With a nod, he turned away. Again he agilely climbed the framework back to his crew, his shirt clinging to his damp, hard shoulders, his well-worn Levi's cupping his extremely fine rear end—

She was staring at his rear end. At the realization, she jerked her gaze off that part of his anatomy, but it was too late—he'd looked back over his shoulder.

And caught her.

His eyes shuttered. She figured he was amused.

Then she looked again, and she realized that, no, that wasn't amusement in his gaze, but *arousal*.

It should have embarrassed her to the core, and as the blood rushed to her face, she acknowledged there was some of that.

And also more.

Her skin felt…tight, as if a size too small. Her heart pounded, echoing between her ears and at all the pulse points. And beneath her sheer blouse and opaque camisole her nipples tightened.

Inside her purse her cell phone began to vibrate again, and yet she still stared at Jake, locked in some weird twilight zone where the majority of her brain cells seemed to have vacated the premises. "I have to go," she murmured, and though he couldn't possibly have heard her, she turned and practically ran up the center aisle toward her car.

THAT NIGHT, she lay alone in her bed, wearing a fall sample of VLL's newest silky nightie. She was hot and clammy and aching and unfulfilled.

Maybe it was the nightie. In the catalog they'd described it as heaven on earth, irrevocably sensual and guaranteed to change the night.

She ripped it off over her head and, nude, lay back down.

Nope, not the nightie. She was still hot and clammy and aching and unfulfilled.

She knew what it was. Or who.

*Jake.*

It was hours before she finally drifted off to sleep.

## CHAPTER FIVE

THE NEXT MORNING Mia found a note on her car in Jake's broad scrawl.

Come see the progress tonight.

Yeah, she'd go see the progress. And Jake. Probably there was nothing that could have kept her away.

At the office, she got swamped the moment she arrived, and she didn't manage to get out of there until nearly seven. A part of her was glad that Jake would certainly be long gone from the theater.

But when she got there, one lone man stood onstage. Jake.

The night was unseasonably hot, even hotter than yesterday. He was in his customary polo shirt, jeans and unlaced boots, crouched low beneath the frame for the hanging garden, hammering away at something. The hammer rose and fell with easy precision. Bang, bang, bang.

Her heart picked up the beat. The long lines of sinew in his back worked rhythmically with the muscles in his arm as he lifted the hammer again and again, mesmerizing her. Then, as if he scented her, he raised his head, and across the thirty feet between them, looked right at her. "Hey." He tossed aside the hammer as he straightened.

"You've had a long day," she said, noting the frame of the catwalk jutting out from the stage.

"Yeah. I sent the guys home—it's just too hot." He swiped his arm over his forehead. "I was getting ready to leave, too." He spread his arms, gesturing to the set around him. "Everything to your liking?"

She tore her eyes off him. The frame for the hanging garden and archway had begun to resemble its final form. She could see the catwalk's width and length, and the proper scaffolding above it. Yes, everything was to her liking, thank you very much—and she stared at all he'd done, stunned. "It's going to be beautiful. I really owe you, Jake."

Something flared in his eyes and he stepped closer. "You keep saying that, and I just might try to collect."

Oh boy. As it had yesterday, and the day before, the air around them heated. Hell, it practically burst into spontaneous flame.

He stroked a damp strand of hair from her forehead. "You're warm."

"It's a million degrees out here."

"It's not just the air."

She caught his hand in hers because she'd just discovered she couldn't think when he was touching her. "Jake—"

"Let's go cool off."

"I know what you're thinking, and you're going to be disappointed."

"Really? I'm talking about going swimming. What are you talking about?"

She felt herself blush. "You know what I was talking about."

"Ah."

"I mean it—you'd just be disappointed."

"Right. Because you don't like sex."

Damn him, his mouth quirked when he said it. He was making fun of her.

And it didn't help that she'd lied to him. She liked sex just fine, *more* than fine.

What she *didn't* like was how none of her sexual relationships had ever worked out, not a single bleeping one of them. Maybe that was her own cynicism, maybe not, but fact was fact.

Once she slept with a guy, he waltzed right out of her life.

She cared about Jake, deeply. Watching him walk away would hurt, too much. So she'd let him think she didn't like sex. So what. It was an easier explanation than the truth, that she wouldn't screw their friendship up for a Jake-made orgasm, no matter how promising such an orgasm might be. "Look, it's no big deal. I just don't get what all the fuss is about."

Now he let out a full-fledged grin and stroked her temple with his finger again, tracing her hairline. "You have no idea what you're missing, do you?"

"Let me guess. You'd be willing to show me."

"Oh, absolutely."

Her engine revved. Yeah, he definitely could show her. She needed a cold shower just thinking about it. "Go home, Jake. The heat is going to your head."

"Is it getting to you, too, Mia?"

Was he kidding? Couldn't he see that her nipples got happy at just the sound of him, or that she broke out into a sweat at the mere mention of sex?

*Yes, hell yes, it was getting to her.* "No."

"Liar," he chided softly, and pulled her out of the sun,

around a set of curtains and into a small alcove where they were protected overhead by staging, but also from anyone happening to walk by.

They were still onstage, with hundreds of empty seats facing them, and yet not a soul could have seen them. It gave the air a shocking intimacy, and every sensual nerve ending hummed with anticipation.

Then he stepped close. Their toes brushed. His breath mingled with hers, and his eyes, good Lord, those eyes. "Jake, honestly." Her laugh sounded a little breathless even to her own ears and she hoped he didn't take it as an invitation. "If this is how you think I'm going to repay you—"

He was slowly shaking his head. "No 'repaying.' What I do for you, what you do for me, comes without a price. *Always,*" he said, and then backed her against the wall and leaned into her with that hard, perfect body. "This is something else, something separate. And it has to be done."

And then he kissed her.

## CHAPTER SIX

JAKE KISSED Mia because he had to get it done, had to in the same way that lungs needed air and French fries needed ketchup. There wasn't much conscious thought about it, other than his hands on her arms, hauling her up closer, and kissing those lips he'd been wanting beneath his ever since his first taste of her the other day.

Mia went utterly still for a beat, and then her hands were fisting in his shirt, whether for balance or because she had to touch him, he had no clue, but he liked it. Liked, too, the helpless little murmur she let out, and the way she clung to him like Saran Wrap.

When he pulled back, he was breathing hard and unsteady, and he was gratified to see her in the same condition. Staring at him, she licked her lips, as if to taste every last drop of him. "Oh, baby," he whispered, and lowered his head again, kissing one side of her mouth and then the other. He was working his way along her jaw when she grabbed him by the hair and brought his mouth back to hers.

And then *she* was kissing *him,* her mouth opening to his in a way that had him groaning. She tasted hot and yet somehow sweet at the same time, and he couldn't get enough. Slipping his fingers into her hair, he changed the angle of her head to better suit him and came at her again, pressing deeper, loving the feel of her hands holding him tight as if she couldn't stand the thought of him pulling back.

Fat chance.

He pressed her back against a wall, losing himself in the moment, as she slid her arms up his chest and wrapped them around his neck. His hands still held her head, his fingers tangled in her soft, silky hair, which fell over his forearms like teasing little fingers, smelling like some exotic scent he couldn't place.

When they tore apart to breathe, he inhaled her, burying his face in the crook of her neck. "God, you smell good. I could just eat you up." He took a little hot bite out of her, making her shiver, and then he licked the spot with his tongue.

"Jake—" she choked out, and her head fell back, hitting the wall. "Hold on."

He had one hand gripping the back of her head, the other low on her spine, which he slid down to palm her sweet ass. "I am." New goal, he thought. Get her in his bed, *yes,* but to make her want it, crave it, as much as he wanted and craved her. Just the thought of her sprawled on his mattress, sighing his name, made him hard.

Or maybe that was the feel of her pressed between him and the wall in a way that had her breasts, her belly, her thighs, everything, all mashed up against him.

In either case, time to back up and give her room to think. And to let it build more for her, to let her become even half as sexually frustrated as he was.

"I have to go," she whispered.

Bending, he put his mouth to her ear. "'Kay."

"Jake." She shivered again and clutched at him. "I *have* to go."

IN TRUTH, MIA DIDN'T actually know *where* she had to go, only that he'd whipped her world into frenzied motion. She felt as if she'd gotten on a roller coaster and couldn't get off.

"Not yet." He slid a thigh between hers, exhaling against her skin. "Mmm."

"Jake—"

He moved against her with that rock-solid body. He was aroused, which sent an all-powerful sort of hunger skittering through her veins. How could this feel so good? she wondered wildly, pressed against the hard wall and the harder wall of Jake's chest, hot as hell, skin sticking to skin, and yet…and yet she squirmed to get even closer.

"Yeah." Lowering his head, he kissed her again—a long, hot, wet, deep kiss that had her lost in him, completely lost.

When he pulled back this time, he cupped her face and stroked his thumb over her lower lip. "Did you dislike anything about that?" he asked.

She stared down at the hands she'd fisted in his shirt and visibly forced herself to loosen her grip as she slowly shook her head. "Don't tease me."

"I'm not teasing, I want to know."

"You know I didn't dislike it. In fact, you know exactly how much I liked it."

He shot her a bone-melting smile. "You'd like the rest, too, Mia. I promise you."

She opened her mouth but he put a finger to it and slowly shook his head. "You've got to go," he reminded her. And at that, he simply walked away, back to the stage. There he picked up some sort of electric tool as he crouched down and began working, whistling.

*Whistling,* while she stood there weaving from her overheated internal system, a desperate overload, a *malfunction.* Befuddled, aroused and pissed off all at the same time, she was torn between calling him back over here to finish what he'd started, and running like hell. Instead, she feigned calmness and dignity and walked slowly, purposely away.

Silently cursing him all the way home.

THE NEXT DAY WAS HOTTER, if that was even possible. Jake started his crew at dawn and after a long hot day at work, they were indeed right on schedule. Mia might well have that last day for rehearsals as she wanted.

After his crew left late afternoon, Jake ran through the plans one more time, checking the materials list to what they physically had left, making sure they had everything they needed.

Alone with his work and thoughts, he yawned. He'd stayed up late last night at his office, catching up on his billings and estimating for the other jobs he'd delayed in order to do this one.

He wouldn't be working tonight, though. Tonight he had other ideas.

When he left the theater, he made a quick stop. By the time he got home with the makings for steak and potatoes, Mia was home, too. A rarity for his workaholic neighbor. Her bedroom lights were on, and as he barbecued, he pictured her up there, getting ready for bed while still obsessing about work, as she always did. She'd be taking her nightly bubble bath with the wild sexy scents that helped her relax. She'd be waxing or shaving or whatever it was women did to feel feminine. She'd probably paint her toenails the pale peach color that seemed to be her favorite. Any of her hundred little rituals he'd come privy to over the past few years, all the things that made her so uniquely Mia.

He took the food off the barbecue, tossed foil over the platter and crossed the grass to Mia's. He knocked on her door, and when she opened it to him, wearing a white T-backed tank top and snug low-slung black yoga pants, her hair falling free and wild about her shoulders, he actually lost his train of thought.

"Jake?"

"Hungry?" he asked.

She cocked her head, appearing to be trying to figure out if he had some deep, hidden reason for standing on her doorstep. *Like maybe collecting the favor she owed him.* "No repaying of any favors tonight," he told her. "Just food. And a game if you want. We never did crack open your new movie edition of Trivial Pursuit."

She bit her lip in indecision, and if he hadn't wanted to bite that lip himself so very badly, he might have smiled in sympathy. She probably didn't think that spending time near him was a good idea, not with the heat they'd been generating lately.

Smart woman.

But though he was incredibly interested in stoking that heat, turning it into fire, he had a plan and it didn't involve rushing her. "Just food and a game, some talk, whatever."

"Like old times."

"Like old times," he promised, and gently nudged past her, leading her into her kitchen.

She went to the refrigerator. "Beer?" she asked, searching. "Or…questionable milk?"

"Beer."

Crouching down to the bottom shelf, she gave him

an enticing view, a smooth stretch of tight, sleek back muscles where her tank rose up and her yoga pants slid down, and a flash of something silky and deep purple, making him nearly groan out loud.

A thong.

She grabbed two bottles and rose, then caught the pained look on his face. "What's the matter?"

*You're hotter than the mercury in the thermostat outside.* "Absolutely nothing."

She came close and handed him his beer, and he made sure that their fingers entangled. At the contact, she stared down at their hands but didn't mention the palpable electricity between them.

He decided not to push his luck by mentioning it, either. Hell, it was enough that finally he wasn't the only one feeling it.

They sat side by side at her kitchen table and ate, with Mia moaning in pleasure over the food. They talked easily as they always did—about his weekly basketball game, her new tires, his brother, who'd just gotten back from a tour in Iraq. And then their neighbor, who'd just gotten engaged.

"Along that same vein," she said, and apparently finally having satisfied her belly, set down her fork. "It's the strangest thing really, but both my partners have recently fallen in love."

"You think that's strange?" Leaning in, he stabbed the last bite of steak off her plate. "People falling in love?"

"I think love's harder to find than everyone thinks it is." Fair being fair, she took his last sip of beer.

He watched her swallow, then lick her bottom lip. "Maybe it's just harder for you to believe in it than most people."

She played with the label on the bottle. "The other night, when you asked me what I was afraid of, you wondered if I was afraid of you falling for me."

He studied her bent head and knew she was thinking, wondering, how could anyone really fall for her, and he wanted to hurt her mother for raising her with that doubt. "Yeah, well, you're not so hard to fall for, Mia."

She lifted her gaze and leveled him with her wide, dark eyes. "And by falling," she whispered. "You mean…"

"Caring deeply, for starters."

"We've never even dated."

"Mia, I've 'dated' a lot of women. I've been in plenty of relationships, in which I've spent less time than I have with you. I know what's out there and I know what's not out there." He ran a finger over hers. "And I know what I want."

*Who I want.*

"Me?" she asked shakily.

"Is that so out of the realm of believability?"

"I grew up with a woman who fell in and out of love with the same ease as she washed her hair. I don't have a lot of faith in what you're talking about."

"You're not your mother. You don't bring men into your life on a nightly basis just for the company. It means something to you. Don't let what she did taint it for you."

"I don't. I'm not a man hater just because the men she brought home nightly were jerks. I'm not disillusioned. A little cynical maybe, but I know what's out there, and that sometimes it can be good."

"No, it can be great," he said very quietly, and stroked his thumb over her palm. "You just have to believe."

She went still, her dark, penetrating eyes searching

his for a long moment before she pulled free. "I'm not saying I don't believe in love. I'm just saying it can be easily mistaken for something else. Like lust."

"Nothing wrong with a little lust."

She laughed and shook her head. "Oh, Jake. What are we doing? What have we been doing all week?"

"Maybe some of that lusting," he admitted, and smiled when she laughed again, as he'd intended. "Do you like it?"

"That's not the point." She squirmed. "I think you should stop."

"Stop what?"

"Making me lust."

"*Making* you?" He laughed, then pulled her close. "Let's see about that," he murmured, and kissed her. She kissed him back for a heart-stopping beat but then shoved free with a rough growl and stood up, pointing at him.

"There," was all she said.

He lifted his hands. "I did not just make you stick your tongue down my throat."

She stared at him, then turned away. "Damn it, I hate it when you're right." She whipped back to face him, pointing at him again, stabbing him in the chest with her finger. "Seriously. This has to stop."

He grabbed her finger. "Be specific."

"Specific? You want specific? Okay, stop leaving me notes that make me want to see you. Stop smiling at me with all that *heat* in your eyes. See? That smile right there! Stop that!"

He tried to wipe it off his face. "Okay, no smiles."

"And definitely stop smelling so damn good."

"I smell good?"

"Oh my God, yes." She shook it off. "Don't distract me. And the kissing—" She glared at him. "That you *must* stop."

"What about the food?"

She glanced at the table, and her empty plate, and he knew he had her. "The food can keep coming," she said, and ignored his soft laugh.

## CHAPTER SEVEN

THE NEXT DAY at lunch break, Jake sat on the stage of the theater, legs swinging as he idly pulled splinters from his palm. His men had all gone to a local café, needing to get out of the sun. Jake had passed, wanting to get some paperwork done. As he picked out his last splinter, he heard the click-click-clicking of a set of heels alerting him to Mia's presence.

Actually, he didn't need the heels, he'd sensed her coming. Hell, he could almost smell her, like a mate. Lifting his head, he watched her come down the center aisle toward him, eyes flashing, mouth grim, looking quite hot and pissed off by it.

Oh, yeah, he thought with equal grimness. Maybe this had started out about getting her into bed, but now... *You are it for me.*

"You left me another note," she said when she got close enough, and in case he didn't remember what he'd written, she waved the paper.

He just smiled. "Yep."

"I thought we decided you wouldn't do that anymore."

"No, you decided."

"Damn it." She lifted her hands to her hair, plunging her fingers into the loose mess, turning in a slow, frustrated circle. Then she faced him again. "I know I said I owe you."

He just arched a brow.

"And it's killing me, okay? Call in your damn favor, already! Do it!"

She was like an M-80 with a lit fuse, ready to blow. With a smile, he jumped down the catwalk and straightened, right in front of her now. "I'm not calling in the favor right now."

"Jake—"

He put his hand to her mouth. "I needed to see you, so I left a note. I wanted to ask about the Greek statues that were delivered today for the show. You're going to need some sort of lift to move them around. Are you going to rent one?"

She blew out a breath. "Oh. Yeah."

He grinned. "But if you'd really rather I call in the favor right now—"

"No!"

"Darn." He took her hand. "Come on, I'll show you the statues. They're going to be great."

The statues were backstage, out of their packaging, waiting to be placed. Four of them. All men, all life-size, all nude.

The first stood like a warrior, legs spread, hands on his hips, chest chiseled, shoulders broad, every other part of his anatomy just as impressive.

Mia stared at it. "Oh my," she whispered.

He pointed to the others. The second and third statues stood rock solid, too, hands folded behind their backs, faces impassive, as if guarding something, their muscles and chiseled features somehow scary and yet haunting.

The fourth statue had one hand out as if reaching for someone, a slight knowing smile on his face. *A man about to get lucky,* Jake thought. "Someone said the models are going to—"

"Brush by them. Interact, maybe flirt." Mia dropped her gaze from the fourth statue's chest to his penis. "Oh, boy. I don't think—"

"Show me."

She looked at him in surprise. "Show you?"

"Pretend you're one of the models."

"Oh, no. I couldn't…" But she walked up to the fourth statue. "Hmm. I guess…" She laid her hands on the statue's chest, then leaned in with a mock sultry expression as if she was going to kiss it. Then suddenly she dropped her head to its chest, letting out a snort which sounded suspiciously like a laugh. "It's a good thing I'm so short and rounded, I could never be a model and pull off that 'don't mess with me' catwalk look as they strut their stuff."

She wore another sleeveless silky tank today, the color of the azure sky, and a white linen skirt that ended well above the knees. She turned around, leaning back against the statue, a grin splitting her face. Her hair was loose, her cheeks flushed as she smiled at him without self-conscious thought or reason, just because she was feeling silly.

He felt the pull of her deep in his belly. And lower. He shifted closer, and her grin faltered. Closer still, and she straightened, reaching out a hand to hold him off. "Wait a minute. I know that look."

Another step, and their toes touched. "Do you?"

"It's your 'you're going to kiss me' look."

"Ding, ding, we have a winner." Jake set his hands on either side of her face, right against the statue's chest, and leaned in and did just that.

At the contact, she moaned deep in her throat. Her hands came up between them.

Half-braced for her to shove at him, he nearly melted when instead she wound her arms around his neck and held on. The scent of her surrounded him, incited, and he sank his fingers into her hair, clamping her head between his hands as he deepened the kiss. When her tongue slid to his first, it ripped a groan from his chest. Raising his head he stared down at her, at her heavy-lidded eyes, her wet mouth, at the pulse tattooing an erratic beat at the base of her throat. "God, Mia."

"I know." They went at each other again. Jake slid his hands down her body and then back up, splaying them wide over her ribs, his fingers just brushing the undersides of her breasts. "You have such a beautiful body, Mia. Let me touch."

She just directed his mouth back to hers and kept kissing him.

"Can I?" he asked against her mouth.

She pulled back, breathing unsteadily. "You're asking?"

"I'm asking."

"Can't you just…do it?"

"I want to hear you say it."

She chewed on her lower lip. Leaning in he sucked it into his mouth himself, then kissed her again, long and deep, his hands itching to palm her breasts. "Mia?"

"Yes," she whispered.

"Yes, what?"

"Yes, I want you to touch!"

He was smiling as he filled his hands with her breasts over the silk. "Okay?"

She tightened her grip on his neck. "Are you going to talk all the way through this?"

"Maybe." He pushed up her tank. Her bra was glossy white and thin, easily tugged aside, and then finally he was touching bare, warm, damp flesh that made him groan. He rasped his thumbs over her nipples, then gently tugged on the hardened peaks.

She nearly strangled him with her hold around his neck, letting out low, desperate mewling noises as he leaned in and kissed her again, sliding his hands down her body until his fingers played at the hem of her skirt brushing her thighs.

She shivered.

"More?" he asked softly, curling his fingers around the fabric, lifting her skirt as he lowered his head and licked at a nipple.

"Um…"

"Tell me," he murmured against her breast, watching the nipple pucker even harder.

"You are. You are going to keep talking." She squeezed her eyes tightly shut when he merely chuckled low in her ear. "Fine. More, damn it."

He tugged the linen up her hips, exposing pale peach satin panties that made him groan, then slid his fingers down the backs of her thighs, lifting her so suddenly that she squeaked in surprise. "Wrap your legs around me— Yeah, like that." Now she was sandwiched between the statue and himself and Jake gritted his teeth at the feel of her warm, damp sex cradling his. He rocked against her, each thrust of his hips building on the unrelenting heat, threatening to burn them both alive. He had both hands in her panties, cupping a bare cheek in each palm, his erection nestled tight between her legs as their hips moved. Dark, needy sounds ripped from Mia's throat, driving him right to the edge. He hovered there, so close to coming his vision began to blur.

Not here.

That was his only rational thought, but as he blinked and dragged air into his taxed lungs, as he looked down into her dazed, flushed face and felt the tenderness overwhelm him, he knew.

He'd taken this as far as he had to make her want him as badly as he wanted her, and he had done that. No doubt, he had done that. He had only to look into her slumberous eyes, down at her beautiful bared breasts, at the rapid, shallow way her belly rose and fell. And the way she gripped him tight, cradling him with her thighs... Yeah, he'd proven that she wanted him. She'd ache all night.

Only somewhere along the way it had become more. Deeper. Somewhere along the way he'd really fallen for her, harder and faster than he'd ever fallen before.

In fact, he could hear bells ringing in his head. Bells? It took him a moment to realize it was her cell phone, and he let out a low laugh. "That's you."

Brought out of the spell, she blinked and stared at him as he slowly let her legs slide down his body. When her toes touched the ground, she shoved her skirt down and reached for her purse, which had fallen at her feet. As she wrapped her fingers around the cell, her pager started to go off, as well, and then the alarm on her Palm Pilot.

"Don't look now but your life is vibrating."

She let out a helpless laugh as she crouched at his feet, pressing her forehead to her phone. "I set my Palm Pilot to go off to remind myself to download some stuff at home, and anyway, it's not just my hardware that's vibrating." She looked up at him. "You've got my entire body doing the same."

"Want to be president of the club?"

"Look, I don't like this, okay?" She shut her eyes. "I really don't."

"Could have fooled me."

"A moment of insanity," she insisted, and rose to her feet. "We're *friends*," she said with a tinge of desperation. "Right? Just friends. God, Jake, that's important. Really, really important."

She was utterly serious. She had it in her head somehow that they couldn't be both friends and lovers. "And you're important to me, Mia."

She stared at him for a long moment, then looked away. "I need a minute."

He needed more than that, but he nodded. "Take as long as you need. I'll be working."

And as he walked away he felt her watching him, probably still wearing that I've-just-been-hit-by-a-Mack-truck expression, the one that made him want to tumble her down and start all over again with the kisses, the touches.

But damned if that game hadn't just become something else entirely.

# CHAPTER EIGHT

MIA SPENT THE AFTERNOON on the stage with Jane, Samantha, Jamie and a handful of others from the VLL offices, going through all their props and set decorations. The area was still under construction, and they were working around Jake and his crew.

Not exactly a hardship.

When she'd first begun, Jake had been high on a ladder doing something with the ancient-wonder archway frame. He'd been thoroughly engrossed in his work and yet suddenly he'd gone still and lifted his head. Even with his gaze covered in mirrored sunglasses, she'd known he'd found her in one glance because her nipples went hard.

He pulled his sunglasses from his eyes and let them hang from their Croakies around his neck, and just looked at her.

At Mia's side, the ever unshakable, unflappable Jane blinked. "Wow."

Yeah. *Wow*. Electricity seemed to zing from Jake's eyes to Mia's body, zapping her with a strong awareness that made her skin itchy and her stomach quiver.

Damn it. Damn him. She'd never before felt electrocuted every time she so much as looked at him. This was new, very new. Squirming in her sandals, she tossed him a little wave that hopefully said "see how unaffected I am," and set out to promptly forget him as she went about her work. She'd ordered miles of midnight velvet that they'd drape around and behind the Greek statues to make them stand out and to give a beautiful backdrop for the models and what they'd be wearing. Sitting in one corner of the stage, she began opening boxes of the material, checking the invoices to her materials list.

But though the material was gorgeous, and her excitement extremely real, she found her mind wandering. All around her came the hammering, sawing, buzzing sounds of the electrical tools of the men, and the chatter of their voices as they communicated to each other in typical male fashion.

"Damn it, I said here!"

"Plug!"

"I'm going to kick your ass, Tom, if you do that again."

"Your momma."

*"Plug!"*

Mia finally looked up. They were all involved in various tasks, working hard in the bone-melting heat. There was a guy at the very top of the scaffolding, holding what looked like a nail gun. He saw her looking up and gestured to his cord, which ran down the ladder and toward the extension cords crisscrossing the stage. The prongs had slipped out and he wasn't getting any juice. She sank to her knees to fix it for him, got a wink for her efforts, then brushed the dirt from her hands.

A shadow fell over her. Out of the corner of her eyes she saw scuffed, unlaced work boots. Faded jeans with a rip over one knee and the other thigh.

And a proffered hand. "Hi," Jake said.

"Hi yourself." She stared at his big, work-callused hand. It was going to be tricky to get back up in the snug skirt she'd worn today, a fact he probably already knew. There was really no way to let him pull her upright without flashing him.

"Take my hand."

All she could see of him was his outline, haloed by the sun's beams like an angel. Ha! As if anything about the man was angelic.

Shielding the sun from her eyes, she looked up at his face as she let him help her up. If there'd been any doubt about whether he'd take the peek, it vanished as his eyes dipped, then flamed.

Instead of letting go of her hand, he tugged her closer and put his mouth to her ear. "I meant to tell you earlier, pale peach satin is my new favorite color."

The low timbre of his voice combined with the way he let his lips brush against her earlobe made her shiver. "Jake—"

"What are you doing tonight?

"Working late."

"So am I. After."

"We'll be tired," she said.

"Not that tired."

She eyed him suspiciously. "What did you have in mind?"

He grinned, the one that lately melted all her brain cells. "No," she said, and he outright laughed.

"I was thinking food," he said.

"Oh." Mollified, she looked at him. "Well if there's food involved."

"Definitely," he said with a straight face, but she knew he was still amused by her.

"Fine. Dinner. Maybe cards or something. Now go away and let me work, you're distracting me."

"I distract you?" He looked disgustingly pleased.

She had to laugh. "Only you would take that as a compliment."

"From you, it's the highest compliment. It means you're thinking about me. That I'm getting somewhere."

"I think about you," she said. "Too damn much. And as for you getting somewhere, where exactly is it you want to get to?"

His smile faded at the serious tone of her voice. Looking over his shoulder at all the people milling around, he nudged her behind the stage and into the alcove from earlier, where they were once again surrounded by the statues. Only feet away were a handful of crews and her own staff, and yet standing behind the curtains, surrounded by the warriors and enclosed in a little world of their own, they might have been all alone.

The memories of what they'd done in this very spot, what they might have gone on to do if her phone hadn't rung, had her cheeks flaming and other parts entirely flaming, too. God, what he'd made her feel. She hadn't imagined, hadn't ever thought… Probably he'd have to only touch her and she'd go *poof,* right up in flames.

"Where do I want to get to?" Jake repeated thoughtfully, sliding his hands down her arms to her hands, which he covered with his. "Anywhere, as long as it's with you."

Hot, and on edge, she stared up at him. "I know what you're waiting for. Me to get frustrated enough to jump you."

"Am I?"

She wouldn't, not when it'd forever change things

between them, and eventually, inevitably, screw things up. Nope. She was stronger than a few raging hormones, no matter that he kissed like heaven on earth and had a touch that could melt the Arctic. "You're waiting for something that's not going to happen, Jake."

He brought their joined hands to his mouth. He kissed her knuckles, then put their hands to his chest. Beneath his thin shirt she could feel the heat of him, the steady pumping of his heart. Why wasn't he kissing her stupid as she secretly wished he'd do? Making her moan with his talented, greedy hands? Making her admit she wanted him?

See, this was her problem with men. She couldn't ever figure them out—they were too unpredictable.

Her entire career was on the line, and *this* was all she could think about. Being with this man, understanding the game and playing it to her advantage so she didn't lose.

So she didn't get hurt, or end up alone. "I've got to go."

"I know." With his hands still holding hers, his long lean body still crowding close, he brushed his mouth along her jaw. "Bye."

She didn't move, just stood there absorbing the feel of him, wanting more, so much more.

"Bye, Mia."

"Bye." But instead of moving, she lined up their mouths.

He let out an almost animalistic sound of arousal, then kissed her, a decidedly *not* short, *not* sweet kiss, and when he pulled back, they were both breathing hard.

Then, with a rather shaky smile, he walked away.

Once again leaving her standing there, pulse pounding, heart going off like a sledgehammer, face flushed, body aching.

"Damn it," she muttered, and when Jake just shot her a grin over his shoulder, she growled and turned away.

He was doing this on purpose, she reminded herself. Making her absolutely crazy on purpose.

She had a sneaking suspicion that the emotion racing through her wasn't just lust, but elation. *Joy.*

Maybe even more.

BY THE END OF THE DAY, Jake and his crew were close to finished. He figured they could be done tomorrow, which was actually a day ahead of schedule. Mia could have her full day before the show for rehearsals.

Still he stayed behind after his crew left, thinking he'd just work a little longer, get them that much more ahead.

He wasn't alone.

There were a handful of others, with Mia leading them across the stage, giving directions as she pointed to the length of the lush plants that had been delivered. Not seeing him off to the side, they all stopped at the base of the catwalk.

The only person in the group that Jake recognized was Jane, who said something softly to Mia. Mia shook her head adamantly. "Not like that."

"Come on, Miss Thing." Jane laughed. "Show us what you mean. Strut your stuff."

"Oh, all right. But take notes, girls, because I'm only doing this once." Shoving her clipboard and phone at Jane, Mia walked to the back of the stage, fiddled with the staging controls, and a curtain rose, exposing the statues that were still backstage waiting to be craned into place. She turned back to face her group. On her face was the "model" expression. Vague. Sensual. She

let out a slow half smile and began to walk the walk.
Strutting. Thrusting out her hips with each step.

Though he'd seen her play at this before, Jake stood
rooted to the spot.

At the first statue, Mia slowed, smiling at it as if it
were alive, running a finger up the warrior's arm. Then
she hip-bumped him, dancing around the back of it, sliding her arms around the torso as she would a lover, gliding her fingers across the belly in blatant sexual
invitation.

Jake's own belly tightened.

Then she sashayed out from behind the statue, gave
it one last come-hither glance and began to strut toward
another, swirling in a slow circle to face statue number
two, moving to some beat only she could hear, running
her hands up her own body as she danced. Jake nearly
swallowed his own tongue.

When she got to the third statue, the one Jake had
pressed her back against to kiss her, she went up on tiptoes, skimmed her hands up its chiseled chest, cupped
its face and kissed it full on the lips.

Jake actually got hard.

Then Mia began that hip-swaying walk again, stopping as suddenly as she'd started, laughing as she looked
at her staff over her shoulder, dropping the model per-
sona with shocking ease. "There. How's that?"

They all cheered and clapped while she dropped the
staging curtain back down.

Skin damp, cheeks flushed, Mia shoved her hair from
her face and, in midlaugh, caught Jake's gaze. She went
still for one telling moment, then shot him a shaky smile.

He felt no less shaky. Christ, he could barely breathe.
He loved watching her, loved being near her. And

though this had been all about fun, it had gone so far past that he couldn't believe it.

Unnerved, still aroused, he ran his fingers through his hair and took a long drink from his water bottle. It didn't help him to face the truth.

He was in love with her.

## CHAPTER NINE

IN FRONT OF HER HOUSE, Mia got out of her car that night, hot, tired and starving.

Jake came to his front door, watching her with a smile. "I have food."

The thought of his cooking made her knees weak. So did his smile, come to think of it.

"Your place or mine?" he asked.

She hesitated only because the last time she'd seen him, after her silly mock catwalk strut, he'd looked at her as if he'd planned on eating her alive.

Her place or his... "Mine," she said decisively, then remembered the spectacular kisses he'd given her in her kitchen. "Yours," she amended, but then thought of *his* bedroom, which she knew was done in dark, masculine colors and had a lovely huge, welcoming bed. *"Mine,"* she said again, and he laughed at her. "This is not funny."

"Baby, you're funny all right, and *much* more."

"Which doesn't solve the problem of whose house."

"Mine," he said silkily, and brooding now, Mia followed him to his door. She stood there on the porch, reluctant to go inside.

Jake leaned a broad shoulder against the jamb. "I wonder who you're really afraid of. Me, or you?"

"Well, I'm not afraid of *you*," she said and grimaced when she realized what she'd just admitted.

She was afraid of herself, and what he made her feel. And that rankled. "Oh, just move." And in tune to his soft laugh, she pushed past him and into his house.

He had some ground beef and seasoning frying in a pan, which smelled so good her mouth watered. Or maybe that was Jake himself, hair still wet from his shower. With his natural ease in the kitchen, he warmed up tortillas, shredded cheese and chopped tomatoes and lettuce, making them each a huge soft taco.

Mia sat on his living-room floor next to him, eating at his coffee table with a Dodgers game on television and the air-conditioning blasting.

Somehow his place always seemed bigger than hers, an illusion due to the lived-in factor his rooms had that hers didn't. He spent a lot of time here, and had filled the place accordingly. There was a large comfortable L-shaped couch made for sprawling out on; several equally large, equally comfy recliners and a coffee table he used a lot more often than his dining room table. There were architectural prints on the walls, not for art's sake, she knew, but because he loved architecture. Not so many personal pictures, but a few—he and a group of friends sailing; he and his brother with their arms slung around each other in front of the American River, which they'd rafted a few summers back, and one of her laughing at some antic of his or another.

She looked good, she had to admit, head thrown back, eyes sparkling as she laughed. Not something she'd done often lately, buried as she'd been beneath the work she loved.

A cop-out.

She could hear Jake saying the words as if he'd spoken them out loud.

And it was true. Her life lately had been a cop-out.

Maybe after this fashion show, she'd do something about it. She'd start with that lazy day at the beach that she'd promised herself. Things would be good. She was so close to making her dreams come true.

And if it hadn't been for the way Jake looked sitting next to her, all clean and fresh from his shower, his hair still wet, his jaw freshly shaven, his body long and toned in cargo shorts and a T-shirt, smelling like some complicated mix of soap and masculinity that had her nostrils twitching, she might have cooled off for the first time in weeks.

Instead, she began to sweat.

"So." Jake handed her the hot sauce. "The statues are going to be quite effective."

He was referring to how she'd modeled this afternoon for her staff, how she'd lost herself in the moment of the work, having fun with her job. With an embarrassed shrug, she met his hot gaze and…inhaled a pepper. Coughing, wheezing, she reached for her water while Jake leaned forward and ran a hand up and down her back until she could catch her breath.

"I know what you're doing," she said when she could talk again.

"Really?" He took another bite of his taco. "What's that?"

"You're making me want you."

"Is it working?" he asked as he ate.

"Yes. No." She had to laugh, and then realized how he always did that, made her laugh. She picked up the glass of wine he'd poured her and sipped at it. "I'm not going to let it work."

He set down his taco, pushed away from the table and turned to her. "You think I'm playing with you?"

His tone warned her that the weather had changed but she looked at him anyway. His smile had dissipated, and in his eyes was a seriousness that caught her breath. A seriousness and a hint of male frustration and tempered impatience.

And genuine desire.

"Look, Jake. I'm really bad at this."

"At what?"

"Communicating about my feelings."

"That's a bullshit but handy excuse."

"It's not an excuse. It's the truth," she insisted. "I haven't had as much practice as you."

Looking amused again, he cocked his head. "What are you saying? That I'm a slut?"

"All I'm saying," she said with another surprising laugh, "is that one of us has had a lot more sleepovers than the other."

"Because the other claims not to like such a thing."

Right. Oops.

He studied her for a long moment, then took the glass of wine out of her hand. He put a hand on either side of her hips and leaned in. Mouth a mere breath from hers, he smiled into her eyes. "Tell me you were jealous and you'll make my night."

"Of Fluffy? Or Gidget? Please."

He laughed and leaned in some more, crowding her, invading her space in a not too unpleasant way that sent her body humming.

"You *were* jealous," he said smugly.

She put her hand to his chest. A mistake. He was big and warm and so close she could see the light dancing in his eyes, and a good amount of trouble, too. "I'm not going to be goaded into discussing your sexual prowess."

"Because we're *friends*."

"Now you're just mocking me."

His gaze lowered to her mouth. His eyes darkened.

And the feelings stirring inside her *definitely* went beyond friendship. Her nipples hardened, and between her legs she went damp. "All I'm saying is that I'm on to you."

"Is that right?" He opened his mouth and took her lower lip between his teeth and tugged.

She felt an answering tug deep in her womb as he kissed away the sting of his teeth.

"I'm not going to beg you to make love to me."

"Even if I ask pretty please?" he murmured, dragging his mouth along her jaw to the sensitive spot beneath her ear. "Really?"

"Sorry." Her voice was a Marilyn Monroe whisper now. "Not gonna happen."

"Hmm," reverberated right in her ear, raising a set of delicious goose bumps down her body, the sneaky bastard. He knew exactly what he was doing to her.

And as if that wasn't enough, he slid his hands up to her waist, gently squeezed and then lifted her, setting her down on his lap. His hands skimmed up the backs of her thighs, urging her legs open so that she could straddle him.

Then he took her mouth in a kiss that had her head spinning. For balance she held on to him, absorbing his heat and easy strength beneath her fingers, pressing even closer for more.

At that, he trembled. The unexpected power of that surged through her, and she lifted her head, staring down at him.

He was sprawled beneath her, long legs stretched out, chest rising and falling with his easy breathing. His mouth was wet from hers, his eyes heavy lidded and sexy as he watched her.

The cat at rest right before the pounce.

She just looked at him, thoughts crowding in her brain. He cared about her. He'd worked his fingers to the bone every day for a week to meet her deadline. He'd fed her, a small thing, but the novelty of someone looking after her felt incredibly…good.

He was her friend.

He said he would remain her friend.

And he wanted more. A more that would involve her heart as well as her body parts. She knew this, and it was in fact the reason she'd held back.

Still held back. God, she hated the fear but it was still there. Maybe someday—

"Hey." Jake stroked a finger over her jaw. "You still here?"

"Yeah."

He looked at her for a long moment, then kissed her lightly on her lips. "You know what? It's late." With a gentle squeeze of her hips, he lifted her off him. "You need to get some sleep. Big day tomorrow."

The last day before the show. He was right, big day, huge day, but…why wasn't he trying to make her beg? Sure she'd said she wouldn't, but damn, he could have tried a little harder.

Because really, it would've only taken one touch, just one more from him and she just might have.

But he stood up and pulled her up, too, keeping his hands light at her hips, looking at her with a smile on his lips. Completely at ease.

*Touch me.*

But her pride stuck in her throat along with her hunger for him. Not a tasty combination. "Yeah." She forced a smile. "Big day tomorrow."

*We could have a big night, as well….*

She bit her tongue just in case it popped out of her mouth. But clueless, whether by design or not, Jake just took her hand and walked her to her front door.

Damn him.

## CHAPTER TEN

JAKE'S CELL PHONE rang at five the next morning, an hour before he'd scheduled his crew to be at the theater. Mourning the half hour of sleep he'd now lost out on, not to mention the great dream he'd been having—Mia ravaging his body for her own pleasure—he reached for the phone. "Holbrook."

"Houston, we have a problem."

It was Mia, and despite her attempt at levity, he could hear the stress in her voice. "What's the matter?" he asked.

She let out a shaky breath. "The crane came to move the statues into place. That's the good news."

"And the bad news?"

"It dropped one of the statues through the catwalk."

"Anyone hurt?"

"No, thank God. But the catwalk—"

"We'll fix it." He was getting dressed as he spoke. "I'll be there in fifteen minutes."

"Jake, it's a mess. The show is tomorrow night. We still need rehearsal time. I don't see how you can—"

"It'll be fixed," he promised, shoving his feet into his boots and looking around for his keys. "The show'll be fine."

Mia didn't say anything. She couldn't. Her throat had been blocked by the big ball of stress wedged there.

*Beach,* she reminded herself. After this show that might now not happen, she was going to the beach….

"Mia? It's going to be okay. I promise you."

She'd woken him up, she could hear the huskiness of sleep in his voice. If she hadn't been panicked, she might have had a lust attack. "You haven't seen it." Her chest was tight, too tight for air. "God, you have to see it. The wood fractured, the supports just snapped. The whole thing looks like a wrecking ball was dropped on it."

"Are you breathing? Because you don't sound like you're breathing."

"I'm breathing," she gasped, letting out a rush of air and inhaling a new gulp of it. "Now."

"Okay, good. Keep doing that. I'm on my way."

Just the sound of him, calm and in charge and sure of himself, made her want to set her head on his shoulder.

"Mia? You hear me? I'll be there in no time."

Startlingly close to tears, she just nodded like an idiot, as if he could see her. She heard his truck door shut and realized he was literally on his way to her, and she found her voice. "Now I'm going to really owe you."

"Hold that thought," he said.

SHE DID HOLD THAT THOUGHT, simply because she knew how he'd like to collect on what she "owed" him. It made her knees wobble, and her heart race, and other things go damp, and she really couldn't deal with that right now on top of her fashion show disaster.

So instead she concentrated on the here and now. Getting down to the wire, and the buzz and tension and highly charged atmosphere around her reflected that. Walking to center stage, she stared down at the gaping hole in the catwalk.

The statue was a goner, splintered into a million pieces across the catwalk and beneath the hole it'd created in the catwalk itself.

And though the hole was rather large and nearly bisected the thing, she thought if she closed one eye and looked at it sideways, maybe it wasn't so bad.

Although maybe it was. She didn't know for sure, and wouldn't until Jake arrived. Compartmentalizing, she went to work on the things she *had* control over. Pulling out her cell phone, she began the sea of calls to find out if she could get another statue delivered today.

She couldn't.

A master of improvisation and thinking on her feet, Mia simply pulled out a pad of paper and began working with the stage and catwalk design, shuffling props around on the sheet here and there, getting a feel for it in her mind so that by tonight, when staff showed up to prepare for the rehearsals, things would look as if she'd planned to have only three statues all along.

Then suddenly she felt warm in the cool morning. Her body sort of tingled, and she knew without looking that Jake had arrived. Turning, she watched him walk down the center aisle, his eyes on her. He wore his usual uniform of Levi's, faded and well-worn, torn in both knees. His light blue polo shirt fit snug to his shoulders and was draped just over the measuring tape clipped at his hip. He was talking on his cell about some blueprints and how he'd be free to start next week, and then spouted a bunch more construction talk as he came toward her, his gaze never wavering from hers. "Gotta go," he said when he got close, and snapping his phone shut, he slid it into his pocket.

"Thanks for coming—"

"It's my job. But first—" He hopped up onto the stage, slipped his hands into her hair and held her face. "You okay?"

There hadn't been a lot of coddling in her life. In fact, there'd been none, certainly not from her mother, and later not from any others, mostly because she hadn't let anyone do such a thing. Fiercely independent and proud of it, she hadn't needed it.

But a very small part of her, a very weak part, liked the way he took care of her. Liked it so much she wanted to grab on and never let go.

And she might have, if it hadn't been for the knowledge that this, what they shared right now, could all go away if she took that last step. They'd sleep together, and it'd be great but eventually she'd lose him, and she thought maybe that would hurt worse than anything she'd ever experienced.

So instead of falling apart and putting her head to his chest, she sucked it up and smiled. "I'm okay. Let me show you, and we'll take it from there."

They turned and looked at the catwalk. The lift operator stood on the other side of it, looking more than a little sheepish.

"Had a problem?" Jake asked him.

The lift operator took off his baseball cap and scratched his head. "If you want a piece of my ass, better chew it now, because once my boss gets here there won't be anything left for you."

"Hey, shit happens." Jake gingerly stepped out onto the catwalk, balancing on the edge, looking down into the gaping hole. He leaped past it, then crouched low and peered both inside and beneath. He got down on his knees, then stretched out on his belly, sticking his head into the hole itself. Muttering something to himself, he then pulled himself all the way in and vanished.

From her perch on the stage Mia couldn't see him, and lifted a foot to step onto the catwalk.

"Don't," came his voice from somewhere beneath her, and she set her foot back down.

Her cell was going off and so was her pager, and she knew the frantic messages were piling up. What would the rehearsal schedule be? When would the designers be allowed onstage with their models? Would they be delayed? Would the show still be possible?

Tightening her mouth she ignored the ringing and waited for Jake. It occurred to her how she'd never been a waiting sort of person, how Jane always joked that on the day God had handed out patience she'd skipped standing in that line because she hadn't had time for it.

But the oddest thing was that she didn't mind waiting for Jake because deep down she knew he'd come through.

He'd always come through.

*Even if you slept with him,* said a small voice. *Even after you slept with him, he'd always come through.*

Before she could contemplate the implications of that thought, Jake's hands appeared in the hole at her feet. Then his head.

And then he was pulling himself up without effort, and straightening to a stand right next to her. He pulled out his pad and began to scribble on it.

"What are you doing?" she asked.

"Calculating the materials we need."

"So—"

"Shh for a sec." He kept scribbling. Then he whipped out his cell phone and dialed, and rattled off a list of materials. "I need an a.m. delivery. Yes, *this* a.m." He listened. "Great. Thanks." When he shut the cell, he hopped off the stage and again hunkered beneath the splintered catwalk.

She couldn't be "shhed" another second. "Jake, damn it. How bad is it?"

"Well, it's not fatal."

"I'm vibrating." She showed him her cell and pager. "With designers wanting to know about rehearsals tomorrow. Delayed? Canceled? *What?*"

"Give me until tomorrow noon."

She hugged her cell and pager to her chest, not even realizing it until he covered her hands with one of his. She knew he could feel her heart pounding, but wondered if he knew her nipples had hardened at the feel of his fingers so close.

"Okay?" he asked. "You can have half a day for rehearsals."

Relief flooded her, and she could barely speak. "Oh my God, Jake. I was so worried."

Under the guise of tucking a strand of hair behind her ear, he touched her with his other hand, too. His eyes heated, and her body kicked up her inner temperature to match. She wore a suit dress today, the color of coral and trimmed in white. She'd known it was flattering and sexy, and had worn it on purpose to see that flare in his gaze.

And she didn't want to face *why* she'd done such a thing. "Are you going to ever collect your favor?" she heard herself whisper.

"Oh, yeah." His crew had arrived behind them. They were climbing onto the stage, milling around. But Jake's eyes never left hers. "Tonight."

The noise level around them increased.

Or maybe that was the roaring of her heart. "T-tonight?"

"Game night. My place."

She let out a shaky breath. Games. *That* she could handle.

If he didn't smile at her.

If he didn't touch or kiss her.

"New game," he said, and her relief backed up in her throat. "Truth or dare."

She stared at him. "Truth or dare? *Why?*"

"Why not?"

Yeah, right, Mia. Why not? She eyed him carefully but though he had a small smile playing around his lips, he was giving nothing away. "Sounds…juvenile."

"Only if you're afraid of honesty for some reason. But that's silly, right? You've always been honest with me."

She swallowed hard. "Right." *Except about the not liking sex thing.*

"Great." He smiled. "Could you back up and give us some room here? We have a lot to do."

"Yeah, sure."

"See you tonight," he said, and for the rest of the day she thought about little else.

## *CHAPTER ELEVEN*

BY THAT EVENING, Jake and his crew had a handle on the catwalk repair.

Mia and her staff were on the stage arranging the props. The long lengths of black velvet, the potted greenery, the three remaining statues were all going to be good backdrops for the models and the lines of lingerie. Jake knew VLL had a huge success on their hands; it was in the hum of excitement hovering over the place as the cameras and lights were set up.

He loved watching Mia in her element, standing center stage, in the middle of the organized chaos, ruling her world. Her face was so animated, the pleasure and passion for what she was doing contagious, and he couldn't take his eyes off her.

Not to mention what the fitted cut of her suit dress did for her hot little bod, which was practically quivering with the exhilaration of the moment. Every time he looked at her everything within him reacted, not just physically, but far deeper than that.

Moving close, breaking into the inner circle of the crazy goings-on and the people around her, he leaned into her, pressing his mouth to her ear. God, she smelled amazing, like sweet woman and hot summer nights and he took a moment to inhale her. "We're done for the night," he murmured. "I'll see you later."

Slowly she turned her head, and he didn't miss the way she closed her eyes as the movement had his lips brushing along her jaw. "It might be awhile before I come."

He stroked a thumb over her full lower lip. "I don't care. Just come."

She sucked in a breath at the double entendre, but someone else pressed close with questions, and he backed away to let her work, convinced that his suspicions were correct, whether she ever put words to it or not.

She *did* want him, and he wanted to know why she was fighting it, pretending she didn't.

Tonight he'd find out once and for all.

TWO HOURS LATER came the knock on Jake's door. He opened it to a tired but beautiful-looking Mia.

"If you have food, I'll love you forever," she said.

If only it was that easy. He led her to the kitchen, where he had her favorite waiting—pizza. He grabbed two plates from the cupboard and met her at the table.

"Thank you," she said, and moaned at her first bite, a throaty, gusty sound that made him hard. She took another quick bite and grabbed his hand, tugging him close. He'd have sworn she'd been about to hug him, just fling her arms around him and pull him close, but she contained herself and just chewed. "My stomach thanks you. Every part of me thanks you."

"Good?" he asked, smiling at her exuberant eating.

"Oh my God, are you kidding? Your crust is to die for." She licked some cheese off her finger. "What do you think it says about us that you do all the cooking and I do all the eating?"

His eyes were locked on her mouth, and the finger

in it. "That I'm smart enough to know that the way to your heart is through your stomach?"

She laughed, and didn't talk again until she'd inhaled three full slices.

"You know, that's one of the things I like most about you," he said, watching her.

She stopped sucking on her fingers. "That I'm a slob?"

"That you don't hold back. That you give life your all. Except in one area, that is."

Her gaze went wary.

"Don't stop eating."

"I'm full."

Liar, he thought fondly. What she was, was scared.

"Why truth or dare?" she asked.

He shrugged. "It's just a game."

She didn't meet his gaze. "Yeah." Her sudden tension was palpable. She must have a few truths she was worried about. "Nervous?" he asked.

"No," she said quickly. Too quickly.

Uh-huh. "Normally I don't aim to make you uncomfortable." He handed her another beer. "But tonight—" he clinked his bottle to hers in a toast "—I think I like you a little nervous."

"I'm not."

He smiled.

"I'm not," she said again and brushed the crumbs off her hands, her expression that of a prisoner heading toward the guillotine. "Let's just do it. Play the damn game."

"Truth or dare," he said softly.

She stared at him for a long moment. "Right here?"

"Where else?"

"Um…"

"Truth or dare? Mia?"

"Dare."

"Hmm." He pushed back his plate and considered his options. "I dare you to kiss me."

Cocking her head, she smiled in relief. "That's all? Just a kiss?"

He had to wonder what the hell she'd been expecting. "Just a kiss."

Standing up, she straightened her pretty coral suit dress, the one that made her skin glow and showed off all her curves. The one with eight buttons from breast to thigh, the eight buttons he'd been mentally unbuttoning all day.

"Easy enough," she said more to herself than to him, and bending toward him, put her hands on the armrests of his chair.

Her hair fell forward, brushing his jaw. Eyes open on his, she leaned closer still. Her dress pulled away from her, enough that he could see the tops of her breasts, just the curves really.

Then he felt the brush of her lips on his cheek. One blink and she was straightening away from him, a little smile on her mouth as she sat back down and picked up her beer.

"Hey," he said. "I meant on my mouth."

"You didn't specifically say," she said primly.

Okay, he thought with a laugh. *Game on.*

"Truth or dare?" she asked him.

"Truth."

She blinked at that and he wondered what she'd have asked him to do. He got hard at the thought.

"Tell me something you've never told another person," she said after a moment.

"A secret?"

She nodded.

He lifted his beer, more to give himself a moment than anything else, watching her carefully. Right for the jugular, his Mia. "Like what?"

"I don't know, something personal. Tell me why you're not crazy about fast food."

"Because I grew up on fast food. Actually, make that scraps."

"Your mother…"

"Worked nights in housekeeping at a downtown hotel."

"And then she slept all day," Mia said. "Never had the energy for kids."

"Right."

"So it's a comfort thing for you," she said softly.

"I guess."

"Oh, Jake."

"I just ruined the whole tough-guy image by admitting that, didn't I."

She didn't smile, as he'd expected her to. Instead, her eyes shimmering with emotion for him, she stood up, and once again leaned over him.

This time her mouth brushed his, once, twice, her lips clinging for far too short a beat before she pulled away.

"What was that for?" he asked, his voice gone a little husky, his hands fisted on the chair at his sides to keep from tumbling her into his lap.

"Just because." She sat back down.

"Hey, was that a pity kiss?"

"I don't feel sorry for you. I feel…proud. You're a great cook, Jake. And a great man."

"Truth or dare?" he asked quietly.

She shot him a nervous smile. "Dare."

Did she really think that would be the lesser of two evils? "Come sit on my lap."

"Is that my dare?"

"Yep." He patted his thighs. "You have to stay here through the next round."

Her eyes narrowed, but she got up out of her chair for the third time, then turned to give him her back and began to sit on the very edge of his knees.

"Nope." He settled his hands on her hips and whipped her around. "Facing me."

She stared down at his sprawled legs, the ones she now had to straddle, then at his belly, his chest and, finally, back into his face. "You just ate five pieces of pizza, I'll give you a stomachache."

"I can handle it." He patted his thighs.

With a soft sound of exasperation, she shifted to sit, but found herself hampered by the snugness of the dress around her legs. "Oops." She smiled. "Can't. Sorry."

"Truth then."

Another sound escaped her, one that came with a low oath, and then she tugged up the hem of her dress from just above the knees to high thigh. As she flung a leg over his, the dress shifted up even higher, giving him a peekaboo flash of pale pink panties.

Hands on his shoulders for balance, she sat perched on his legs, hers spread to accommodate his, chewing on her lower lip. Her feet didn't touch the floor, they swung a few inches above his tile, and everywhere her inner calves and thighs touched the outside of his, he burned.

He burned in other spots, too, and his hands tightened slightly on her hips. "Comfy?"

Her high-heeled sandals fell off her feet and hit the tile. "You're sort of bony."

"Bony?" One quick tug, and her pale-pink-covered crotch was flush against the V of his jeans, and the unmistakable erection behind it. "How's this for *bony*?" he growled and slowly rocked his hips to hers.

"Oh…my."

"I'm so damn hot for you I'm dying with it." Sliding his hands up her body, he took her hands in his, entwined their fingers, then brought their joined hands behind her back, low on her spine, which pressed her forward even more, nudging the hottest, neediest part of him against the hottest, neediest part of her.

An electric arc of pleasure and pain struck him, and he leaned in at the same moment she did, their mouths meeting, opening on each other as he tried to claim her as his own. Then her tongue touched his and pleasure skittered down his spine, pooling in his groin. He forgot about the silly game, forgot about the fashion show, forgot about everything but the woman panting softly in his arms.

As he rocked his hips forward into hers, she let out a sexy little whimper and flexed her hands in his. The hem of her dress slid up even farther now, to her hips, exposing more of her panties, the ones he wanted to pull off with his teeth because she looked so damned sexy he couldn't stand it. And yet there was something almost sweet, certainly vulnerable about the way she sat there, so open for him. From beneath the sheer material of her panties he could see the outline of her, so utterly, erotically feminine he wanted to drop to his knees and worship. "Truth," he grated out.

She blinked, slow as an owl. "You want to keep playing?" She was breathing a little roughly, which excited him all the more. "Like this? Now?"

*"Truth."*

She swallowed hard and looked at his chest. "I gotta tell you, I was hoping you'd say dare."

His laugh sounded like a groan even to his own ears. "Next time. Truth, Mia."

"Okay." She swallowed. "Why do you bother?"

"With…?"

"Me."

What? Why did he bother? Was she serious? He looked into her face. She appeared to be holding her breath. *Totally serious.* If she didn't know why he bothered, then damn, he hadn't done his job, and he hated that. He tipped her chin up with a finger and waited for her to meet his gaze. "I'm glad you're sitting down because this one's a doozy."

She looked even more nervous now. "No. No doozies. I take back the question."

"Too late."

"Jake—"

"I 'bother' because I'm falling for you."

# CHAPTER TWELVE

"You…" Words failed her as she looked at Jake in shock, utter shock.

Jake looked right back, eyes glittering. "Yeah. I'm falling in love with you." His hands slid up her back.

Mia expected him to tunnel his fingers in her hair, yank her forward and kiss her, reminding her of this almost chemical-like attraction they had for one another. She did not expect him to gently cup her face, stroking her jaw in a way that brought a lump to her throat.

"And because of that," he said in a low voice. "You're important to me. So damned important."

Still speechless, Mia just slowly shook her head. Her world was reeling, her heart drumming so fast it felt as if it were coming out her ears.

Jake surged to his feet, and with her still wrapped around him like a pretzel, headed down the hall, shouldering open his bedroom door, stalking straight toward the huge king-size bed in the center of the room.

*He loved her.*

"Your turn, Mia." He dumped her on the mattress, and before she'd bounced twice he was on her, stretching his big, long body out over hers.

*He loved her.* God, she couldn't wrap her brain around it. "Um—"

"Truth or dare?" Again he entwined their fingers and pulled her hands up over her head. Dipping down, he kissed her throat as he shoved a muscled thigh between hers.

While she struggled to make sense of the three little words he'd just uttered as if saying "Let's have more pizza." If she'd been standing, she'd have staggered at the implications. If he loved her, what was it that they were doing? If he loved her, then this wasn't a game. *Right?* "Jake—"

"Truth. Or. Dare?" He closed his teeth on her throat, nipping where he'd just kissed. Then he touched his hot, silky tongue to the spot.

"Truth," she gasped, arching up into him.

"I've known you for two years." Another lick. "You've dated. You even had a relationship during that time, though granted it was low-key and long-distance."

Oh, God. She knew where this was leading, and went still, only her heart thundering out of control. "Yes."

"I never gave it much thought because I didn't like to, but you haven't gone two years without sex."

When she didn't answer, he lifted his head and looked down at her.

She let go of the breath she'd been holding. "Is that your question, whether or not I've had sex in the past two years?"

"No. I've seen you at work, Mia. And at home. In the kitchen moaning over some food I've made you, or yelling at the Lakers game on television. You're a passionate woman who gets a kick out of life, so my question is, do you really not like sex?"

"Jake."

"Simple question. Simple answer. Yes or no?"

"Nothing about that question is simple."

"Would you rather take a dare?" He took a light bite out of her jaw and rocked his hips to hers. "Because believe me, I've got one."

He was still hard, deliciously so, and she arched up to meet him.

"See, that's what I mean," he said, a little hoarse now. "You melt beneath me. Your heart's racing and your nipples are hard. I'll bet you're wet, too. Are you wet, Mia?"

She licked her lips and dragged air into her taxed lungs. "The answer to your first question is no. No, I don't really not like sex. Double negatives, I know, but you're making it hard to think."

Lifting his head, he looked down at her.

"I like sex," she whispered. "I like it a lot."

"Why did you lie to me?"

The question for the ages. She'd held back from him all this time because she'd instinctively known, even in the beginning, that this, with him, would be different, special.

So with Herculean effort, she'd kept this light, kept it just a friendship, all to ensure it wouldn't ever end.

And now he'd single-handedly taken them to the next level, *and* he wanted to know why she'd lied. She had no idea how to tell him. "Truth or dare?"

He blinked. "What?"

"You can't ask two questions, so now it's your turn," she said. "Truth or dare?"

His eyes smoldered. "So we're still playing."

"You started it."

"Truth," he grated out.

"Did you mean it?"

He didn't ask what. They both knew what she wanted to know: Had he really meant what he had said earlier? That he was falling in love with her?

"Yes," he said fiercely, and caught her mouth with his. "I meant it." He punctuated each word with hot, openmouthed kisses along her throat. Sliding his long fingers into her hair to hold her head steady, he plundered her mouth again, in a hot, deep, wet kiss that rocked her world and brought her humiliatingly close to doing as she always said she wouldn't—*beg*.

"Now you again," he said, panting. "Truth or dare?"

She looked into his eyes and saw the heat, the passion. The desperation.

And knew at least that she wasn't alone in this. Whatever she was feeling, he felt it, too. And he'd even put a name to it. Oh God. "Dare."

"There's no going back," he said roughly. "Not after this."

*"Dare,"* she repeated boldly, while quaking on the inside. He looked so intense, so utterly fierce. Everything within her quivered in anticipation, and she put her mouth to his throat. He was warm, slightly damp and smelled like heaven.

"Dare then," he practically growled and yanked his shirt off over his head. "Are you ready?"

Her eyes locked onto his body, gloriously hard and defined. She loved his chest, and the small mat of dark hair in the center, with the line leading down, down, down, vanishing into his low-slung jeans. And God, his stomach. She could spend a day just looking at the rippled abs, the way his jeans gaped, giving her tantalizing peeks of forbidden flesh. She stroked her fingers there, just above the waistband, and moaned when his stomach quivered. With a stomach like that, he could probably thrust into a woman for hours without tiring. "I'm ready."

"We make love. Right here, right now."

She lifted her gaze to his.

"And forget the damn game," he all but growled. "This is just you and me and what we want to give each other. Free will."

His love was there for her to see, and also his need. A little part of her, the part that had held back all this time, wanted to give in. Do it. Try it. He won't hurt you. He'd never hurt you. "Yes," she whispered, and almost before the words were out of her mouth, he'd unbuttoned the front of her suit dress down to her naval, shoved it off her shoulders, pinning her arms to the sides while he fingered her bra.

She knew he was looking for a hook, but there was none. "It's like Velcro," she managed to tell him. "It's a new design. Jamie did it, he's one of my partners."

"Mmm. Nice." The next thing she heard was the sound of the Velcro giving way and then he was peeling the material from her breasts.

"God, Mia. I love your body." He leaned in to taste her, and all of Mia's fantasies about what it'd be like with this man paled in comparison to the reality. Thoughts of the game vanished, as did any possible repercussions of the recklessness of letting her heart into the fray as he kissed his way over the curve of one breast, flicking her nipple with his hot tongue. Her breathing came rapidly now, and she clutched at him. "Jake."

Against her, his hips were still oscillating in a slow,

maddening grind, rocking her to the heavy bulge behind his fly, driving her closer and closer to climax.

"Mia." He bit very lightly down on her nipple and tugged, eliciting an electrified moan as she writhed beneath him.

"Mia."

*"What?"*

"You liking this?" He did it again, another light bite with his teeth, and she could only strain against him.

"Are you?" he asked patiently.

"I told you, I *like* sex."

"That's good but that's not what this is." More rocking of his hips.

Her toes curled. She was on the very edge here.

"We're making love, Mia. Say it."

She might have killed him right then but she could feel how incredibly hard he was, could see the cords straining in his neck, the tic in his jaw. He was dying, too. "Fine! Yes! We're making love. And I like it, okay? Now stop stopping!"

"Just making sure," he said very silkily, and tugged off her dress, leaving her in only her Velcro tearaway panties.

"Your jeans," she panted, tugging at them.

He stripped so fast her head spun. Then he kissed her again, melding his mouth to hers, his tongue probing, his appetite for her clearly as rapacious and all-consuming as hers was for him. She continued to arch upward, meeting his thrusts, her hands frantic over his broad shoulders and the tense, hard muscles in his back, then lower, sinking her fingers into the hard muscles of his butt.

He broke from the kiss. Breath rasping, he slid down

her body and ran a finger over her bikini bottoms. "Pretty," he said, and slid his thumb beneath the elastic at her hips.

With a Velcro-sounding riiiiiip, they came apart.

He smiled. "Love this stuff." Then he scraped the panties away from her. The smile seemed to back up in his throat when he looked down at what he'd exposed. Swallowing hard, he traced the hypersensitive crease at the top of her thigh. "Want to know what I see?"

*No.* She wanted him to touch her, wanted him to send her screaming over the edge. "Jake—"

"I could look at you all day." One stroke of his finger right over her center, and she gasped. *Just a few more,* she thought. *Please.*

*"Mine,"* he said, and stroked her again.

Mia thought she couldn't get any more tense without shattering into a million pieces.

"You look good enough to eat, did you know that?" Another purposely accurate stroke of his finger, which came away wet from her own arousal. Slowly, purposely, he outlined her, skimming right over where she needed it most—

"How about it, Mia? Want to be my dessert?"

Fisting her hands in the sheets at her side, she let out a frustrated breath. "Not again. You are not going to talk all the way through this."

With a chuckle, he bent and blew a breath over her, making her cry out.

She was going to beg and she didn't care.

"I might," he admitted, and lifting his head, watched her as he mercilessly held her on the very brink. "I just want to make sure you're enjoying this."

"Damn it, Jake. We all know I lied and why. I like this. I *love* this. Now please, Jake. *Please.*"

He obliged with flattering haste, all kidding out the

window, leaving an intensity in its wake that stole what little breath she'd managed to retain in her lungs.

Surging up, Jake went after the jeans he'd tossed on the floor, coming back with a condom in his hand. He took one look at her shamelessly sprawled on his bed and groaned. "Ah, man, look at you." He stroked his hand down her stomach and sank a finger into her, groaning roughly as she cried out and arched into him. "You're it for me, Mia," he whispered, and bent over her, brushing a kiss where his fingers had been. "You're all I ever wanted. Come for me."

And with one lick of his tongue, she did. Completely. Utterly. Lights exploding in her head, blood roaring in her ears, the whole shuddering, shivering bit. "I need you inside me," she panted when she could speak at all.

Not arguing, he ripped open the condom packet but she took it from his hands. "I want to do it."

"Hurry," he ordered, no longer her amused, lazy lover but a man nearly past his limit. He was hot to the touch, and though hard as steel, he felt silky and velvety and smooth, and she lingered as she stroked the condom down his length thinking that she'd have liked to taste—

With a growl, he tumbled her back to the mattress, slid his big hands to the backs of her thighs, lifting her high as he thrust home.

The sensation of him sinking in deep, filling her, warming places she hadn't known needed warming, nearly overwhelmed her. She'd been here before, not with him, but with other men, and it'd always been good.

But what she felt in this moment, in Jake's arms, her gaze locked on his, his body surrounding her, filling her, was so far beyond good it stunned her. More like sucker punched. Tears filled her eyes, and with him filling her to overflowing she stared up into his equally thunder-struck expression. "Jake…"

"I know." His voice was thick, rough, and not just with desire but something else, something that put a name and a face to the feelings burgeoning in her heart.

"It feels so…" Struggling for the words, she blinked, and a tear slipped down her cheek. *"Real."*

Touching his forehead to hers, he nodded. And then he rocked his hips, seating himself inside her more fully, deeper.

Holding on tight, she arched up. "Don't stop."

"I won't. Mia…it's never been like this for me." Another thrust that drove her up against the sheets. "Ever."

"Me, either."

He groaned, low, raw, deep, and began to move. She could only hold on through the sensations battering at her as he held her, filled her, leaving her a sweaty, shaking, writhing mess hovering on the edge of pleasure again and again, then finally, *finally* tumbling her over. And over.

And over.

He fell with her, her name on his lips.

WHEN SHE WOKE UP, dawn was peeking in Jake's windows.

Show day.

Her heart kicked, not just because of the monumental career day it would be, but because she was wrapped in the arms of a man hard asleep against her.

For a moment, she froze. She always woke alone, but this was…incredibly good. Incredibly right. And she snuggled in closer to Jake, thinking she could get used to this.

Very used to it.

It wasn't just how amazing he looked, sprawled in his bed, tanned and tough, body defined in the way of a man who spent most of his waking hours in hard physical labor. She knew his eyes, if they were to open right now, would smile from just seeing her and his lips would curve to match. He had a way of looking at her, as if she just might be his whole world. The knowledge of that had changed her forever, had made her feel both strong and weak, and…wanted.

Loved.

A miracle. He was her miracle. God, he felt so solid, so warm, and she ran her hands up his sleek smooth back, loving how the muscles flexed as he stretched.

"Mmm," rumbled from his chest as he stirred and cracked open a beautiful sea-green eye. He saw her watching him, and just as she'd imagined, he smiled. "Hey," he said. "Whatcha doing?"

"Looking at you. You're so beautiful, Jake."

"Yeah?" The next thing she knew she was flat on her back, his legs spreading hers, his silky hot erection nudging against her. "Like you." He dropped his mouth to hers for a kiss. "This I could get used to, waking with you smiling at me." He kissed her again, and it was no simple kiss but a raw statement of need as he slid inside her.

She sighed and held on as he began to move within her. He fulfilled her like no one else, which was her last thought for a good long time.

IT MIGHT HAVE BEEN two minutes or an eternity later, Mia felt Jake's mouth brush her temple. "I love you," he whispered on a thread of a breath when his body finally relaxed.

"I think I'm finally getting that," she said, and stroked

her hands down his damp back. "And something else, too. I love you back, Jake."

He went utterly still. Then, still breathing unevenly, he lifted his head. "Say that again?"

She smiled. "Did I ask you to repeat it when you said it to me?"

His eyes narrowed. "Humor me."

"I love you." She bit her lower lip. "In fact, I think it's possible I've always loved you. I don't know why I resisted facing the truth for so long."

"Because you're stubborn as hell?"

"Hey."

"And smart." He kissed her chin. "And sexy." He kissed her nose. "And beautiful." He surged up to his knees and pulled her up to face him. "You know what this means, right?"

"Um…that *you* have to sleep in the wet spot?"

He grinned. "That you'll have to face yet another truth. We belong together."

She felt her eyes widen as her heart kicked. "So that means…"

"You'll have to date me for more than the food I bring you. Maybe you'd even consent to some sort of exclusivity."

"You mean…"

"Maybe we'll even work our way up to cohabitation."

"Oh my God."

"Is that 'oh my God' he's lost his mind, or 'oh my God' he's onto something?"

He looked touchingly unsure, and she leaned into him, everything suddenly so right for the first time…ever. "Definitely onto something. Now, how about getting back 'into' something." She grinned. "Like me."

He reached for her with a matching grin, his eyes bright with emotion. "Oh, yeah."

With a joyous laugh, she tumbled him back down to the sheets. "Are you going to talk a lot this time, too?"

"Maybe." His hands came up to hold her hips as she straddled him, and when she wrapped her fingers around him to guide him home, he groaned. "God, I love you, Mia."

She closed her eyes as he entered her, then opened them again, feeling so complete, she could hardly believe it. "Now *that* you can keep on saying."

"Deal." Then he rolled her over the bed, stretching his body out over hers, looking into her face as he took them both to the beginning of their forevers.

# EPILOGUE

Sizzling Nights, *global fashion show*

MIA STOOD BACKSTAGE at the famed Greek Theater, holding hands with Jamie and Samantha as the models lined up, ready to strut their stuff. Above them the night was glorious, the dark velvety sky littered with stars. The theater itself was filled with fashion royalty and peasants alike, hushed in anticipation as the lighting changed, signifying the beginning of the show.

In tune with the rocking music, the first model brushed past the three partners, moving through the archway of the hanging gardens, appearing to the audience for the first time. Beneath the ancient wonder, the tall, leggy blonde began to walk forward, wearing no other than Jamie's own lingerie design, a silky black teddy designed to steal one's breath.

At the sight, the audience went crazy and Jamie sucked in his own breath, making Mia hug him hard. "We did it." She grinned and hugged Samantha, too. "Can you believe it?"

"There was never any doubt in my mind," Jamie said, making the three of them laugh giddily as he grabbed one of the bottles of champagne lined up for after the show. He popped the cork while Samantha reached for three flutes.

They each took a glass, holding it up to each other in a toast. "To a great year ahead of us," Jamie said. "And a great big fat checkbook for Velvet, Leather & Lace."

"To the two years of backbreaking work behind us," Samantha toasted. "And all we've been through together."

"And to the here and now," Mia said. "And how the three of us have become six."

They all drank to their good fortune, both in business and in love, and grinned dizzily as the audience continued to go wild.

"I think this means we can charge more," Jamie said thoughtfully.

"And work less," voted Samantha.

"And finally really live our lives." Mia nodded her head to the front row, where Marsh, Lorna and Jake sat, cheering them on. It was amazing that love, once such a terrifying unknown for each of the independent workaholics, had finally brought it all together. "Nowhere to go but up," Mia said, and lifted her glass.

*Everything you love about romance...*
***and more!***

*Please turn the page for Signature Select™*
*Bonus Features.*

## Bonus Features:

# BONUS FEATURES

## Velvet, Leather & Lace

# Suzane Forster's
### Travel Tale...
### A Day in L.A. with Suzanne

When I think of the City of Angels, which is what many natives call Los Angeles, the first words that come to mind are not angelic. They are *big*, *adventurous* and *dangerous*. Just the way we like our men, right, ladies? Of course, that's only one aspect of the city, but it is very apt.

Los Angeles is about an hour north of my home in Newport Beach, which can easily turn into two hours on a heavy traffic day, so just getting there can be an adventure. And if you've ever visited Southern California, you've probably witnessed one of our car chases. It's not unusual to turn on the TV and get a helicopter's view of a perpetrator trying to outrun several police cars on one of L.A.'s famous freeways. You could easily think you were watching a Jerry Bruckheimer movie, except that it's really happening.

But L.A. also has a kinder, gentler side. Really, it does. And I like that in a man, too. Is there a better combo than tough and tender? For me, the gentler, more inviting side of L.A. has mainly to do with its great variety of restaurants and its wonderful food. The city is famous for its delicious fresh fruit and produce, and my idea of the perfect way to start a day in L.A. would be breakfast at Marmalade Café in Farmer's Market on 3rd Street.

One of my favorite menu items is a frittata that features some of the market's freshest produce—steamed carrots, broccoli, cauliflower, rutabagas, mushrooms and caramelized onions, gently nestled in a jacket of fluffy whipped eggs, and oozing rivulets of Swiss and cheddar cheese. Their pumpernickel raisin toast is scrumptious with either whipped creamery butter or cream cheese. Did I mention that everything is calorie free?

> *But L.A. also has a kinder, gentler side.*

After that it's fun to stroll through the market, checking out the shops, the displays of fresh flowers and the artisans' booths, where unique and original handmade treasures can be found. It's the perfect place to find one-of-a-kind gifts. Luckily the market is just large enough that a stroll restores your appetite, and at the east end, you'll find the Gumbo Pot, a fast-food restaurant that offers New Orleans' beignets, so decadently delicious they really should be illegal. These come warm from the oven, filled to the brim with chocolate and liberally dusted with confectioners' sugar. Be sure and tuck your napkin under your chin!

For a late lunch, it's a short drive (or a long walk) down Fairfax to Canter's, which has my vote as one of the West Coast's great delicatessens. Lunch is a steaming bowl of matzo ball soup and a sandwich so thickly layered with either roast beef, corn beef or pastrami, that I can't begin to get my mouth open wide enough. These are sandwiches you have to sneak attack, working your way around the edges until you nibble them down to size, and my personal favorite is the corned beef on marbled rye, slathered with yellow mustard. None of that fancy, spicy stuff for me. My husband, Allan, is a pastrami fan, and for side dishes, we both love the potato salad and poppy seed coleslaw.

A great place to spend the afternoon is the Third Street Promenade in Santa Monica, which is several blocks of open-air shopping and restaurants. You can easily while away a whole afternoon there, and you're only a couple blocks away from the ocean, if you want to walk barefoot in the sand and get your feet wet in the surf.

Dinner is a chance to experience yet another side of L.A., the fun, sexy, seductive side. One lively place is a restaurant called Samba, where shimmying samba dancers, decked out in beads, ostrich feathers and little else, dance in the aisles while the waiters serve luscious drinks and skewers of Brazilian steak, dripping with savory juices. When we were there, the dancers were limber and lovely, but strictly female. As we left, I gently suggested to the management that they think about equal opportunity when hiring future dancers.

And before I forget, there's the city's renowned garment district, which is the backdrop for my story, "A Man's Gotta Do." I won't recommend any restaurants because you'll be too busy shopping for designer duds at fabulous discount prices to think about food. But just imagine the appetite you'll have when you're done. Bon appétit! I do hope you'll get a chance to visit some of my favorite haunts on a future trip to the City of Angels, and meanwhile, please enjoy "A Man's Gotta Do"!

## TIPS & TRICKS

# THE ART OF SEDUCTION

*Unleash your inner seductress and hold him captive with these enticing lovemaking tips.*
by Claire Sibonney

Sumptuous foods, candlelight, massage...even exercise can help you set the mood for passionate lovemaking. No matter what your love style, unleashing your personal power of seduction is easy with this sensual essentials guide.

Are you a temptress or a tease? Brazen or bashful? No matter what your love style, unleashing your own personal power of seduction can be easy to do. But if you're feeling lovelier than ever, and not getting any love, you may be going about it the wrong way. Your solution could lie in something as simple as a well-laid-out plan.

Snow Raven Starborn, a San Diego–based author, covers all the essentials in *Seduction*. A culmination of Starborn's sensual secrets, it presents twenty-three different scenarios for you to practice with your lover. Choose from a variety of fun-filled activities, including menu suggestions, color-scheme offerings and aromatherapy—all designed to stimulate his senses.

**Feeling Sexy:**
No matter how carefully you orchestrate your seduction, feeling sexy is the first step in getting your lover to give you what you want. Start with a trip to the hairdresser, a little makeup and some naughty lingerie, but if you're still not happy with what you see, you may have to increase your romantic investment.

Going to the gym may not always be as fun as getting a manicure, but you'll feel better for it. Follow these sexy exercise essentials and unleash your inner seductress: hip and inner-thigh stretches (for flexibility), squats (for lower-body strength), dips (for upper-body tone) and buttock crunches (for a well-defined backside).

But it's not all about the physical you—the emotional art of seduction is often just as arousing. Practice feeling comfortable in your own skin, says Starborn. Take some time every day to reinforce all the qualities you love about yourself and the ones he should love, too. Think about these positive traits while you're serenading your imaginary lover in the shower or jogging in the park. Better yet, take a yoga or dance class to practice your self-confidence in front of others.

## Setting the Scene:
After you've made yourself irresistible, it's time to focus your attention on developing an enticing, warm and sensual lovemaking environment. Set an intimate table for two with rose petals scattered about it. Light dozens of votive candles in every corner and select your favorite sensual and erotic music to complement your romantic meal. Draw a warm bath and add drops of your favorite scent or drape a canopy over your bed. Think of the entire picture you're painting for your seduction: "Men don't really notice the atmosphere in little bits," says Starborn. "They notice the environment in its entirety. They think of it as a place that's 'oh, so comfortable.'"

## Making Memories:
Regardless of where you are in your relationship, there are an infinite number of

activities to include in your seduction. They can be as innocent as a walk on the beach or as daring as a game of naked Twister. In *Seduction,* Starborn tailors each activity to the mood you're trying to achieve.

In "The Welcoming Seduction," intended for first-time intimacy, Starborn suggests candlelight portraits. Reminiscent of another famous artistic love scene—in *Ghost*—replace clay with fine paper and warm-colored charcoal, and unleash your inner artist. Sketch the profile of his face or the contour of his buttocks—it's completely up to you. For more intimately acquainted lovers, Starborn describes "The Confident Seduction." The activity includes a hot-oil sensual massage, with tantalizing instructions on relaxing and warming up your lover. (By end of the massage—if you're lucky—the roles get reversed and you're the one getting pampered.)

**Pleasing His Palate**
Most women have already figured out this shortcut to a man's heart, but in seduction, it is to be taken all the more seriously. Choose exotic foods that are as sensual to the palate as they are playful to eat. Oysters, sushi, fruits, cheese, strawberries and chocolate make excellent fare.

As Starborn illustrates, it's very important to coordinate your meal with the activity you have planned. If you're performing a striptease, your meal should be extralight. "If you feel bloated and self-conscious, you're not going to feel like getting naked," says Starborn. However, if you're planning an afternoon seduction that doesn't involve taking off your clothes, feel free to indulge your appetite: a picnic in the park with the works. Finally, one of the most often ignored details of seduction is the morning-after. As with the main meal, Starborn offers both homemade recipes and eat-out varieties, depending on your mood. Whether you decide on a cheese omelet with orange juice and champagne or crepes at a French bakery, the most important rule is to end your seduction as pleasurably as it began.

**More Tips and Tricks:**
*Color Scheme:* When planning your personal seduction, choose a color scheme to complement the emotions you're trying to stir. If you're introducing a passionate activity, you may want to keep him in check emotionally, says Starborn. In that case, stick to cool colors such as purples, blues and greens. If the aim is to keep him warm and comforted, choose rich colors such as oranges, reds and browns. You

can apply these colors to all aspects of your seduction—from the color of your outfit to the cocktails you serve.

*Pulse point Oils:* Aromatherapy, or "aromasexuality," as Starborn calls it, can produce an amazing effect on your lover. "Women don't usually realize that men respond so well to scent," says Starborn. "They pick it up and it becomes part of the atmosphere." The options are so diverse, you could pick a new aroma for every type of seduction. Depending on the scent, you could dab it directly on yourself or in the environment: in a candle, a bath or on your pillow. If you're not yet familiar with aromatherapy, but have your own signature scent, you could try mixing an undernote of something new with an overnote of your usual fragrance.

*\*Originally published online at eHarlequin.com.*

# A Day in the Life...
## of Jill Shalvis

*We asked Jill to give us a glimpse of what a typical day looks like for a busy writer. She recorded an actual day while writing her story!*

14  The alarm goes off at 5:50 in the morning. That can't be right because I'm in Hawaii, alone on a beach with nothing but the waves and a cute cabana boy offering me a mai tai...

Oh, wait. That's a dream.

My reality... I've got a dog on my feet (they're numb), a husband still dead asleep and an eight-year-old with her nose right next to mine, her eyes wide-open. "Mommy, I spilled the milk all over the floor. And I sorta spilled the cereal, too."

The dog perks up at this, leaps off the bed and vanishes into the kitchen to lap up the spill. The dog is my new favorite family member.

Four kiddie fights, three missing shoes and two hours later, I'm finally alone. I sit in the big leather chair in the living room and pull my laptop on my lap. Hit the on button. Open Word.

Stare at a blank screen.

Come on, I think. I need to get going on this sexy novella about one of three partners who have a successful lingerie catalog. My heroine is the designer of the catalog. She knows firsthand how the lingerie feels and looks. Hmm, maybe that's the problem—I can't remember what sexy feels like. I get up and pull out my pajama drawer. Big T-shirts, flannels and lots of cotton.

No silk or satin or lace in sight.

I dig deeper. Surely at one time I had something sexy, before kids, before ten years of sleep deprivation.... Ah, there it is. A black teddy. It looks as if maybe it'll fit on my big toe. Somehow I suck it up and get the thing on, but if I move it's going to split in half.

Note to self: Don't move.

I page my husband with "Help, can't start my car," thinking he'll come home and I'll surprise him with the black lace. Sexiness will follow suit.

Then I sit back down at the computer to wait. The screen is still blank. How is that possible? Surely I typed something the last time I sat here...

The doorbells rings. Oh, boy. Grab robe. It's my neighbor, whom my husband has called for me because he can't get home. I stammer some excuse and shut the door. Go back to computer, trying with all my might to get into this heroine's head. I'm going to feel sexy, damn it, if it's the last thing I do.

I put my fingers on the keys, dip into the imagination and...nothing. *Nada.* Zip. Damn. Turn on *Sex and the City* for inspiration. When did single men get so cute? They weren't that cute when I was single....

The dog chases away the FedEx man. I'm not feeling too bad about that; it was probably just some work I didn't want to do anyway.

Try again. Look at my blank screen. Come on, surely I have something sexy to add to this story!

The phone rings. Thank God. I leap at it for the distraction. Only, it's my ten-year-old who has fallen on the ice at school and needs an emergency-room visit. Her third this year. Heart clutching, I tear off the robe and jump into jeans and a sweater. Spend the next two hours discussing a broken elbow. Pick up the other kids. Feed everyone, get one daughter to jazz class and the other to a basketball game. Feed everyone some more. Supervise the homework. Referee more fights. At nine o'clock, silence finally reigns. I jump into the shower, and then grab one of my husband's T-shirts. Feel like a physical and emotional wreck. Didn't get any pages done!

"Hey," my husband says, perking up when I fall onto the couch in exhaustion, "like the look."

I open my mouth to get defensive but see a real warmth and genuine affection in his eyes. Hmm. Maybe there's nothing wrong with a little cotton. Maybe sexiness isn't in the material at all, but in the heart. "Hold that thought," I tell him, and reach for the laptop as he groans and reaches for the remote.

Here's a sneak peek...

18

# *SAVING ALLEGHENY GREEN*
## by
## Lori Wilde

*Nothing solves an identity crisis like a nice murder....*

# CHAPTER 1

AT TEN MINUTES after midnight on a muggy Saturday morning in late July, my kid sister, Sistine, shot her rat bastard boyfriend, Rockerfeller Hughes, with a .22-caliber pistol.

Rocky and Sissy had been drinking, which was not an unusual occurrence. Particularly in Rocky's case. His favorite beverage of choice being a shot of Jack Daniel's dropped into a mug of A&W root beer.

Sistine didn't hurt him. Well, not much. There was blood, sure, and he was howling loud enough to rouse corpses, but in truth she shot him in the foot, and he was wearing steel-toed Doc Marten boots so it wasn't quite as awful as it sounds.

Still, it was a mess, and some neighbor ended up calling the sheriff.

That's one bad thing about living in a rural river community like Clover Leaf, Texas. Everyone's got their nose in your business 24/7.

Like any sensible person with a day job, I was in bed. Sleeping. Or rather, trying to sleep. Between Rocky and his ragtag band of wannabe musicians playing a miserable riff of "My Mama Didn't Raise No Ho" in the garage and Sissy screaming at a decibel far above top-of-the-lungs, I was finding it difficult to achieve theta state.

I had been struggling to restrain myself from intervening in their argument, having learned from experience meddling in Sissy and Rocky's battles was a fool's mission. But Aunt Tessa, dressed in a gauzy white flowing robe, à la Aimee McPherson, came running into my bedroom, her healing crystal charm bracelet jangling as she moved.

"Ally," she cried, "get up. We need you. Rocky's been shot."

"Huh?" Pushing hair from my face, I sat up. The room was dark save for a shaft of moonlight spilling through the Home Depot miniblinds I had installed myself.

"Sissy shot Rocky. With your granddaddy's pistol. You better come quick. Someone must have called the cops. Probably that sanctimonious televangelist next door, because I can *feel* the sirens."

Reverend Ray Don Swiggly, the latest Sunday-morning television huckster to make millions off spreading the supposed gospel, had recently built a palatial summer home on the edge of the Brazos River right next door to our house. Being of the New-Age persuasion, Aunt Tessa had vast theological differences of opinion with the good reverend and expounded on her convictions whenever anyone would listen.

I cocked my head, not wanting to get into a long-winded discussion about the Reverend Swiggly when there were more urgent matters at hand. "I don't hear any sirens."

"You will."

I let it go. With Aunt Tessa sometimes you just had to trust. It was easier than trying to figure her out. I threw back the covers, hopped out of bed and grabbed my practical terry-cloth robe with the frayed hem. Okay, so I looked like a neglected housewife. Not everyone could pull off flaky chic like Aunt Tessa.

"Where's Mama?" I asked. "And Denny?"

"Your mother's in the pottery shack. I don't think she knows what's going on."

"Good. Keep her there. You know how she gets in a crisis." I gave Aunt Tessa the assignment not only to keep Mama from freaking out, but to give my aunt something to do. Tessa had as much of a tendency to slip into theatrics as Mama did. "What about Denny?"

"He's still sleeping."

"Are you sure?" Sissy's eight-year-old son had witnessed far too many of his mother's escapades.

"I'm certain. Come on." Aunt Tessa hustled me down the hallway.

We took the stairs two at a time then flew through the back door and out onto the stone walkway leading to the freestanding garage built years after the house was constructed. A million lights blazed and a knot of Sissy and Rocky's drunken friends, scraggly-haired young men and scantily clad women, clotted around the garage door.

I recognized Tim Kehaul. He was one of Sissy's many ex-boyfriends and the only guy to ever dump her. Tim had discovered rather late in life he preferred strong, hard masculine muscles wrapped around him in the night to soft, feminine limbs.

Tim possessed a cherubic face, sensational cheekbones and thick bronze hair that curled tightly against his head like a cap.

"Ally." Tim shyly smiled. "Strange doings."

"Hey, Tim," I said, too distracted to really notice him or wonder what he was doing there.

Tim rarely came around, since he didn't like Rocky, and Sissy hadn't forgiven him for taking up with his own sex. The fact that Tim and Rocky lived right next door to each other in the same trailer park two miles upriver must have caused friction between the three of them. But I gave up asking questions about Sissy's tangled sexual history. Sometimes it's best not to know.

I elbowed my way through the crowd and hollered at Aunt Tessa over my shoulder to take care of Mama before I plunged inside the garage.

Rocky lay on the floor, baying like a hound caught in a bear trap. His too-tight, blood-flecked Grateful Dead T-shirt had the neck slashed out in a deep V, exposing more of his chest and an old scar crisscrossing his throat than I cared to see. For reasons that escaped me, Rocky cut the neck out of his shirts.

Sissy sat with his head cradled in her lap, tears pouring down her face. "I'm sorry, Rocky. I didn't mean to shoot you," she wailed.

"Yes, you did. I'm having you arrested," he said through gritted teeth.

*Thank God. Maybe she'll break up with him.*

I flicked my gaze over his body, searching for the wound, and stopped at his feet. Blood oozed from the toe of his boot and pooled on the cement. Or rather, what was left of his boot. Bits of leather had gone flying and were stuck to guitars and drums. What a mess.

"Ally! Thank heavens!" Sissy exclaimed when she realized I was in the room.

"Your crazy sister shot me," Rocky whined. "Can you believe that?"

"Shut up. Both of you." I sank to my knees beside Rocky.

"Don't touch it." He howled, even though my fingers were nowhere near his blasted foot.

"You know I'm a nurse," I soothed. "Hold still so I can examine you."

"You might be a nurse, but you're her sister and you hate my guts." He jabbed a finger at Sissy. "For all I know, you'll make it worse on purpose."

"I admit it's a tempting thought," I said dryly. "If you'd rather bleed to death." I shrugged and started to get up.

His face paled. "No. Wait. Don't go. Is it really bleeding that bad?"

"I can't tell until I take your boot off."

"It's going to hurt, isn't it?"

"Like a son of a bitch," I said cheerfully, and loosened his boot laces.

"The cops are comin'!" Tim yelled from the yard, and the next thing I knew engines were revving and the police sirens Aunt Tessa had predicted several minutes earlier screamed in the distance.

"Oh, jeez, Sissy." Rocky gazed balefully at my sister. "Run your hand in my back pocket and get out those joints. I can't get busted for possession again. They'll revoke my parole."

"You brought marijuana into my house after I distinctly told you not to?" I shouted.

24 "It's not your house—it's your garage," Rocky quibbled.

I jostled his foot. On purpose.

"Yow!"

"Sorry. My hand slipped."

Rocky glared then turned his attention back to Sissy. "Come on, babe, get the joints."

"Not if you're going to have me arrested. You know I had every right to shoot you," my sister told him.

"Sissy." I frowned at her. "No one has the right to shoot anyone, no matter what that person might have done."

"He's got a wife," Sissy muttered.

"What?" I glared at Rocky.

He looked sheepish. "It's no big deal. I haven't seen her in a year."

"He's lucky," Sissy said. "I was aiming somewhere a bit higher but I missed and the bullet ricocheted off the clothes dryer and got him in the boot."

Rocky rested a protective hand over his genitals. "Okay, sweetie, baby. I was wrong. I'm sorry. I shoulda told you I was married when we started dating."

"Damn straight."

*She's gonna dump him, once and for all. Praise the Lord and pass the ammo.*

The sirens were getting louder. The crowd once assembled in my yard had vaporized.

"So get the joints out of my pocket, please." Rocky rolled calf eyes at Sistine and I knew she was falling for it. "I'll tell the cops it was an accident. I promise."

"Do you want me to flush 'em?" Sissy asked, rooting around behind him, frisking his bony butt. She came up with a crumpled plastic bag containing six fat hand-rolled marijuana cigarettes.

"Hell, no. Hide them in here somewhere."

My gaze caught Sissy's. "Don't you dare."

"Sheriff's Department." A commanding voice spoke from the open doorway. "Nobody move."

Law-enforcement officials poured into my garage, guns drawn. They surrounded the three of us, locking us into some surreal, redneck militia melodrama.

We were screwed.

I caught my breath and glanced toward the door.

A tall, muscular, mustachioed man trod across the garage toward us. He looked like a Rambo/Terminator cross—hard gray eyes, jarhead haircut, service revolver strapped to him more snugly than a spare body part. The twinkling star on his chest revealed his identity.

Sheriff.

The famed former U.S. Marine MP, Sheriff Samuel J. Conahegg so highly lauded in the *Clover Leaf Gazette.*

He'd been elected on the strength of his promise to scour the local government of corruption. His predecessor had run off with the county clerk, bucktoothed, knock-kneed Mavis Higgins—who was reportedly a real hottie in bed despite her uncanny resemblance to Olive Oyl—and two hundred thousand dollars of taxpayer funds.

Conahegg was known not only for his tendency to go for ride-alongs with his deputies at any time without notice, but for his utter lack of mercy. Zero Tolerance was his middle name, and from his ramrod straight stance, I could believe it.

"What's going on here?" he asked, his voice a strange mixture of barbed wire and honey.

My heart did a crazy, swoony dance.

Why? I had no explanation. I'm not given to instant attraction to strangers. And most certainly not to domineering, uncompromising types.

His gaze took in Rocky with the shot toe and Sissy

holding the bag of illicit weed. Then he looked at me. I shrugged and lifted my eyebrows.

Nobody said a word.

The sheriff turned to one of his men. "Call for an ambulance, please, Jefferson."

"Will do, sir." Jefferson sprinted from the garage.

"The rest of you can put away your weapons." Conahegg waved at the four remaining deputies. They obeyed his command, sliding their guns into their holsters while sending us malevolent stares.

"You." The sheriff flicked a finger at me. "What's your name?"

"Al…er…" My throat was dry as a crusty gym sock. I tried to swallow. Twice. And finally got out "Allegheny Allison Green."

"Is that your real name?"

"Don't blame me. I didn't pick it." I might be attracted to him, but damn if I'd let him know it.

"What happened here?" He jerked his dimpled chin in the direction of Rocky's toe.

How to explain?

Rocky and Sissy were no help. Rocky had closed his eyes, feigning unconsciousness. Sissy peered assiduously at the floor, as if, if she stared long enough, it would open up and suck her right down.

"He got shot," I finally answered.

"So it appears." Conahegg squatted beside Rocky. "Hurts pretty badly, does it?"

Rocky didn't move.

"Hmm," Conahegg mused, stroking his chin with two fingers and a thumb.

None of the stalwart deputies had spoken, nor even moved. They stayed positioned at the ready, their faces expressionless.

"What I don't know," the sheriff continued in his oddly engaging tone, "is how he came to find himself toeless."

"A gun went off?" I ventured.

The sheriff jerked his head around and drilled me with eyes gone deadly sharp. "You're not that stupid."

Ulp!

He both complimented me and scared me in one breath. I had to give him high marks for perceptiveness but low scores on charm. Still, something about him magnetized me in a way no man had in a very long time. Just my luck. I finally get the hots for someone and it's the kind of guy I could never get along with.

The sheriff shifted his body away from Rocky and toward me. Instant sweat popped out on my skin. I could feel it trickling down my neck.

"Let's start again, shall we?" he asked.

I nodded.

"All right." He paused to glance at his watch. "At exactly ten minutes after zero hundred hours we received a report that someone was shooting off a gun at this residence."

He'd brought his military precision with him to his job as sheriff. You could see it in his posture, read it in his face. He was probably not an easy man to work for. He would demand perfection from his employees, and mete out just punishment if his orders weren't followed to the letter. He possessed an enigmatic power gleaned from years of hard self-discipline.

I shivered.

"We're outside the city limits," I pointed out, forcing myself to stop thinking about the strange pull I felt toward him. "It's not illegal to shoot a gun here."

"To discharge a weapon, no. But to shoot a person, yes."

"It was an accident," Rocky said.

Conahegg and I stared at each other again, our eyes striking like two flint rocks sparking off each other, before we glanced over at Rocky.

"Sh…sh…she didn't mean to do it," Rocky stammered.

"*You* shot him?" the sheriff asked me, a bemused smile flitting over his lips. It almost looked as if he admired me, and for one short second I wished I had shot Rocky.

"No." Rocky shook his head. "Her." He pointed at Sissy. "She was showing me her granddaddy's gun when she dropped it and the thing went off."

The sheriff reached over and gently pried the bag of marijuana from Sistine's fingers. His gentleness with her surprised me. He touched her chin, lifted her face. "Is that true?"

Tears glistened in my sister's eyes. She shook like a kitten abandoned on the roadside.

"It's all right," he said softly. "You can tell me anything."

Oh, he was good. Too good. Sissy loved male attention and she'd go to the ends of the earth to get it. Although how he had sensed that about her I had no idea.

"Uh-huh," Sissy whispered. "It was an accident."

"What about this?" Sheriff Conahegg crushed the bag of joints in his fist. "How did a nice girl like you get possession of a nasty weed like this?"

Sissy's gaze flicked from the sheriff to Rocky.

*Come on. Tell him the truth. Rocky's the biggest pot hound in three counties.*

Sissy took a deep breath.

We waited.

"I found it," she said.

"You found it?" Conahegg shook his head, disappointed in her answer.

"Yes."

"Where did you find it?"

*In Rockerfeller Hughes's back pocket!*

"I don't remember." Sissy was studying a guitar lying to one side of the garage as if her life depended on memorizing every fret.

"Are you aware of the penalty for marijuana possession?"

"No." Her voice was barely audible. Sissy might

talk tough and act tougher, but when she's in trouble she reverts to kid mode.

Silence ensued. You could even hear the frogs croaking down by the water. Conahegg rose to his feet and swept his gaze around the room.

The garage was unbearably hot. From where I sat crouched over Rocky's foot, the smell of fresh blood kept assaulting my nostrils and my knees ached from the cement floor.

"May I stand up?" I asked. "My leg is going to sleep."

He nodded.

I stood.

Or rather, I tried to stand. My legs wobbled like rubber bands and I stumbled sideways into that hunk of granite passing for a human being.

Conahegg's hand went out to catch me.

The contact was electric.

No kidding. You read that clichéd comparison in romance novels and you assume it's an exaggeration. I mean, I'm a nurse, for crying out loud. I touch people all the time. Save for static electricity, you don't ever feel a jolt, a shock, a current.

Except I did.

And I had no clue why. It scared me. Big-time.

I jerked away. Fast.

"Are you okay?" he asked.

*Oh, sure, other than the fact you fried all my internal organs, I'm peachy.*

"Need to get the circulation back in my legs," I

said, jogging in place, more to shake the sensation of Sheriff Conahegg's touch than to bring blood to my lower extremities.

"Ally?"

The sound of my name drew my attention to the garage door occupied by my mother, Aunt Tessa fluttering at her side.

"I tried to keep her in the pottery shed," Aunt Tessa explained, "but she heard the sirens."

Mama floated over, hardly noticing the sheriff's deputies with guns strapped to their sides. "Honey?" As always, she looked to me for explanation and reassurance. "What are these people doing here?" Her voice still held the sugary sweetness of her Carolina girlhood.

"Ma'am." Super Sheriff turned on his heel and held his hand out to Mama. "I'm Sheriff Conahegg and we received several complaints of disturbing the peace."

"Oh, dear." Mama pushed a wisp of graying brown hair back into the loose bun atop her head. "Why, I know you." She smiled. "You're Lew Conahegg's boy."

"Yes, ma'am."

"I remember when you wore short pants. Your father and my husband used to have offices side by side on the courthouse square. Green's Green House and Lew Conahegg, Attorney at Law."

Really? I didn't remember that.

"That's been awhile," Conahegg said.

"I'm so sorry to hear about your father's passing."

"Thank you, ma'am."

"Well," Mama continued, "you'll have to excuse the noise. My daughter's boyfriend and his band like to practice here in our garage."

She waved a hand at the abandoned instruments. I was beginning to wonder if she'd even noticed Rocky lying on the floor, suffering from a gunshot wound inflicted by her youngest daughter. Mama had the amazing ability to focus upon only what she wanted to see and ignore the rest.

"So I've gathered." Conahegg nodded. He still held Rocky's bag of weed in his hand. As if he'd just become aware of that, he shoved the pot into his pocket.

"Goodness, Rocky," Mama said, finally catching on. She lifted up her long skirt and stepped over his injured foot. "What happened to you?"

"Accident, Mrs. Green."

"You've got to be more careful, dear. You weren't imitating those musicians on television who smash their guitars, were you? That's not a nice way to treat your instruments."

Everyone looked at me.

I shook my head. No point in explaining reality to my mother. I'd learned that a long time ago.

"Mama," I said. "Why don't you let Aunt Tessa take you inside and make you a cup of tea."

Mama brightened. "That sounds nice. Tessa?"

But as Mama spoke to her sister, a strange expression crossed Aunt Tessa's features.

"Ung!" Aunt Tessa cried out, and all gazes swung in her direction. Her right hand went to her throat and her eyes stared vacantly ahead.

My heart sank into my shoes. No not now. Not a visit from Ung. Uh-uh. Please God.

Not in front of Conahegg.

But I was not to be the beneficiary of divine intervention. The gathered deputies watched in fascination. I'd seen it before. Many times. I admit, the first time you see it can be quite a show.

The expression on Aunt Tessa's face changed from empty indifference to lively animation. Her lips curled back, a combination smile and grimace. Her eyes widened until they seemed to encompass her entire face. Her nostrils flared. Her cheeks flushed with color.

"I am Ung!" Aunt Tessa growled in a deep voice.

Conahegg shot me a "what-in-the-hell?" expression. I couldn't blame him. Aunt Tessa's transformation into her twenty-five-thousand-year-old spirit guide, a cavewoman named Ung, is quite a spectacle.

Aunt Tessa spread her arms wide. "I speak from spirit world. Heed warning." Her eyebrows dipped. She crooked a finger and lurched toward Rocky.

Reflexively he raised his hands, shielding his face. "Get her away from me. She's creepy."

"The warning is for you!" Tessa-turned-Ung cried. "Much evil. Beware!"

Chills chased up my arm.

Granted, I don't often believe in Aunt Tessa's New-Age, Shirley MacLaine crapola but occasionally Ung will make a prediction that comes true. Of course, it's not much of a stretch to figure out that a dope-smoking, unemployed musician who cheats on his girlfriend with his wife and vice versa is going to end up in trouble.

The sheriff, who by the way had magnificent forearms, tugged me to one side. "What's this all about?" he whispered.

"You got me."

"Who is that woman?"

"My aunt."

The sheriff rolled his eyes. "Why does that not surprise me?"

"Are you disparaging my family?"

"Looks like they're doing the job all by themselves," he commented dryly.

I planted my hands on my hips. Who did he think he was? I mean besides sheriff. He had the power to put us behind bars on one trumped-up charge or the other, but he certainly didn't have the right to bad-mouth my kinfolk. We took enough guff off the locals. You expected more understanding from your elected officials.

"Hey, come on. Do something, man. Get her off me," Rocky cried.

Aunt Tessa was hovering over Rocky's prostrate body, trembling from head to toe. "The evil forces are strong," she croaked. "Run. Run. Run for your life."

"That's enough!" Conahegg said, and motioned for a deputy to intercept Aunt Tessa. "Where is that ambulance?"

As if on his command, the ambulance pulled down the graveled river road and into our yard, siren wailing and lights flashing.

Aunt Tessa crumpled in the deputy's arms, her face slack. On the floor, Rocky was sweating buckets and my idiotic sister sat rocking him in her arms and cooing into his ear. Some people never learn.

"What do I do with her, Sheriff?" the deputy asked. Aunt Tessa was dishrag limp, and she often stayed that way for an hour or more after channeling Ung.

"I'll take her to bed," Mama said, surprising me with her helpfulness. "Come on, Tessa." She guided the deputy, Tessa in his arms, out the side door.

"We'll need statements from everyone involved," Conahegg said at the same time two paramedics trotted into the garage.

"Everybody else took off," Rocky said. "'Cept for my darling, Sistine."

*Oh, brother.*

"I'd never leave you, tiger," Sissy whispered.

No, but you'd shoot him in the foot, I thought rather unkindly.

There have been many times in my life I could

have sworn I was a changeling. When I was a kid, growing up with a head-in-the-clouds, fairy-tale-believing, troll-doll-making mother; a florist father who collected butterflies and a cavewoman-channeling aunt, I harbored sweet fantasies that Gypsies had stolen me from my rightful parents—usually a practical-minded accountant and a devoted stay-at-home mom—and left me on the Greens' doorstep.

Although I never came up with a proper motivation for such rash actions on the part of these anonymous Gypsies, I quickly determined my place in the scheme of things. I was in the Green family to take care of everything. To attend to the routine chores no one else seemed inclined to do, like paying bills, holding down a steady job, cooking dinner, cleaning the house, washing the car, changing the light bulbs. That sort of thing. If it hadn't been for me, the family would have unraveled long ago. Especially after Daddy died.

"I'd like you to come to the station with us," Sheriff Conahegg said to me.

"But I didn't witness the shooting."

He took me by the shoulder—that red-hot grip again!—turned me around, ducked his head and whispered in my ear, "Maybe not," he said, "but you seem to be the only one in the place with a lick of sense."

I smiled. Swear to God I did. And flushed with pride. I *was* the only one with a lick of sense, but nobody in my family saw me that way.

SNEAK PEEK BONUS FEATURE

In my bizarre-and-proud-of-it clan, I was known as the dull one. Ally would rather clean the dishes than strip naked and dance in the rain. Or Ally is such a snore—she has always got her nose stuck in a book instead of actually living. Or Ally doesn't have an artistic mind—she only cares about making money. My family never seemed to appreciate that because I did the boring, mundane things, they got to be eccentric.

The paramedics loaded Rocky onto the stretcher and trundled him into the back of the ambulance. Sissy begged to ride along but they wouldn't let her. She stood beside me, sobbing into her hands.

The deputies scattered, searching for witnesses to interrogate, leaving me and Sissy and Conahegg in the garage.

"Well, ladies," Conahegg said. "May I have the honor of escorting you to my squad car?"

...NOT THE END...

*Look for SAVING ALLEGHENY GREEN in bookstores September 2005.*

# LAUNCHING AUGUST

Fall in love all over again with classic stories
by *New York Times* and *USA TODAY*
bestselling authors.

**Fantasy** by Lori Foster
Available August 2005

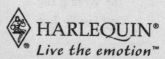 

SAGA

Coming in August…

A dramatic new story in
The Bachelors of Blair Memorial saga…

*USA TODAY* bestselling author

# Marie Ferrarella

# SEARCHING FOR CATE

A widower for three years, Dr. Christian Graywolf
knows his life is his work at Blair Memorial Hospital.
But when he meets FBI special agent Cate Kowalski—
a woman searching for her birth mother—the attraction
is intense and immediate. And the truth is something
neither Christian nor Cate expects—that all his life
Christian has been searching for Cate.

**Bonus Features,
including:
Sneak Peek,
The Writing Life
and Family Tree**

*Where love comes alive*™

**MINISERIES**

Coming in August...

*USA TODAY* bestselling author

# Dixie Browning

# LAWLESS LOVERS

Two complete novels from
The Lawless Heirs saga.

Daniel Lyon Lawless and Harrison Lawless are two
successful, sexy and very sought after bachelors.
But their worlds are about to be rocked by the
love of two headstrong, beautiful women!

**Bonus Features,
including:**

**The Writing Life,**

**Family Tree**

**and Sneak Peek
from a NEW Lawless
Heirs title coming
in September!**

*Where love comes alive*™

If you enjoyed what you just read,
then we've got an offer you can't resist!

# Take 2 bestselling
# love stories FREE!

# Plus get a FREE surprise gift!

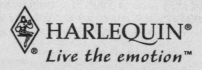

Signature Select™

## SUZANNE FORSTER

has written nearly thirty novels and has been the recipient of countless awards, including the National Readers' Choice Award for SHAMELESS, her mainstream debut. She's received recognition for outstanding sales from Waldenbooks and Bookrak, and her twelfth novel, CHILD BRIDE, was a top-selling Bantam series romance. Her romantic thriller THE MORNING AFTER hit top spots on several bestseller lists, including the *USA TODAY* and the *New York Times* extended lists. Suzanne loves to hear from readers. You can e-mail her at sueforster@aol.com.

## JILL SHALVIS

has been making up stories since she could hold a pencil. Now, thankfully, she gets to do it for a living, and doesn't plan to ever stop. She is the bestselling, award-winning author of over thirty novels. She has hit the Waldenbooks bestseller list, was a 2000 RITA® Award nominee and is a two-time National Readers' Choice Award winner. She was nominated for a *Romantic Times* Career Achievement Award in Romantic Comedy, Best Duets and Best Temptation, and writes series romance for both Silhouette and Harlequin.

## DONNA KAUFFMAN

was first published with Bantam's Loveswept line in 1993. After fourteen books, she went on to write contemporary single titles for Bantam. In 2001 she returned to her category roots and had her first release from Harlequin's Temptation line. Donna is also currently writing for Harlequin's Blaze line. She enjoys creating characters that like to push the edge a little! Donna lives in Virginia with her husband and rapidly growing sons. She also has a rapidly growing menagerie of pets.

## Available in August

Three old friends who have lost touch over the years. One chance reunion and an opportunity to rethink the choices each has made. Cut through the layers and get to the heart of deep-lasting friendship in this daring new novel by an award-winning author.

## CUTTING THROUGH

by *New York Times* bestselling author **Joan Hohl**